About the author:

Robert Crole, M.A. M.Sc. was educated at Edinburgh Academy, Gordonstoun School, Oxford and Edinburgh Universities. As well as teaching in Edinburgh and Wiltshire, he has worked in Africa and Australia, and served in the Royal Navy in the Mediterranean at the end of WWII. With a family background from both England and Scotland, he enjoys the best of both worlds in the Scottish Borders, and draws on the vocabularies of both in his writing.

Abbeys Hold Dark Corners
Robert Crole
isbn no. 1 873708 12 2

Published by Alba Publishing
20 Dounehill
Jedburgh TD8 6LJ
Tel. 01835 864556

Cover Illustrations: Patrick Benson

Printed by Kelso Graphics

ABBEYS HOLD DARK CORNERS

A Murder Mystery set in the Scottish
Borders

By ROBERT CROLE

ALBA PUBLISHING

AUTHOR'S NOTE

This is a work of fiction set in the Scottish Borders. All the characters in this story are entirely the creation of the writer's imagination. No criticism is in any way implied of Historic Scotland which handsomely conserve our four, tragically ruined Abbeys or of the Lothian and Borders police who maintain our law and order. The Abbeys are faithfully portrayed with the exception of the Bell Stair in Melrose Abbey where a door has been replaced by a grill for the sake of the plot and an imagined stair inserted over the tower crossing. By coincidence the stair has been opened to the public while this work was in composition. Blackhouse Tower has been slightly embellished and the track to it is a private road. Otherwise architecture and geography have been generally respected.

For Hugh
15th June, 1958 - 4th November 2000

'O see ye not yon narrow road
So thick beset with thorns and briers?
That is the path of righteousness
Tho' after it but few enquires.

'And see ye that braid, braid road,
That lies across that lily leven?
That is the path of wickedness,
Tho' some call it the road to heaven.

'And see ye not that bonnie road,
That winds about the fernie brae?
That is the road to fair Elfland,
Where thou and I this night maun gae.

The Ballad of Thomas the Rhymer

Contents

ACCEPTING THE INEVITABLE

'What is this life bot ane straucht way to dede.'
William Dunbar, c.1500

'I have been thinking,' said Daphne Stone to her husband, Roger. He looked warily at his wife. As an Intelligence officer in one of those government departments that was at one time secret, he was used to cautious approaches and devious screens.

He put down his crossword puzzle.

'Yes,' he said, apprehensively.

'I have been thinking it is time we had a holiday. Now that Mary and Daniel are at university, we could take off on our own.'

His silence encouraged her to go on.

'You know whenever you choose where we go, like sailing to France, we always end up in trouble, and last time it was murder in Hereford. This time I should like to pick, suggest,' - she caught his eye and giggled - 'a really relaxing place. Not beaches and sun, which I know you can only take for two days. I think we should go to Scotland. The Seymours are always pressing us to visit them in Northumberland and we could start with them and then go on to the Borders.'

'Sounds a good idea.' he nodded. 'I have some leave due. We could take the car and find some country pub to stay in. Go hill walking.'

She looked away. 'Well, I thought, Roger, we should go on bicycles.'

He groaned inwardly. He had seen it coming. She had been taking her old bicycle out of the garage and he had noticed her riding tentatively down the street.

She continued. 'I am putting on weight and,' she would have liked to say it will be very good for us, but she knew that this was not a wise approach to an Oxford graduate who would immediately ask what do you mean by 'good', -

1

'and, it's very beautiful country,' she finished rather lamely. 'I've just read an article which says the best way of touring is by bicycles and bed and breakfasts.'

'I am sure that ought to be beds and breakfasts in the plural. More emphasis on the beds.'

She let that pass.

'Look, I found this in your quotation book:

"O Caledonia! stern and wild,

Meet nurse for a poetic child." '

'But his next words are,' Roger replied, fighting a rear-guard action' "Land of the mountain and the flood", so on bicycles it will be all uphill and pouring with rain.'

'Nonsense!' she said, 'if there is uphill, there must be downhill as well, it stands to reason. And the booklet says Kelso has less rainfall than London. We shall meet all kinds of interesting people in the Bs and Bs. Besides, McConachie lives there. Didn't you tell me that he had returned north and you always wanted to meet him again?'

'I don't know where he lives,' said Roger. He thought of that friendly face of the stolid Scots policeman he had worked with in the south. A fellow he recalled with great affection. You never felt that he was other than plodding away, yet with an uncanny instinct for getting to the truth, seeing both the wood and the trees. 'Yes, I should like to see him. I expect that he has a quiet life up there and spends all his time fishing.'

He returned to his crossword to avoid making a decision, but Daphne was not finished yet.

'Look,' she said, 'I got all these brochures and there are four marvellous Abbeys to visit, built by King David in the twelfth century to civilise the Scots.'

'He didn't do very well then,' said he sardonically.

She held out the pictures to him.

'But they're all in ruins!' he exclaimed.

'Yes,' she admitted, 'but very beautiful ruins. Look at Jedburgh, that's the first one. Almost all the church is there, although there is no roof.' She pointed to what had been a handsome building with its three storeys of nine windows and pinnacled tower. 'They once dug up a headless torso there, the brochure says, must have been murdered.'

She hoped this kind of detail would encourage him.

'Then there's Kelso. It says that they only discovered recently from old plans in the Vatican that what they thought was the east end was really the west. There's only the remnants of the tower and the entry porch.'

'Not much of it left, looks a bit sinister,' said Roger, reluctant to show too much interest.

Daphne knew that her husband was beginning to accept. 'Here's the one I like best, Dryburgh, it has a lovely position on the River Tweed. Haig and Sir Walter Scott are buried there. And it has a splendid layout of monastic buildings on a small scale. Also,' she glanced carefully at him, 'the brochure says there's a first class hotel beside it.'

He realised that he was being gently led along.

'The fourth one, that's Melrose. It was a Cistercian house. The booklet points out that each of the four belonged to a different order.'

'I can see it's got a nave, a transept and half a tower,' he said, ' and a large graveyard,' he added. 'You know, I have always wondered about these old churches. You go in and just see altars and fine mullioned windows, but the monks must have been able to climb up to the galleries and towers, even if it was just to clean the windows or mend the bell ropes. There must be internal staircases and secret passages.

Daphne could see the fish was nearly landed.

'What are those three, pointed hills in the background?' he asked.

'Those are the Eildons,' she replied. 'They had a sort of Rip van Winkle there, Thomas the Rhymer, who came back with weird prophesies of gloom and death.'

'It all looks peaceful enough but I seem to remember from my schooldays that the Borders had a pretty bloody history. The English kings had a hobby of burning Abbeys in their spare time, particularly Henry VIII. He sent an army of mercenaries under the Earl of Hertford to try and persuade the Scots to marry Mary to his son Edward, and they massacred everyone. Do you think we shall be hospitably received?'

'I shall guarantee no dead bodies,' she said, in which she was to be proved entirely wrong

So it was that three weeks later they took their car to the Seymours, enjoyed a night of hospitality in a comfortable country house before being dropped by their host at the bicycle shop.

'You're quite mad, Roger,' he said, 'fancy being talked into this by your wife.'

They regarded each other as they emerged from the hire shop in their cycling gear. Roger wore a red bobble cap, Daphne could see the grey on his sideburns. Otherwise his face looked like his son's, she thought, the same wide set eyes, turned up nose, and mouth ready to smile.

'You look like Daniel,' she said.

He laughed back. 'You're not looking that old yourself, Mrs Stone,' he said, surveying his wife's rounded figure, concealed in a blue anorak and trousers. 'Let's hope we still have some spring in our heels, when we reach harbour tonight.'

'Otterburn's first port of call,' she said.

'I don't know, my dear, if you studied the map when you measured the distances because it is all uphill to Carter Bar.'

'Just think what it will be like running down to Jedburgh,' she laughed.

CLOUDS GATHER OVER THE BORDERS

'From Carter's ridge the traveller's eye
Might fancy smoke against the sky,
And make him ask if death still stalks
Amidst the Abbeys' vaulted walks.'

Robert Lake, 2000

I

Major Alistair Peter McAlistair, retired, lived in a small house on the edges of a Cheviot village. He was a man of order and in the thirty years of his military career, his life had been dedicated to it. Orders to be obeyed and order to be achieved. Papers on his desk or corpses in the field were objects to be categorised and arranged to be placed in the necessary containers. His trim, stocky figure, his small, immaculately groomed moustache, his attention to the details of dress had occasioned his regimental nickname of Apple Pie from the initials of his Christian names. He had not found it amusing when he had heard one of his junior subalterns using it, he thought they were mocking the particular creed he sought to inculcate into them.

He sat in his neatly ordered study, looking down the valley, glanced at his watch and realised that at five minutes to six, he had to wait before he poured himself his evening drink. He did not take in the view but brooded in his mind.

It was always the Ministry in London that had blocked his promotion. First they merged the regiments which made officers like himself redundant. Then they had said that he had to move on to let younger men come in. In the end he had accepted that it was time to go.

They had retired happily enough, he and his wife, Maisie, to the Borders. He knew she always represented the other side of his life, someone whose whimsy and sense of poetry balanced his extreme precision. She had accepted the respect for military punctuality and order that he required without surrendering to it. Even within their innumerable homes, there had been corners where what he called confusion was allowed to reign provided it did not overlap with his dominions. Her disorder was categorised.

At long last they had acquired their own home, Innisfree, she had called the cottage, from some poem, she had said, as the old name of Hillview seemed unimaginative. He remembered she had read him the poem and he had approved. Rhyming provided a sense of completeness.

The move had gone well, too. They were old hands at fitting their belongings into houses but this time it had had to be done more carefully since it was for good. Maisie had hesitated so often and so long about each piece that he had grown impatient, and lost his temper.

He regretted it now. He looked again at his watch, crossed to the corner cupboard to take out the glass, the one with the regimental crest on, and poured himself a whisky, spirit to the level of the unicorn's nose and water to the top of the horn.

He looked at the photograph of Maisie on the table. The cancer had been mercifully swift and the hospital clinically efficient. She had accepted the onset of death, contented to have seen him established in their own and final home but she had not finished the layout of the garden. Not too many straight lines, she had said, in her last clear moments. Their two children had come north from London for the funeral and the burial at Morebattle. Everything had been properly conducted. Then he was left to his daily round, cooking his meals and walking the dog. The black labrador, Keltie, stirred at his feet as if in sympathy with his thoughts.

It was not as if his life was empty. There were always things to do but somehow they had become bland in their routine efficiency without sparkle. He looked again at the photograph. Maisie had a pixy like face, he sometimes had called her gnome. In his rare moments of humour, he would say that he had a gnome in his garden, and he thought again of how much of the warmth in his life had stemmed from her.

Keltie nuzzled his knee; it was time for her evening walk. He drained his glass and placed it carefully beside the decanter on the tray. He could see that he would need another drink. Maisie usually had her gin before supper with his second.

He put his supper into the oven, called to Keltie, opened the front door with its curtained draught excluder, almost Maisie's last achievement, and went out onto the village road. There was rarely any traffic on it, although it led off into the hills and ultimately to Northumberland. The world outside was green and quiet, the evening air was misty and still. She would have liked it, he thought, but going back into his empty house, he realised that its peacefulness made his solitude wearisome.

With his second drink he leafed through his diary. There were the regular shooting dates but there were many empty days. The funeral of his wife had turned his thoughts to cemeteries. His last posting had been to the War Graves Commission in France. He recalled those pleasing lines of stones and crosses and for a time he filled his thoughts with recollections of the carefully tended graveyards of Normandy, where anything out of place could be immediately restored.

Perhaps there would be a need for his kind of experience in the Borders. After all, every village had its War Memorial, and most their cemetery. Then there were the abbeys, the four of them, with their neglected gravestones. He would begin with them.

II

John Brearley was the owner and manager of a small tourist coach company. He had served a stint in the army. Good training for life he called it, where he had taken advantage of every course he could get himself drafted into, from driving to computer literacy quite apart from all the usual things like shooting people which you expected to learn.

On leaving he had done yet another course to pass as a bus driver, and had then set himself up on his own with his Real Tours Company. Real comfort was what he reckoned to provide at real prices and that meant American visitors.

There were not so many now that the rate of exchange for the dollar had fallen but he had a good season with repeated tours to the Scottish Borders. His army buddy, Gus Macdonald, had somehow found himself working in a tourist agency in Dallas and it had not taken him long to link up with the Real Tours Company. He came over regularly.

'J, ' he said, 'you deliver the goods and I'll deliver the people. There's good money in this.'

Although John Brearley had never been over fond of military discipline, it had taught him how to manage groups of people of all sorts, tactfully and efficiently. He also learnt that even the best of hotels were eager for his custom. That is why he found himself heading north in the newest of his coaches and with the latest of his tours.

'Summer in the beautiful country of Sir Walter Scott has to be seen to be believed. Enjoy the magic of the romantic history of the Scottish Borders with all the comforts of modern coach travel and luxury hotels. Look at the majestic ruins of Melrose Abbey by moonlight, watch the leaves turning colour in the riverside woodlands beside Dryburgh,' as his brochure put it.

Nor did he neglect culture. With the same enthusiasm as the hoteliers, local entertainers and even lecturers from distant universities were persuaded with suitable rewards to offer their services, although requested not to overstretch their audience.

Gus worked closely with him acting as courier and co-driver. They were both experienced in the art of pleasing, of pouring oil on troubled waters, and it suited them to play down their positions, to carry bags and render subservient services, an attitude which led to substantial tips at the conclusion of the tour. He and John would hand over their tourists to the hotel at the end of each long day and relax in their own company.

'Gee,' said one their last trippers, 'Gee, they're just great. You hardly notice them, but they're always there when you need them.'

This time they had done some of the London things, they could readily vary the menu there, and Kenilworth and Chatsworth on the way north.

'You missed out Stratford, John,' - he always introduced himself and Gus with their Christian names - complained the largest woman of the party, Mrs Oldberger, wagging her finger at him. It gave her the excuse of comparing everything they saw unfavourably and loudly to the Shakespearian sites they had missed.

'I don't think that you will be disappointed by the Border Abbeys,' he replied. 'They are just the right places for some real drama.'

III

'Bloody workfare, bloody job creation, bloody government, bloody trippers leaving their flaming litter everywhere.' That was what Shelagh Thornell had come to expect every working day whenever her husband, Jim, came back to their Hawick home, He would go on through tea and slump himself in front of the television binding coarsely away. Here was he, a trained wool spinner, best in the mill the manager had said, here he was bloody good at his job, sweeping graveyards.

As she looked out of the window, she realised that he had recently seemed quieter. There was a time when she would have given as good as she got, but it did not seem right somehow when he had lost his job through no fault of his own.

He had been a changed man since he had been finally laid off from the mill. Twice he had been made redundant. A skilled wool worker, he had worked twenty years with the same firm until it closed. Taken on again, he had hoped to see out his time but once more there had been the meetings and the rumours and the talk, all leading to the same thing and this time not much in the way of compensation.

They said at the 'Broo' that he had to work; some fellow from Edinburgh had set up a scheme to clean up the Abbeys. So there he was, he an experienced mill hand, sweeping the paths and picking up the litter like a common scavvie. She could understand how he felt but he still took it out of her, although now she came to think of it, she had had a few weeks' peace. Was it all going to start again? She peered anxiously though the window, but with his helmet on and his beard she could make nothing of his expression. James Thornell stood outside the gate of the narrow strip of garden that fronted their terraced house, wrenching the motor bicycle back on to its rest. She braced herself just in case. He came in without a word, stripped off his helmet and jacket. She was almost more worried when he did not explode. He sat down in his chair, and picked up the paper while she made the tea.

'It's just bacon 'n black pudding again,' she said hesitantly. 'You'll mind that ye didna gie me ony much in the way of the housekeeping last week.'

He grunted, fumbling in his pocket and handed her a fiver in silence. Seeing her surprised look, 'stroke of chance,' he said 'found it among the stanes at Melrose.'

They ate in silence until she felt she could safely go on.

'Is it the horses?' she asked. He did not reply immediately.

'Aye,' he said, 'I met a feller in ma dinner hour who gave me a tip, so I gave him what I had, and it came in first.'

He looked away. She bit her lip. Jim once before had taken to the bookies and she did not want to see it start again.

'Can we no just stick to the lottery, Jim?'

He rose and picked up his helmet. 'I've to deliver something,' he said and without further word, picked up his helmet to go out.

'Whaur ye'll be on Monday's morn?' she asked.

'Jed,' he said, ' bloody Jed, woman, ye ken that.'

She sighed. She knew it was a different abbey each day on a four day round, but she only made him up a piece for Dryburgh where he could not pick up a pie. She watched him go out, check the panniers on the motor bicycle and drive purposefully away. He'd be at Jed on Monday.

IV

The police car drew up outside the house on the council state, The one half of the semi had wooden boarding across the windows and the other looked dirty and uncared for, weeds and old beer cans filled the small garden strip.

The constable studied his notebook.

He said to his companion. 'This is the place, man, number eighteen.'

He knocked officiously on the door while they glanced around. It was the sort of area in Newcastle where the police always glanced anxiously around. There was no immediate reply although they could hear movement from within, so he hammered again more loudly.

A face appeared at the window and then eventually the door was opened. A man appeared half-dressed in shirt and trousers, wiping soap off his face.

'Good morning, gentlemen of the law.' he greeted them with mock solemnity, while still contriving to block their entry. 'Wot can we do for the representatives of the Northumbrian constabulary at this hour of the morning?'

'Come off it, Sammy,' said the senior officer, 'it isn't you we are interested in to-day, not unless you want to make a confession to us, in which case,' and all three chorused, 'anything you say will be...'

'We want to interview Steve,' said the other policeman.

Sammy without appearing to offer any impediment to their entry, yet contrived to do so.

'Steve?' he said interrogatively.

'Steve Moran,' said the younger man brusquely. 'Come on, We know he lives here. May we come in?'

The pair made as to enter while Sammy made a

sweeping bow with little obsequiousness. 'Welcome, O fuzz.' he announced loudly.

'Which is Moran's room?' The police officers began to suspect that they were being stalled.

'First on the right, upstairs,' said Sammy, 'but I don't think he is in.' He smirked as the younger constable threatened to push him out of the way.

After that they did not really expect to find Steve Moran in his room. There were other cubicles in the hostel let out to DHSS tenants but these were locked and apparently empty, and they could not force entry without a warrant.

'There is only my 'umble self 'ere,' said Sammy, 'but if Steve comes 'ome, I shall tell him you called.'

'You tell him, Sammy, we want to ask him some questions and he could help by coming voluntary like to the station. If he helps us, man, we can help him.'

'My foot,' said Sammy, or something like it, as he watched the car drive off.

Steve emerged from one of the upstairs rooms and made sure the coast was clear.

'Ta, Sammy,' he said, and went back to his own room to finish dressing. He was not as fussy about shaving as his friend, and he came down to the kitchen where he sat looking miserable and scruffy, drawing on the last of half a cigarette.

'Wot d'yer think, Sammy?' he said at last.

'Steven my boy, it is clear our friends know about what you were up to last night, that is, someone has shopped you. You can't stay here, 'cos they have this address and yer can't stay in Newcastle 'cos the DHSS won't pay for other flipping digs like. Yer'll 'ave to git out. And if the fuzz really know about yer flogging snow, I should say, git out quick.' His diction faltered on longer speeches.

'Yer better go and be a 'omeless person in Scotland, besides the papers are always saying, there's a bit of a drug problem over the Border which might solve yours.'

'Don't you get at me too, Sammy,' he snapped at him, 'I've got enough on my flipping back without you sticking your knife in.'

He went upstairs to pack, checked how many snorts he had left. If he mixed in some chalk he would have enough to push in town as well as to have some for himself. Sammy went out and returned to report that there was still a police car at the exit to the estate.

'Yer'll have to foot it across the park, Steve. I tell you what I'll do. About six o'clock, you get all ready. I go to the end of the terrace and drop a match into the big litter bin, casual like. The coppers will come see what's aboot, and you scarper out the back.'

'What the hell are you doing here, Sammy.' said the constable at the wheel of the car as it braked abruptly beside the blaze.

'Practising for Guy Fawkes night,' he replied.

Steve Moran took the bus to the airport, there was no point in trying to hitch before that. He had spruced himself up as best he could and carried a small canvas bag. He would have liked to have had a rucksack to look like a proper hiker but it was not a normal part of his possessions, and inconsiderately none of the other occupants of the hostel had left one out to be borrowed.

He had a few quid in his pocket, and that would last him until he could register at a Scottish Social Security office. Sammy had said 'They don't tell the fuzz nuffin, confidential like it all is. Anyways, don't suppose our lot talk to their Scotch oppos, different language like.'

With these comforting thoughts, he took to the highway, and within a few minutes was picked up by a truck heading north. 'Can't take you far, mate,' said the driver, 'just to Otterburn, but you'll get a B and B. there.' He sized up his companion. 'Going far?'

'Going to see my aunt in Jedburgh,' Steve said rather unconvincingly, and the driver took it as such, and was glad to set his passenger down in the village before turning off to his yard. He said afterwards to the plain clothes constable that he thought there was something funny about the fellow.

Steve still felt all right, he did not need anything, the quick lift had given his confidence a boost. He knocked at the first house that had 'vacancies' displayed.

He thought he better try a different explanation. 'I'm going to see about a job in Edinburgh.'

'Are you in a car?' she asked. 'There's private parking round the back.'

'They didn't send me the fare,' he said, 'so I've had to hitch.'

She was a little reluctant to take him. He could see her hesitating.

'Just the night,' he said, 'and the notice says you have vacancies.'

'All right,' she said, 'just the one night.' She took comfort from the presence of the man who had arrived with his wife on bicycles, much more the sort of people she preferred to lodge.

She watched the latest arrival sign the book. He seemed to have difficulty writing his name. Imagination was never Steve's strong point and the police later were able to identify Steve Smith without too much difficulty. Anyway she had described him clearly, 'a small man, not very well shaven, who looked ill with wild eyes that stared at you. He didn't eat much breakfast, and I always give my guests quite the best breakfast in Otterburn.'

AN UNHAPPY DISCOVERY AT JEDBURGH

'Before the cross was the body laid'
The Lay of the Last Minstrel: Sir Walter Scott

I

'He's a junkie,' said Roger to his wife next morning as they had seen their fellow guest take to the road and tucked into the famous breakfast. 'You can tell by the eyes, and I don't think he will go far without needing a shot of whatever he takes to keep him going. Probably see him in the ditch, he headed north.'

'I'm surprised our landlady took him in,' said Daphne, 'but she did say it had been a desperately poor season and she needed every customer she could get.'

They paid their dues and prepared themselves once more for the road before mounting a little stiffly onto their bicycles. These were a sturdy pair of machines and, as they had found out on the climb from Corbridge, fully equipped with a good range of gears as well as panniers for their light luggage.

From time to time they could ride together but as the traffic increased they were forced to stay singly and could only exchange shouted comments.

'I see what they mean by going up north, it isn't the same as going up to London,' remarked Roger, changing into an even lower gear.

'Can't hear.'

He tried again as a lorry passed.

She shook her head.

'It doesn't matter. Is it uphill all the way?' he laughed to himself.

'He was in that Forestry Commission lorry,' she shouted back.

'Who?'

15

'That horrid man from the guesthouse.'

'Good luck to him, wish we were.' He spoke rather breathlessly. 'How far to lunch?'

The bleak, grass moors of the army ranges rose to the right of them, while to the left they could see the dark, endless woodlands which surround the Kielder Lake. As they ran down the dip in the road to Catcleugh Reservoir, Roger noticed the junkie coming out of a copse ahead of them.

'He hasn't got far. I expect the Forestry truck stopped here.'

'Let's stop here, too.' said Daphne, 'I don't want to come up with him particularly.'

At the picnic area the sky was light and the air fresh. 'Bliss was it in that dawn to be alive but to be young is very heaven,' declaimed Roger through his ham sandwich. 'Not that it is dawn and perhaps we aren't so young.' He glanced affectionately at his wife. 'But we are alive.' A group of lorries growled past on the main road and they watched as their man stood vainly thumbing at them.

'I hope he appreciates the good clean hill air that he's breathing,' said Daphne.

'Probably be too much for him,' said Roger, unkindly, as they saw Steve Moran clamber into the front of a large truck. 'That should take him into Scotland, it'll be heading for Jedburgh at least.'

Daphne felt relieved. The man seemed to offer something offensive, something intrusive into her country idyll and she preferred to have him removed from the scene.

They resumed their climb. At some points even the mountain gears were of no avail so they dismounted happily to plod up the last steep slopes to Carter Bar.

'There you are,' said Daphne. 'Worth while, isn't it.'

They propped up their bicycles against the large, convenient stone and sat on the verge to survey the scene. Green, undulating hills stretched before them, plunging into secret valleys. Only in the misty distance could they see signs of habitation where the white houses of a village caught the fitful sunshine. The wind was gently herding clouds across the sky, one moment allowing the light to brighten a hillside or a wood, the next leaving it in shadow.

'Can't see any abbeys,' said Roger, 'but I'm afraid our English armies did not leave much of them.

There was a sudden alarming noise behind them, a kilted figure emerged from behind the stone. But it was only a piper warming up his drones to offer them a skirl on his pipes as a welcome to Scotland

Then a small coach and a Land Rover drew up beside them to remind them of the road. 'I think we better go on if we want to find a bed and get a meal in Jedburgh. We can visit the Abbey to-morrow.'

'Watch your brakes,' said Roger. 'Scotland, here we come.'

II

John Brearley brought his coach to a halt in the lay-by, announcing to his party that they had reached the border between Scotland and England. The buzz of conversation had increased as they had climbed the curving road to the ridge and now they all dismounted in excitement. The few who had been there before eagerly pointed out landmarks they thought to be familiar. Brearley generally chose to drive the coach as he was more experienced than his colleague with the difficulties of the British roads. Macdonald took the Land Rover that they brought with them for special journeys and smaller expeditions. It gave them independence as well as anonymity when required.

They always stopped at the Border, even in driving rain and mist; it allowed the party to stretch their legs, to fuss about with their cameras, and to enjoy glimpses of what they could make out through the smur of the promised land. Brearley as usual remarked softly to Gus as they watched all the camera clicking. 'If you can't see the hills, its bloody raining, and if you can see them it's about to rain.'

He shepherded the party, the twenty-one of them, back aboard, drove them down the winding road criss-crossing

the river with its red cliffs into Jedburgh, where Gus pointed out the stark features of the Abbey, then took them to
their hotel, twelve miles distant. There were the usual problems of luggage and rooms, the search for possessions lost
under the seats of the vehicle and the checking of meals for
the three vegetarians. Mrs Oldberger , in a loud voice, chose
to announce at this moment that all she wanted was to get
tucked into a good piece of Scotch beef, preferably on the
bone.

'Your introductory lecture to-night is at 8 o'clock in the
conference room,' Gus reminded them. 'It is shown on your
schedule,' pronouncing it skedule so that there could be no
mistake, 'Ian McShea will introduce us to the Myths and
Legends of the Scottish Borders.'

Later that evening, John, Gus and the lecturer settled
down over their drinks at a nearby inn. McShea looked out
of place; he wore a black leather jacket to substantiate his
working class origins and a kilt to evince his Scottish ones.
The two couriers took off their blazers, loosened the ties
under their collars, and stretched out their legs under the
table prepared to relax.

'Kissed 'em all good-night, J?' asked Gus.

'I don't know that I fancy any of them,' Brearley replied,
draining his glass, and ordering another round. 'They're
much as usual.' He dealt with the passports on the tour and
took the trouble to check the details, flicking through the
visa stamps.

'What are they like this time?' asked McShea.'

Brearley set the glasses down before replying.

'There are the four women school teachers, probably
camp, three old couples, doing their tours in search of culture or long lost Scottish ancestors, and the usual lot of widows or divorcees like Mrs Oldberger who having exhausted
their men, now clutter up the world. Then there's that fee-
ble looking git, Dwight Graham Jnr, retired attorney, he
calls himself, so bloody loaded with cameras you'd think
he'd fall down and break up, and then that younger fellow,
Harry someone. He flicked open the passport. 'Harry S.
Webb, who's always reading and asking questions which

the guides can't answer. Can't say I fancy any of them. Then there's the two young couples who brighten things up.'

He glanced quizzically at his partner. He himself had a strict rule that he never became involved with any of his touring group but he was never sure about Gus, or even in which direction his sex drive took him. He had after all opportunities to follow matters up back in the States. For Brearley, business and women had to be kept apart, especially in his business. Even the woman who shared his bed and his computerised accounts was only able to reach halfway into the machine.

They continued to chat over their drinks. There was a sociable hum from the crowd in the small bar. Glancing around and at the clock, Brearley at last pulled out the next day's programme from his brief case.

'Time, lads,' he said. It's Jedburgh tomorrow, usual day, Abbey, hotel lunch and Queen Mary's House. They all lapped up what you gave them tonight, Ian. You'll meet us here the day after tomorrow for your spiel on Kelso. Business as usual.'

They exchanged glances. McShea picked up his brief-case and moved slightly unsteadily to the door to take himself back to Edinburgh.

'I hope the bugger's all right on the road, J.' remarked Macdonald as he watched the man depart.

'So do I,' said Brearley, as he, too, took up his briefcase and retired to bed

III

Steve Moran was groping his way around Jedburgh. He was not feeling all that well. He kept reassuring himself that he was clear of Newcastle but now he was in a world that he did not understand. He remembered his almost hostile reception by the woman in Otterburn and thought that he had better shave. Anyway he could do with another snort.

'Toilets' he looked for and following the signs discovered that he had to pay to enter. Inside, there was hot water and a clean basin. His small, wizened face broke into a smile. Sammy was right, Scotland would be O.K.

He fumbled in his bag to find his razor, and, using the soap provided, contrived a shave with a shaky hand. He took the bag with him into the toilet cubicle, checked the contents of the envelopes carefully, put a pinch to his nose, and, after dusting himself down, emerged with renewed optimism to face whatever landlady he could find.

He wanted somewhere not too conspicuous near the town centre. At the first house he tried, the man said that they were full, but he should try the second door along where his wife's aunt sometimes did a B and B.

'Aye,' she said, 'come in and I'll show you the room. I canna do tea, but you'll get that in the toon.'

It was small but clean, almost cheerful with the evening sunlight filtering through the gauze curtains. Moreover it was cheap. Steve did a quick check on his money. He would be all right for a day or two but he would need to sell.

He thanked the woman, signed her book with a little more confidence but no more accuracy than in Otterburn, waited until she had returned to the kitchen before, within the privacy of the room, unpacking the bag and transferring an envelope to his pocket. It was still just light as he made a tour of the town. There was only really the one main street running up to the abbey and the castle jail. What he was looking for was a bar that appeared only semi-respectable. He made his way though the door, as if searching for someone, but soon realised that this was not Newcastle. There was not the bustle of the end of an urban working day. He wondered if there was a dance that evening and examined posters and notice boards unsuccessfully. Then he remembered it was Sunday. Eventually he settled into a pub corner with a vodka and packet of crisps, prepared to wait.

The room was L-shaped and furnished with bare wooden tables. Round the corner from him was a piano at which sat a short, stout man toying with the keys. Between him and Steve was a young man with an effeminate face rolling his own cigarettes. When Steve rose to refill his glass, he re-seated himself nearer the youth.

'Can you give us a tune, man?' he said to the pianist to break the silence. The man strummed once more on his keyboard.

'What do you fancy, Geordie?' He struck up with the Bladon Races. ' Something like that?' Steve let the corner of the white envelope stick out of his pocket and saw the youth's eyes wander towards it.

A few more men came in. They were each wearing the same coloured blazers with a crest on the breast pocket. The noise increased as they ordered their drinks. When others came in similarly dressed, the room was filled with large creatures with loud voices. Steve realised that it was a rugby team. Not his scene. He pinned his hope on the youth.

When the glasses were refilled the singing started at the bar with the pianist picking up the tune. Some beer spilled as the team jostled at the counter, loud laughter interrupted the song, and there was some kind of punch-up in the corner until the landlord intervened.

It was time to go. Steve pushed the table away from him.

'Gotta have a piss,' he said, glancing at his companion. The boy nodded and followed him to the gents. They delayed until the place was empty.

Steve pointed towards the toilet cubicle and they went inside.

'A tenner,' he said, 'it's the real stuff, pure.'

The youth examined the contents of the envelope carefully and hesitated.

'Come on, come on, pal,' Steve urged him, terrified of imminent incursion into the toilets. 'A fiver, then.'

The deal was completed and they made to come out. But it was too late. A large rugby forward, bomb happy, surged through the swing doors to see them emerging.

'Dirty bastards,' he shouted, and two of his team mates joined him. 'Dirty bastards,' he shouted again, punching

Steve in the stomach.

In the end it was not clear who was hitting who. The rugby players were happy to have an excuse for a fight, and finally Steve found himself in the street with the noise of battle continuing inside. He did not wait to see the fate of his customer, but stumbled into the first dark alley to be violently sick. He fingered his head carefully, remembering that he had struck a washbasin when he fell.

He put his hand into his pocket and felt for the five pound note: it was not there. He fumbled desperately in his other pockets. All his money and the envelope had gone.

He realised that he was not well. It was not just the result of the scrap, he had been used to finding his way out of those situations, his doctor had warned him that his much abused body could tolerate little further strain. Suddenly there was a surge of noise and light into the street behind him, and a shout of 'dirty little poofter, where are you?'

He forced himself to stumble on. The sound of his foot-steps encouraged his pursuers, who turned, baying, in his directions. He could not even remember where he lodged if he had had the courage to face his landlady.

Another dark alley presented itself with a light at the end. He plunged in and halted abruptly when he saw the large notice saying 'Police and Sheriff Court.'

'O Gawd, no!' He groaned, and ran on. To his right there was a wall with railings and, against the sky, the clear outline of the ruined Abbey. The rabble behind him had halted, perhaps daunted by the police station, though he had no time to think of that. But there was movement again in the street below him as he circled the wall. There was a corner where the ironwork met a hedge. With the last spur of fear he hauled himself onto the parapet and scrambled over the railings to lie helpless in the rank grass of the graveyard. He could run no further and, fortunately for him, the rugby team decided honour had been satisfied and returned to the bar.

As the evening fell silent in the town, he shifted himself slowly from the dampness, groping his way on all fours towards the stonework of the old building. He picked his way over the foundations of old walls. The shape of the tower rose above him while the remnants of the transepts protected him from the falling rain and offered him a sense of security from his enemies. He crept into the shelter of a tombstone, wedged himself against the wall as best he could and collapsed into the long sleep of total exhaustion.

IV

'I'll tell you something,' said the retired custodian of Ancient Monuments with whom Daphne and Roger had found lodging, as he saw them breakfasting, 'I'll tell you something as you are educated folk. If you want to see the Abbey, dinna gang in by the fancy path the Edinburgh offeecials have set up. When you come through the vestibule, tak the one marked way oot. It will bring you up by the cloister and tak you into the west end, where it says processional route, and then, yince you're in, you can stand and see the hale line of the building in all its glory, nave, choir and crossing, richt through to the east end.'

Jedburgh Abbey stands or in completeness stood, on a rise above the Jed Water. The body of the kirk is the best surviving of the four Border Abbeys. Except for the east end, the yellow stone structure of the building, the nave with its aisles, the triforium and clerestory with their nine windows remains as an entire but roofless shell. Of the transepts where Moran had sought shelter, the north one is a private tomb and the one to the south has collapsed. Only the foundations of the canons' habitation are left and it is across these by ramps and bridges that the visitor is led.

The Real Tours coach decanted its Americans into the Abbey car park from where Brearley conducted them to the entry point at the foot of the hill.

'Gee,' said Mrs Oldberger as she looked up at the powerful outline catching the morning sun, 'Gee, ain't it just great, so peaceful.'

'So sad,' said one of the teachers, 'Such a symbol of

man's destructiveness,' and she meant man's.

The group crowded into the small shop and ticket office to busy itself among the shelves, while Brearley identified himself.

'Real Tours have a group concession,' he said loudly, 'and will provide you with the guidebook which should be enough. On our return here there will be time for you to browse.'

As his party collected to ascend the ramp, Daphne and Roger, who preceded them, followed their landlord's advice and took the path in reverse order, heading for the Abbey's west end.

There were few other visitors at this early hour. As they passed the western edge of the cloister, now but a herb garden, a stocky figure moved briskly past them. Military, thought Roger later, with a narrow moustache and precise dress., but they barely noticed the gardener at work among the gravestones.

The couple stood in respectful awe at the Abbey's main entrance below the intricate rose window in the gable and admired the long, narrow nave and the rounded arch of the crossing under the tower. Then they climbed the slender, spiral staircase that lead to the clerestory to reach the halfway gallery. From there they could see the whole length of the church as the sun streamed through the upper windows to fill the skeleton building with light.

The silence they were enjoying was broken by the arrival of the tourists at the transept door, there was a surge of chatter and a brandishing of cameras as they burst in and fanned out. They moved for the most part into the nave, taking in its sad majesty, but a few advanced beneath the tower towards the east.

It was always disputed who saw it first, Mrs Oldberger was certainly one of them but she said Dwight spotted it and held her back. When she let out a shriek, Brearley came up quickly to see what the trouble was, and he, too, could see the body on the ground, face downwards with the arms stretched out like a cross. It was a man's body and it looked very dead, and it lay with the tiny plaque 'Place of High

Altar' at its head.

'Just stay where you are, don't come forwards,' he shouted. He had one rule about bodies, not to go near them. For one thing many of those he had dealt with were booby trapped, and for another it never paid to get entangled with the law. He could not afford the time.

Attracted by the sudden agitation Roger and Daphne descended to join the murmuring crowd collected between the four great pillars supporting the fabric of the tower.

Roger peered over the shoulders of the women to discover what they are looking at. He could see the two men holding back their party with some difficulty. Realising that the group was foreign, he suggested that he should go and seek help from the office.

'This'll be just great,' said Mrs Schumacher, inching forward with her camera. 'Dead body we found in ruined Scotch Abbey.' Brearley kept begging them to keep back.

'You can see he's dead, people just don't lie like that. We can't do anything. Please stay where you are and let me do the talking. None of you want to have to give evidence of the finding of the body. For Christ's sake don't go near it. He's dead, you can't do anything.' The last thing he wanted was this kind of complication with his tour.

Summoned by telephone, Constable Brian Hedges came swiftly out of the Jedburgh Police Station that stands on the corner of the Abbey grounds. He could see the crowd at the end of the building, but determined to act correctly, he proceeded down the hill to pass through the office to remount by the ramps.

He pushed his way through the women to where the men were screening the figure on the ground.

'We had just come in, constable, when we saw this, this body.' said Brearley. 'I could see he was dead so I have kept everyone away.'

Hedges bent over the corpse to be sure and stepped back to extract his portable telephone from its pouch. The station sergeant summoned a doctor and passed the details to Hawick before joining Hedges.

'You had better take down all the names and addresses,'

he said to his constable. Brearley quickly explained that they were all in his party, except these two, he pointed to the Stones. 'I can give you a list of my Americans,' he said, 'but you will understand, sergeant, I do not want this -' he was going to say bugger up, but changed it 'to cause any inconvenience to my party. It would be very bad for your Borders tourism.'

'Quite right, sir,' said the sergeant. 'Mustn't do anything like that. You say your going on to Queen Mary's House and lunching at the hotel, just check with us before you go.'

Mr and Mrs Stone explained that they were on a bicycling tour.

'I do not suppose we shall want to take any statement from you since you were not one of the finders of the fatality,' he said.

'Who are you?' He asked Thornell who had joined the throng and stood at the side with his hoe. Thornell explained who he was and what he did in the Abbey grounds. 'Hae you seen this mannie afore?.' The sergeant lapsed into his doric, when he realised that he was speaking with a local.

Thornell peered down at the corpse.

'At's a Magpie's scairf, he's wearin, Newcastle United colours. I came in nine o'clock to stairt ma wirk and I never saw that mon before.'

Interrupted by the arrival of the doctor, the sergeant turned to greet him while Hedges made a note of Thornell's name and address.

'He's dead, all right,' said the local G.P., happy to be summoned from the tedium of his daily round of chronic cases, 'can't tell you much more. I'll leave that to your own surgeon.' He moved the head slightly. 'He seems to have a gash on his temple but that does not look lethal. But I should say he did not die in that position, He's been stretched out to lie in the shape of a cross. Funny that, given where he's lying. He doesn't look the sort of fellow to want an altar as a pillow.'

By the time the detective sergeant and the police doctor came from Hawick, several coach loads of visitors were thronging the entrance lobby and its approaches. After a further examination of the corpse which showed no unnatural cause of death, the detective in charge consulted the Procurator Fiscal who agreed to the removal of the body and the reopening of the site. It was only later that they regretted their swift reaction.

The police investigators found a DSS card in an inner pocket of the scruffy jacket in the name of Stephen Moran, of No 18 Bellingham Terrace, Newcastle upon Tyne, and those in the morgue quickly discovered the unmistakable white grains in another. By late afternoon and after a few telephone calls, the shabby details of the dead man's life were laid bare. Subsequently the night's encounter with the visiting rugby team became known.

Meanwhile the Jedburgh sergeant caught up with Real Tours and, having made sure he had their names and the plan of their itinerary, wished the Americans an enjoyable tour. Only the inquisitive Harry S. Webb ventured to ask if anything had been discovered about the dead man.

'A man from Newcastle,' said the sergeant, 'seems he just dropped dead. Probably hypothermia.'

'Funny way to drop dead,' said the retired attorney, rather hoping it had been something more dramatic.

Mr and Mrs Stone, calling at the police station, found they were free to proceed but gleaned little more about the event. As they set out for the twelve miles to Kelso, Roger glanced up at the Abbey ruin casting its shadow towards them in the evening sunlight.

'I expect the custodians check the place last thing at night, so our friend must have climbed in later. I can see where you could get in with a bit of a scramble. He goes into the ruins, stretches himself out and dies. Bit odd to lie face downwards with your arms splayed out. We must have been with those Americans about the first in this morning.'

'I'm glad we took the advice of going round in reverse otherwise we should have stumbled on the body.' said Daphne.

'I expect it gave the ladies from the U.S.A. the thrill of a lifetime.' said her husband sardonically.

'I don't know about that,' suggested Daphne. 'Don't they spend their time shooting each other over there.'

KELSO'S DARK PORCH

*'A huge ruin frowns over the pleasant market town, more like
a fortified castle than the residence of peaceful monks'*
**Hill Burton in Baronial and Ecclesiastical Antiquities:
Billings, 1852.**

I

There was nothing like an untoward event to bond the
party together. Brearley always watched anxiously at the
outset of a tour to prepare for inharmonious rifts or unde-
sirable liaisons that would upset its smooth running. It was
generally the single women who were responsible; some
deep-seated emotional disturbance would trigger wholly
unreasonable outbursts over the most trivial of mishaps.

While he drove the coach back to the hotel, he listened
to the conversation among the passengers who were happily content with their encounter with death and the reassuring stability of the local police, now captured on film. Even
Mrs Oldberger could think of no similar incident in
Stratford.

She leant forward with a waft of exotic perfume from
the seat behind him, her ringed fingers resting by his shoulder.

'John,' she said, 'do you think that those Scotch policemen really told us everything? I just can't think of anyone
lying down and dying like that. There must be something
deeply significant in that position, something religious, I
would say. You know we have all these cults in the United
States and this is the kind of thing they do, commit suicide
high on drugs. Only they generally do it in some sort of
group.' She sounded regretful as if the Abbey had let her
down.

She breathed heavily behind him. 'Now, I reckon if Will
Shakespeare had been around, he could have made a darn
good play of it like that one with all the killings in it, what
was it called, the one you took us last time.'

29

He was not really listening to her, tuned into other talk at the back of the bus. 'You mean Titus Andronicus? Lots of blood in that.'

She leant back and he was free to resume his consideration of the party. The three, elderly married couples were all right. As long as he kept them comfortable, they would be contented, and they did not look as any of them would take ill or drop dead. The modern requirement of medical certificates by the airlines helped eliminate that risk. The two young honeymoon couples would be no trouble, although you never knew, they'd be too wrapped up with themselves. God knows why they came on this sort of trip. Mr and Mrs Peter Bryant and Mr and Mrs Michael May, the matches, he called them, Bryants and Mays, and laughed inwardly at his joke. The five lone and older women, widows or divorcees, perhaps, murmured amongst themselves. The youngest, Margaret something or other was still attractive enough to excite men, but he only had the two that were unattached. He did not like the Henry fellow, too nosey, the tall attorney was harmless enough, visible across the aisle, fussing with his cameras.

He listened to the higher pitched chatter of the four female school teachers at the rear. He could hear the short, dark woman with the square, almost masculine face, Jane Marshall, laying down the law about something. He never liked domineering women. The other three, the tall blond, Ruth McKinley and the two rather slighter women, tended to follow her but he sensed there were already tensions arising among the four of them.

He had to take a group of twenty one because of a last minute cancellation and, while he could carry the surcharge on the single occupation, it did lead to complications in sharing accommodation. One of the teachers was Mrs O's niece so they liked to share, the two men were together and he had left it to the other single women to sort out who had the room on her own.

The seating arrangements in the dining room, too, could cause trouble. Early on in the tour he generally arranged for one large table to accommodate everyone until the party split into groups of its own choosing. He had to observe closely that there was no loner left in isolation, or in the case of frictions, that the parties were discreetly kept apart.

That evening seemed set to be peaceful. The day's events provided a topic of conversation. After they had repaired to their rooms to pursue their own devices, they came down to meet in the hotel drawing room. Initial uncertainties were wearing off: the older couples congregated together in the comfort of armchairs and mahogany tables while the younger ones went into the cocktail bar. John Brearley made it his duty to flit between them.

'You can go easy on your before dinner Manhattans, ladies,' he said to the elderly, 'Real Tours is standing you wine at dinner tonight.' While among the younger and the unattached in the cocktail bar, he would say, 'lay a good foundation, Real Tours will throw in some real wine at the table.' Mrs Oldberger, clad in her fully fashioned, magenta frock, had followed him through and wagged her finger at him.

'You naughty man, John, encouraging the young to drink,' as she took a swig from her evening gin and smirked at the company.

'Aunt, don't you look just great,' said her niece, Molly, dutifully, after all, her trip was being paid for. She looked ruefully around, already the companionship of her three fellow teachers was beginning to pall, and she to regret that she had persuaded them to come with her. She envied the completeness of the Bryants and Mays chatting in animation in the corner.

It was Brearley's habit to mix briefly with his party at the end of the day, to listen to any complaints and try to smooth them out. There would be the usual kind of 'I don't want to make a fuss, John, but...' when one couple found that they did not enjoy the same view from the window as an other, or 'I simply must have a different mattress for my back, it always gives me the gyps in the fall.' He would listen sympathetically, which was most important, and solve those practical problems that could be resolved.

Tonight while he kept Mrs Oldberger at bay, he was

edgy. Up to a point the disturbance at Jedburgh did no harm but he did not like involvement with the police. He could hear Jane Marshall's deep voice again. 'No way, Beth,' she was saying, 'you know we agreed that you and Ruth would take turns to have your own room, and it's your turn tonight.'

'I wanna be with you, Jane,' said the other, and Brearley could see out of the edge of his eye, her almost tearful countenance. The one called Beth, Beth Havers. Brearley recalled, put her hand onto Jane's and he could sense rather than pick out any words, that she was telling them to talk more quietly.

When he returned to the drawing room, it was Mrs Sorenson who button holed him. Her husband, Niels, had taken on the position of senior statesman of the party, and he approached with his wife.

'I do hope, Mr Brearley,' she said anxiously, ' that you are giving us enough time at Abbotsford. I know all these ruins are said to be most interesting historically, but a lived-in house with the authors descendants still occupying it, is really what we want to see.'

Her husband standing beside her joined in.

'Yeah,' he said. 'A've been reading Sir Walter's novels, one by one, since last fall, while Elma, that's my wife here,' he added unnecessarily, 'has been studying his poetry. You just try her on the Lay of the Last Minstrel.'

Mrs Sorenson needed no further encouragement.

' " The way was long, the wind was cold,
The Minstrel was in form and old."' She began.

'I think, my dear, you meant to say infirm and old,' her husband interrupted gently but it gave the manager the opportunity to contrive an instant look of appreciation before replying.

'Yes, yes, of course,' he said. 'We shall have all Saturday at Abbotsford. Real Tours regard this as quite the high spot of our Borders Tour. From your reading both you and your wife will know that all these places we visit play an important part in Sir Walter's writings, particularly his verse. I shall ask our lecturer to make a point of drawing your attention to this in his talks. I hope you will not hesitate to ask him.'

After another tour of tactful inspection, John Brearley left them all to enjoy the good evening he enjoined upon them and retired to his separate lodging place. He and Gus stayed at a small inn about a mile away.

'Like a walk, Dwight?' asked Harry Webb, following Brearley's route from the bar window. 'We have a bit of time before dark.'

The older man said, 'Yeah, why not, give us an appetite for our dinner. I guess we have about half an hour.'

They made their way down the drive to the main road where they could see Brearley some way ahead of them.

'You been with Real Tours before?' Harry asked.

Dwight nodded. 'I came with my wife last year, but she took ill and we hardly left the hotels. She died right after we got back to the States and she said to me the night before she passed away. "Dwight, you go back and complete that tour, right properly, just in remembrance of me." So this is a kind of memorial trip.'

'That's just great,' said Harry, and then after a pause, 'is it just the same as last year?'

'I can't rightly tell you as I was so tied up with Jessica, that's my wife, being sick, so all the trips are new to me.'

'Do our two couriers never stay in the hotel with the tour?'

'Can't ever remember it but Jessica was that sick.'

They followed the road for a while, watching idly as Brearley entered the roadside inn, and noticing a car drawing into the car park.

'I think that that is our lecturer, what was his name, man in a kilt....?'

'McShea.'

'That's it. We are due another talk tomorrow.'

Their conversation continued blandly. Harry Webb seemed to be asking the questions, but Dwight Graham Jnr had one he hesitated to ask without longer acquaintance. He wanted to say,

'Harry, why do you carry a gun? I saw your shoulder

holster in the mirror when you were dressing.'

But he did not: and as the evening darkened and grew cold, they turned and made their way back to their own hotel.

II

Major Alistair Peter McAlistair sat broodily in his study, far gone into his melancholy. It had been an ill week. On the Monday the worst had happened. He had taken Keltie out as usual in the evening up the road to the sharp corner. As they had returned, with the dog no more than a few feet from his heels, a four wheeled drive vehicle had come too fast round the corner, struck the animal violently and sped on towards Northumberland.

He bent over Keltie, the need for action stemming his distress, and saw that the dog's back was broken. There was little he could do. He had always put down his dogs himself. There was no other traffic within sight or sound, no-one to help. He ran back to his cottage to fetch the pistol he kept for the purpose, and with only one short moment of hesitation shot Keltie through the head.

He collected a sack from the woodshed to carry the body into the garden where he buried it swiftly and efficiently.

It was only when he poured himself out the second of his evening whiskies that the tragedy of the event hit him and he wept, looking down on the emptiness of the carpet and aware of his utter solitude.

He tried to recall the car number. He did not think it had an S in it for Scotland but that did not matter, his whole hating of the English whom he perceived as the destroyers of his career now redoubled in his mind. Each day that he visited one of the Abbeys, he pictured the scene of its repeated destruction by the vandal armies from the south, raping a fair and peaceful land. They were the hideous forces of disorder that the monks and their monasteries had sought to hold at bay.

Now this had happened, the ultimate hit and run. The

fragile routine of his daily life threatened to fall apart. He had to become more rigorous in maintaining it, more attentive to his daily visits to the Abbeys, more assiduous in pressing the authorities to keep the graveyards in order.

He took another whisky, the one he usually took with Maisie when he brought the dog back in, and brooded once more. At any rate, the visit to Jedburgh had gone well. He had found that fellow, Jim someone, at work collecting litter and trimming the grass round the stones, perhaps his correspondence with Edinburgh had achieved something.

But it was not enough, there had to be order. He had heard the group of visitors arriving from the coach park. On another occasion had they been from England, he might have let fly at them. When he recognised them as American, having done what he felt he had to do, he had departed.

Tomorrow was his day for Kelso.

III

In the morning the party from the States gathered in the hotel conference room for their lecture. Ian McShea started punctually at nine o'clock because he had to be back at the University before midday as he kept his extramural activities to himself. When he began his talk a few latecomers arrived with intrusive apologies.

He enjoyed the freedom from close academic scrutiny that these occasions allowed, describing the development of the monastic system in the Borders and their contribution to the economy. It was not difficult to hint at the corruption of the church and the rapacity of all subsequent landowners. With more justification he described the iniquity of the sixteenth century destruction of Kelso by English armies.

'You will see in Kelso all that is left of what was once one of the greatest abbeys in Scotland, dedicated to the Saints Mary and John' He dealt with its founding originally in Selkirk and its translation to Kelso, its elaborate building by Norman craftsmen over a hundred years in the twelfth and thirteenth centuries and then with the stages of its destruction at the hands of English armies in 1523 and 1542. Finally it was almost totally brought down in Henry VIII's "Rough Wooing" when in 1545 twelve monks and ninety laymen held it against the Earl of Hertford's army until his guns made a breach in the church, forcing them to retreat to one of four towers.'

He went on. 'Burton in his 'History of Scotland' states. "The assault was given to the Spaniards but when they rushed in they found the place cleared. The nimble garrison had run to the strong square tower of the church and there they again held out. Night came before they could be dislodged from their last citadel" so the besiegers had to "leave the assault till the morning, setting a good watch all night about the house, which was not so well kept but that a dozen of the Scots in the darkness of the night escaped by ropes out of the back windows and corners with no little danger of their lives. When the day came, and the steeple eftsoons assaulted, it was immediately won and as many Scots slain as were within." '

He looked anxiously at his watch, mindful of the wary eye of his prowling head of department in Edinburgh.. 'I think I had better stop there. Those church defenders all came to a nasty end four hundred and fifty years ago, so you should not, I hope, find any dead bodies there today.' His audience dutifully gave a weak laugh, after all, yesterday's discovery had enlivened their tour, and trooped into the waiting coach.

McShea collected his papers and his briefcase from Brearley and departed.

Gus Macdonald generally presided over the party's visits in Scotland. He had the sharp features and tongue of a Glasgow Scot, and a leathery complexion from his years in the Texan sunshine. He could change his speech readily from an adopted Americanism to his native dialect. On these tours he enjoyed showing off his brogue.

Leaving his partner to follow later in the Land Rover, he settled into the driving seat of the coach, adjusted the microphone and began.

'Ladies and gentlemen, today's schedule is that Real

Tours will take you this morning to Floors Castle, then return you to Kelso to leave you to lunch where you wish and explore the town. It has excellent shopping facilities and the Abbey is open all day without a custodian. We shall pick you up at five o'clock in the coach park to return to the hotel unless any of you would like to stay on, in which case we shall arrange to pick you up later.'

'But we shall take you first across the river to show you where the Teviot joins the Tweed. In the old days, there was a large castle and an active town between the two rivers. It was called Roxburgh.' He pointed as the coach drew up. 'You see yon mound on the left, that was where the castle was, there are only a few bits left, and behind it was a town, they say the fourth largest in Scotland at the time, and of that there is nothing left.'

'What happened to it?' asked the attorney.

Gus was happy to be asked a question that he could answer.

'That's a good question, Mr Graham,' he said. 'The answer is that the Scots pulled it down because they got fed up with the English occupying it, and Kelso grew up to replace it.'

'Now,' he went on, 'if you look the other way, you will see Floors Castle, one of the greatest noble houses of the country owned by the Duke of Roxburghe, and,' he added with the little smile anticipating laughter, 'he spells his name with an 'e'.'

'Why does he do that?' asked the attorney who was sitting at the front.

Gus was not sure. 'I think because he is a duke,' he managed.

There was a collective sigh of satisfaction from his listeners. Mrs Oldberger felt that although it was not up to the high cultural standards of Stratford, it was at least a return to patrican levels.

'Real Tours will take you to the castle this morning for a full visit. The house,' he glanced quickly at his notes, 'was built by the architect and playright John Vanbrugh in 1718 and then in the middle of the nineteenth century handsomely transformed by Playfair into what you see now.'

He moved onto happier ground. 'I want to tell you to two things about it. The first is that if you have seen any of the Tarzan films, this castle was used as the setting for his ancestral home as Lord Greystoke. Do you remember it?'

The older members of the party murmured encouragingly, one said loudly and triumphantly to his wife and their neighbours, 'Me Tarzan, you Jane', while the younger ones smiled politely.

'One other thing,' Gus continued, 'You see that thorn tree in the park.' He could not but it did not matter. 'It marks the place where, when the Scottish King James II was besieging Roxburgh Castle for the last time, his cannon called the "Lion" blew up and killed him.'

'The books say,' and Gus prepared himself for dialect not within his normal capacity. It was a struggle but always impressed his customers.

' "But quhill this prince, mair curieous nor becam him or the majestie of ane King, did stand neir hand by the gunneris quhan the artaillerie was dischargeand, his thie bane was doung in twa with ane piece of ane misframit gun that brak in the schutting, be the quhilk he was strickin to the grund and dieit haistilie thereof, quhilk grettumlie discuragit all his nobill gentlemen and freindis that war standand aboot him." '

The effort won him a round of applause.

'Gee, isn't that just great,' said Mrs Oldberger, 'sounds straight out of that play by Shakespeare about Scotland, What was it called, John?'

The schoolteachers at the back followed Jane's example in applauding. Even Dwight Graham Jnr and Harry S. Webb were impressed, although the attorney could not refrain from remarking that everything they heard about the Borders always seemed to end in violent death.

IV

No such thought troubled Spike Jones in the town as he prepared for the day. He was a youngish man who had drifted north from London, working as a bartender. He would live in rough digs until he found a girl to share with. Generally after a while they would fall out and he would move on. He had picked up Kathy in Newcastle and she had suggested they went back to her home town in Kelso.

'Dad's deid,' she said, 'and ma Mum wilna mind if we share the bed. There's only twa in the hoose.'

When she met him he had a spike of hair carefully tended above his forehead to give his hatchet face a full Mohican look, but when he applied for a job at The Feathers, the landlord had said.

'I'll gie you a job, just a trial, mind, but ye'll hae to tak the thing off, we're no keen on that sort of fancy hair style in the toon.'

He retained his nickname without its inspiration. That was five years ago and with his shaven head, earrings and easy nature he had settled happily into the life of the town. He did not have to rise early in the morning and could join Kathy contentedly after his evening's duties. It was the pleasant existence of providing people with what they wanted.

Not long after he had felt established, a man in dark glasses had come into the bar which happened to be empty and chatted to him, he did not give his name, but had a kind of Scottish accent, Spike thought. They had arranged to meet by the riverside the next day when he was off duty.

'Spike,' he had said, 'would you like to do us a favour which would do you no harm either. You're the sort of man who ken what folk want. We could drop you off some stuff,' he stressed the word and caught the barman's eye, 'and we can arrange to collect the cash from you.'

'We play fair and will let you have the first lot free, then you let us have the lolly before you get the next package. You keep ten percent, but,' and he looked hard at Spike, 'but we have no time for pikers. You play straight and we play straight.'

Spike was not averse to the odd joint and he was often asked for the real stuff. He had nodded. This was a proper bit of business that he could handle.

'You'll know many of the right people, won't you, having a key job like yours?' the man continued, 'I know a shrewd operator when I meet one.'

'We won't meet again, better not, but I'll telephone you with time and place where you drop off the cash, we collect and leave you the next lot of stuff.'

Moving into the discreet shelter of some trees, he had scribbled down Spike's number and passed him a small parcel. They parted and Spike went home with a new sense of importance.

V

Jim Thornell parked his motor bicycle under the trees by the old graveyard behind the Abbey, When he had started on his round of work, he thought that he might earn more if he included the area in the job but they would not let him.

The grounds of the Abbey itself were small, once the grass had ceased growing, there was not much to do. They had asked him to start painting the railings when autumn set in. With the grass cut, he would leave the mower out of the shed with a spanner handy and smoke out of sight round the corner from the tower, ready to appear mechanically concerned when voices or footsteps alerted him.

In his boredom during his dinner hour, he had met Spike and, later, Kathy. After a few more encounters, Spike had said.

'Could you do me a favour, Jim, and take a package to Bill in Hawick? Here's his address and here's a fiver for you.'

Later in the evening he met Jim where his motor bicycle was parked under the trees in the square, and his bicycle panniers took back to Hawick more than the newspaper.

'Just take this to Bill in Hawick. Here's his address. You don't need to know what's in it. Here's a starter.'

'A clever fellow like you'll know a lot of folk in Hawick,' Spike had said later, tapping the side of his nose. 'But don't ask questions. The first lots free, but you bring me back the ready and I'll see you all right.'

Kelso days, Mrs Thornell began to recognise, were those when Jim came back with money and very often late. She did not like the horses but he seemed to be on a winning streak.

For Spike and Kathy time was not generally a problem. Opening and closing was what mattered to him but she had noticed the occasional, early morning phone calls that stirred him early from his bed. She asked no questions when that morning the call came through.

'Is that you, Spike?' the voice said.

She could hear his 'Yeah, yeah.'

'Put your packet in the usual place at six, tonight and then come back at ten. Same as the last run, and all divided into the amounts I asked for. Can you manage those times exactly. We don't want any cock-ups.'

'Yeah,' he said again, 'no problem.'

But it was to be one of those days when time was to be the problem.

Their small bedroom had coomed ceilings and with little space they had set a dressing table in the single window recess. Lifting the floorboard at the side he could reach into the eave recess to stash both the packages he received and the cash he collected. With a crude notion of concealment he occasionally spilt some of his wife's perfume over the skirting to put off those sniffer dogs he saw on the television.

He waited until Kathy had gone down stairs and then with his knife lifted the board and made a long arm to extract a tin. He checked the money inside and transferred the notes to a sponge bag. They always asked for notes of twenty pounds or less and it made a bulky packet. It was easy for him to change the larger ones in the bar till since it was usually he who paid the day's takings into the bank.

Spike's philosophy of life was an easy one. Right and wrong did not bother him. If a fellow dealt straight with him, he would deal straight. If he thought he was being deprived of his dues, he would happily cheat. He liked to feel useful, he got a kick out of dodging the law. The man dealt fairly. 'Take your ten per cent,' he said. Spike counted out the notes again, took his share and placed it in another tin under the boards. It was there for a rainy day, perhaps they would have kids, he thought. No mortgage, no trouble with his mother in law, though he could not give her that formal title. They were not short of a bob or two, and he could give Kathy a slap-up dinner some place.

Concealing the large bag under his blue anorak he made his way to the pub where he locked it in a drawer. He cleared up the usual debris from the night before, and prepared to open for lunchtime.

'Can you rin the place your own the night?' asked the owner. 'Mary and I have to go to Edinburgh, Meg's been taken sick.'

Spike hid his frustration. He could not object to the man going to look after a daughter. He knew the man's wife did not drive. Why did it have to happen today of all days when he needed to have the time to reach his rendezvous?

'Yeah,' he managed, 'Yeah, no problem.'

Later he made an excuse to go out. He crossed the large square in the centre of the town. A touring coach was unloading a voluble bunch of visitors outside the hotel. He could recognise the loud voices as transatlantic. The side of the vehicle carried the slogan of Real Tours, Real Comfort. For a moment he thought he recognised his original contact amongst them but it seemed unlikely. He walked up Bridge Street towards the Abbey but it was thronged with visitors. He clearly could not go in early. The man had said exactly six o'clock. The trouble was he had to go in twice, once to place the cash and then to return for the package. The whole point of the scheme was that the parties never saw each other. He would have to hope for a lull at the bar in the evening.

After lunch at the hotel, the Americans assembled in the

town's handsome square before dispersing, some to go to
the Abbey ruins directly, some to abandon culture in favour
of the shops and some to enjoy the riverside walks.

Macdonald rather wearily directed the elderly towards
the Abbey a hundred yards away.

'Yes, there's no custodian, you don't have to pay. The
bookshop will have the postcards,' he repeated.

Mrs Sorenson, having discovered that Sir Walter had
been at school in the town was determined to find the
building itself, and he had to remind her that she was probably two centuries too late.

He had not Brearley's easy manner: by the end of the
morning and lunch in charge of the party, his temper
became frayed. He let his eye follow Margaret Lake who
attracted him; she hovered on the pavement as if she was
waiting for some company. He fretted. His partner was due
to bring in the Land Rover to take over the shepherding if
required.

He turned back into the hotel. He remembered that
when he paid the bill for lunch that he had to remind reception that when Americans put down their knives at a meal
to eat with a fork alone it was not a signal for the waitress
to remove the plates. It was little details like that which
kept his tourists happy. Not all the party had departed. He
looked up in surprise to see Harry S. Webb talking in the
lobby to Mrs Oldberger. They stopped as he approached.

Are you not going to see the sights, Mr Webb?' he
asked.

'I was just finding out what Mrs Oldberger here recom-
mended,' he said, and took his leave. Macdonald caught
her eye, but she avoided his glance. He completed the set-
tlement with the hotel before returning to the vestibule
from where he observed Webb joining the Lake woman to
set off together. On Brearley's arrival, Macdonald led him
tacitly back into the hotel and to the bar.

Come five o'clock half the party was ready to leave
town while the others were set to enjoy an urban evening.

'It's a cute little place,' said Mrs Sorenson to the managers who had joined them all in the square. 'But I could

not find a sign of Sir Walter's school, and the Abbey is not up to much. My book says that he was living at Sandyknowe near that tower, what's it called, John? Are we going there?'

Brearley hastened to reassure her. 'The day after tomorrow, Mrs Shorenson.'.

Her husband thought that he could smell the liquor on the man's breath. Having followed his wife's earnest researches through every street of Kelso, he felt he could do with some refreshment himself.

'I sure think that we should head home and put our feet up,' he said. To the relief of the Sorensons and other elderly members of the party who chose to go back to their hotel, it was Macdonald who drove them.

'Gus will bring the coach back to the car park for ten o'clock,' said Brearley, to those remaining, 'and I shall collect any of you from the hotel. I don't suppose I shall have to make a sweep of the bars!'

'Now then, John,' said Mrs Oldberger, frowning at him, 'don't go putting ideas into these young heads. Molly and I have found a concert for 7.30 in that cute little octagonal church to keep us out of harm's way.'

The two men, Dwight and Harry said that they wanted to look at the river to see what the famous fishing waters were like, and Margaret joined the Bryants and Mays, setting off briskly and pointedly to avoid the company of the school teachers. Jane Marshall was not all that put out; she took the arms of her two companions and led them off.

'Let's go see if Scotsmen really are drinking men,' she said, shepherding them towards the nearest hostelry in the High Street. 'Perhaps we won't get served.'

'Don't go looking to see what they have under their kilts,' said John Brearley, coarsely, returning thankfully and clutching a brief case, to his quiet hotel corner.

VI

Back at the bar, Spike was preparing for his evening

duties. The pub opened at five and it was usually quiet until seven, but he felt that this was going to be one of the busy nights, just when he wanted time. He ran a concerned eye round the saloon with its gas log fire which had saved him the labour of bringing in fuel, the parade of bottles, the lines of carefully polished, gleaming glasses, the brass handles of the beer taps and the orderly disposition of the mats on the tables. He took a duster round the edges of the wooden panelling and gave a rub to one of the horse brasses that seemed tarnished.

His counter led also into the rougher public bar which, with its cruder, wooden furnishings and dartboard provided a different if more homely atmosphere for some of his regular customers. He wondered for a brief moment, brief because wondering was not really part of his nature, he wondered why he bothered with this other line of business. For kicks, he would probably have answered. Sometimes the contented round of small town life irked him, inwardly he missed the pace of the city, the wail of suggestive sirens, and the quick, sharp repartee of urban backchat.

Some workmen came in, thirsty on their way home, nodded their greeting and he served them in the public bar. The couple, pleasant English-sounding, who had arrived the day before for bed and breakfast, came in for their key. With ear alert for the bar doors, he searched out the key of their room from the kitchen.

'You can put your bicycles in the shed. The boss is away but 'e'll lock 'em up when he gets back later. Make yerself at home. You know we don't do tea but there's 'eaps of places in the town.'

'We'll perhaps look in later for a drink when we come in,' said Roger, remarking to his wife as he went upstairs, 'doesn't sound like a native, does he? Quite pleasant to hear the sharp tones of a cockney voice again.'

Spike saw Thornell come in and served him a beer. Looking down at the glass, as it foamed up, he was able to murmur 'nothing on tonight unless you can wait.'

He wiped the glass clean and set it down on the mat.

Jim Thornell also spoke downwards as he counted out

the coins in the palm of his hand. 'Aye,' he said, 'I'm a bit strapped, you know, and I winna be back for a week. Whit time?'

Another customer interrupted them, and he stepped back.

'Say, half past ten, Jim.'

Thornell nodded, he could give Shelagh a ring and say he would be late. He glanced around and took his drink to one side.

A neat figure pushed the door firmly open and entered. He wore a well cut tweed suit and a cloth cap to match.. He had one of those thin Scottish moustaches that barely seemed worth the trouble of shaving around them. Small, alert, blue eyes looked around with swift inspection.

'Evening, Major,' said Spike, 'The usual?'

'Good evening, Spike,' Alistair McAlistair replied curtly.

As Spike turned to measure the malt whisky into the optic, he remarked. 'Ye're running late today, Major.'

McAlistair made no reply, placed the exact amount required, and took the proffered glass and a quick sip. There was a pause until Spike, sensing that the edge was off the man's evident irritation, ventured: 'You are usually in at dinnertime, lunchtime, like.'

The Major grunted, glanced at his watch and drank again.

'Bad day,' he said, 'MOT for the car and a bloody puncture on the way. Then had to have two new tyres. Garage only just finished. Thrown out my programme completely.'

'Yer shooting oppo was in as usual and asked for you.'

Spike turned to deal with another customer. He liked the Major, touch of class about him, but fidgety, like now, always looking at his watch as if he had a train to catch. Spike, reminded, saw the bar clock behind him showing ten minutes to six. It would take him five minutes to reach the Abbey and even then he sometimes had to wait until the place was free of visitors.

He caught McAlistair's eye and served him quickly with his second drink.

'Major, could you sub for me a few minutes? I have to

go out. Just see no-one breaks the place up and say I'll be back in half a mo.'

'I can't serve drinks, you know, never done it. Pity none of my children are here, they all seemed to have served time behind bars.' He surveyed the room behind him, nodded, rather pleased with his own little joke, and adopted a gently commanding attitude.

Spike donned his anorak, retrieved the bag from the drawer and moved as swiftly and unnoticeably as he could through the town's narrow vennels, across the old graveyard towards the ruined Abbey. He could now always make the excuse of looking for his friend Thornell in his shed at the back. He was fortunate, there were no other visitors. Once within the galilee porch under the shadow of the dark, forlorn tower, he edged into the small transept, and with a final cautious peer around, slid his package into a recess at the end of an old altar. With relief he returned briskly to his duties.

McAlistair greeted him and made a gesture to a number of newcomers, standing expectantly at the counter. Spike could hear American twangs in the speech of the three women nearest him. There was a dark haired one with a butch look, he thought and a tall blonde at whom he threw a second glance and addressed.

'Wot do ye fancy, my dears?' he said in his most welcoming tones.

'Do we have to come to the counter or do we get served right at the tables?' It was the darker woman who spoke. 'We have had to wait ten minutes.' The others shuffled uncomfortably behind her.

Spike, who had been ready to apologise for the delay made as if to answer a shout from the public bar, but thought better of it, contenting himself with asking again what they would like.

'Real Scotch whisky,' demanded Jane Marshall.

'What would you suggest?' added the blonde, sensing that they were antagonising the barman.

It was the following morning that they discovered

Spike. It was the custodian who found him, dead, sprawled across the low tombstone, just to the right inside the porch, his arms stretched out. Cross-like, said the custodian as he gabbled to the police on the telephone, explaining that he had gone in early as he had left it to Thornell to lock up the night before.

The police arrived with a wail of car sirens, a rare sound in the usually peaceful morning in Kelso. There had not yet been a report of a missing person, but word had soon spread last night that the barman had failed to close up at the Feathers.

By the time the townsfolk had woken to their morning routines, the dead man had been identified, it was reckoned he had been shot, the area had been fenced off and the full process of police procedure and investigation was under way. The custodian was enjoined to silence but there were not many in Kelso who did not know such details as he could give or imagine by dinner time.

VII

Inspector Ian McConachie of the Hawick C.I.D was a tall and bulky man: he seemed to take up a lot of space without being conspicuous. His appointment as the administrative head of the Borders detectives had delayed the retirement that he wanted. They had said to him that when several of the younger men were being seconded overseas for the unenviable and probably impossible task of establishing civil discipline in alien lands, he would have to be retained. The posting was made tolerable because it was to his wife's home territory, and also held out the prospect of fishing in the Borders rivers. The sight of running water and rising trout was enough to nurture the great passion of his life and make the humdrum routines of office life more bearable.

With his cap on, his round face appeared youthful and benign around a trimmed moustache. Bareheaded, the fringe of grey hair left to him betrayed his age and experience. He knew what they said about him because now they had to show him his confidential reports. 'Safe pair of hands, completely reliable,' which he had come to realise meant that further promotion was unlikely. When they wrote 'a highly respected senior officer,' he knew also that it meant his superiors were happy to have him as a dependable subordinate on whom their careers could successfully rest.

He suspected that he was considered out of date, but without making great play of it, he kept track of the latest technology, while still believing that an understanding of people was the essence of a good policeman and led to the solution of most crime. But he kept his office impersonal: the metal cabinets, the large desk with the two telephones and a computer screen on a small consul were unrelieved by domestic touches. Work was work for McConachie, and home was home.

That Wednesday morning he was sitting dutifully at his desk working his way through the usual routine papers in his in-tray. Just occasionally his thoughts ran ahead to Saturday when he would be free to fish. As he placed yet another return in the out-tray, he saw in his mind the long pool on the Teviot which was his favourite haunt: August was never the best month, but it was approaching September, he reflected. His hand twitched to make an imaginary cast, before he brought himself under control and directed it towards the next demanding file.

A knock on the door interrupted his checking on the morning's deployment of his small team. His junior constable came in and stood rather awkwardly in front of the desk.

'Yes, Gordon, what can I do for you?'

'It's a bit personal, sir,' the young man stammered. McConachie looked at him in mild surprise, while Detective Constable Goddard continued to look embarrassed.

'Come on, man,' said the Inspector at last. 'What's the matter?'

'I don't like to complain,' said Goddard, although it was

exactly what he was doing, 'but I am being sexually harassed.'

McConachie was taken aback, in his experience Borders' folk generally managed to sort such matters out. He allowed himself a look of concern, but checked his humour, he had been instructed to take these complaints seriously.

'I don't want work with that girl, Jackie Kennedy, again.'

'Why, what happens?'

'Whenever she has the chance, like when I am driving, she...'

At this point the internal telephone rang on the desk in front of him, and the Inspector, with a gesture of apology, picked it up.

'Sir,' he said. His face took on a grave expression. Goddard could hear the Divisional Commander's voice without being able to make out the words.

'Very good, sir. I'll come in before I go.'

McConachie replaced the receiver. For a moment he looked blank before he recalled the thread of the interrupted conversation.

'Kelso police have reported that a man has been shot in the Abbey. You had better come with me to investigate. We can talk about your problems on the way. Would you go now and check Monday's incident reports. There was something about a death in Jedburgh Abbey. Obtain all the details you can in five minutes and meet me at the car.'

'Yes,' said his senior officer. 'Kelso police say definitely not suicide. Fellow called Elwyn Jones, worked as a barman. For some reason they have suspected him of pushing. I have taken the liberty, Mac, of asking Edinburgh to send down one of their drug squad. They are always on to us about the report of drugs in our schools, so I want to show that we are doing something. I felt that you would be happy, too, working with a really up to date officer. I have arranged for the man to phone directly to your car.'

VIII

Sergeant William Evans of the Lothian and Borders Police presided over the anti-drugs squad room at the Headquarters in Fettes Avenue, Edinburgh. He was a short, dynamic man with red hair and a red beard, fiery in appearance and by nature. They generally called him Foxy, sometimes Taffy but if they ventured further to add the tag: 'Taffy was a Welshman, Taffy was a thief,' he would threaten them, mockingly with the Race Relations Act. 'The Welsh,' he would say, 'are a race, a proud race and we won't have anything derogatory said against them, will we?' But only his intimates would try it on over an evening drink.

This morning as he flicked through the Scotsman a triumphant smile showed his uneven teeth through his Barbarossan face.

'Look,' he said, 'look, boyos,' although half the staff in the room were women, 'just look at this article. It shows that the real language of the Borders is Welsh. None of this Gaelic or English, genuine Welsh. I can almost read it myself.' He passed it round.

'There's another bit, too, about drugs. You had better all read it. I think it's based on research in England but it suggests that school children are switching from Ecstasy to heroin. We had better be prepared to comment on that at the Super's meeting.'

They met daily first thing in the morning to report on any incidents in the previous twenty-four hours and to obtain direction for the next. The undercover officers had phoned in to pool their current information.

The team duly filed in to the conference room, leaving one of their number to man the telephone, and took their places at the table, where the burly Superintendent rested a heavy file.

'You'll have seen that piece in the paper. It really confirms what we already have noticed in Edinburgh. Schools and universities are being targeted by the dealers.

You'll mind that in the last three months we have had two incidents in Scotland where primary school children have been found with heroin in their satchels, or whatever they carry nowadays, not in the Lothians, I am happy to say.'

'We have again asked all headmasters to look out for any signs of drugs in the secondary schools, giving them details of the physical signs of drug taking, and we may have to extend this warning to the primary schools as well.'

'The universities are more difficult territory. We are not only concerned about the student population but we also have to be aware that the staff have to be considered as well, although probably cannabis is the main drug used. Recently in two raids on Uni' discos, we have found some E, but also horse. Any comments, sergeant?'

'Yes,' said Evans. 'We had a brief discussion, sir, before meeting, and it is our general impression that the students are now scared of E, and looking for something different and more reliable. They're all after the kicks but not pre-pared to risk E, after all the publicity of deaths.'

'This is what the talk is, but there is also an increased amount of heroin being recovered from the small time deal-ers on the streets. At one time they were flogging cannabis, then Ecstasy, but now it seems there is some major source of heroin, particular supplying the students and they won't talk.'

The Superintendent glance round the table but the team had nothing to add.

'And to-day?' he looked to the Sergeant.

'There's three at the courts, God knows when they'll get clear - as usual the courts are our main consumer of man power, and woman power,' he caught the eye of one of his female detectives. 'Brown is lecturing in schools, and Mctavish and Random are following up two investigations arising from last week's disco raid. We are also waiting for analysis reports from forensic of various samples taken.'

'Call for you from Hawick, sir,' said the duty officer. The Superintendent picked up the phone, his face grew serious as he listened.

It was the Divisional Commander speaking. 'Look,' he

said. 'I have just been on to your C.I.D. and they think that I should let you know what has happened. We have had two fatalities here, which may have drug links. The first was a small time, Newcastle pusher, Moran found dead in Jedburgh Abbey, doesn't appear to be suspicious but there were traces of heroin in his pockets. You'll have seen our report.'

The Edinburgh Superintendent had not, but he was not going to admit it. The Hawick officer continued.

'Moran was found at the altar with his arms stretched out like a cross but he seems to have died from natural causes tho' I have not yet had a final report. The second is death by shooting, body found in Kelso Abbey, bullet through the head, no weapon so that rules out suicide, and,' he paused to take a breath 'and the man, a local bartender, was also laid out like a cross.'

'It's no just the kind of thing we are used to down here. A report has gone in to your people who may want to take over. Meantime I thought that I had better check with you. The second man has been identified as a fellow called Jones, lived with a local girl, English, nothing very positive against him.'

'You can see with two deaths in two abbeys in the space of two days, there's a fair old stooshie here, and with the possible drug connection, we have a very hot potato on our hands.'

After a few more questions, the Superintendent said that he would send someone down if necessary. 'I'll discuss it with my sergeant here.'

He called Sergeant Evans back into his office to brief him, looking at him qiuizzically to see the man's reactions.

'Very rum, sir,' said the sergeant, 'and what was that about being spread out like a cross?'

'Yes, Taffy, that's what I was told, it seems to establish a link between the two deaths.'

'Sounds as if we have a religious maniac loose, the names mean nothing to me, but I can check our records in case my memory is at fault.' He thought of adding, 'now you would not expect a fellow called Jones to be involved in drugs, would you?' but it did not feel the right time for humour.

'There's a thing, ' he said, returning to the central office, 'Borders police got two stiffs, in two days, both laid out like bloody crosses, and in two bloody abbeys. How many more have they got?'

He looked at W.P.C. Random. 'You've a degree, Meg, haven't you, how many?'

'Stiffs, days, or abbeys, Serge?' she answered pertly.

He made a face at her.

'Two, she said. 'So that makes four, all burnt down by the English.'

'Serves them right for not being good, chapel going Christians. Perhaps we shall have to offer to send you down, Meg, to investigate. It sounds as if they are going to need a bit of history and religion.'

'You had better go down to Kelso, Taffy.' The Superintendent came in, interrupting. 'I have given you an outline of what has happened. You can ring Inspector McConachie in his car. He's a bit old fashioned in his views but a good policeman, you should have no difficulty in getting on with him. Give him a ring. Hawick still think there is a drug link, you'll know how we are concerned about their schools. You had better take someone with you who understands religion. It's not my strong suit and I don't suppose it's yours either!'

Evans made contact with McConachie, arranging to meet him in Kelso. He collected Random and what reports from Hawick he could find, which he skimmed through as she took the A68 over Soutra Hill. Mid afternoon, they reached the town where they met the Inspector under the sombre ruins of the western towers of the Abbey.

'You'll get a park at the back,' he said. 'We have set up a caravan investigation centre in the side street and I can brief you there.'

'The dead man, Elwyn Jones, known locally as Spike, worked as a barman at The Feathers. He was last seen there about ten o'clock last night. The landlord came back and found him missing and was understandably pretty cross as the place was unattended. Jones was found by the custodian at nine o'clock this morning. I'll show you where in a moment. He had been shot in the head, killed instantly says the medic, probably dead about twelve hours. His arms were spread out like a cross and rigid. We have interviewed his common law wife, Kathy Bourne. They live with her mother.'

'She says that she did not always wait up for Jones in the evening and had gone to bed and to sleep. Only in the early morning did she realise that he had not come home.'

'The custodian did not lock the gate last night. It is left open during the day without supervision. There is a man who comes to cut the grass and keep the place tidy, James Thornell, and we are trying to get hold of him. Meanwhile we are asking anyone who was here yesterday to come forward. This centre should pick up the locals who pass regularly, but as you can see the Abbey is right in the middle of the town.'

'I expect there will be considerable visitor traffic as well,' said Evans, wanting to offer some Edinburgh wisdom.

'Aye, just that,' said McConachie, pushing his cap back to scratch his head. 'Just that, so we are checking all hotels and B and Bs. It will take time, but you can see the ball the press will have to-morrow. Headline stuff, two deaths, two abbeys.'

'Good for the tourist trade,' said Evans.

'Mebbe that,' said the Inspector dryly, 'But I think that we could do without this kind of attraction.'

The sergeant waited, he was not sure where he came in.

'Moran,' went on the Inspector, 'was a known small time dealer wanted for questioning in Newcastle. He had traces of heroin in his pocket and we know that he tried to flog some in Jed. We still think that he died of natural causes but when he was found by a bunch of tourists, American they were, we did not have time to examine the grounds properly before the Abbey was reopened. Now that this fatality has been found stretched out in the same way, we have to think if that there might be a link. If so, is it drugs?'

'Yes,' said Evans, ' drugs and violence run together, like birds of a feather.'

McConachie looked up, slightly surprised at the poetic streak in his companion.

'You had better see the place now, Taff,' he said, 'and then I should like to take to you to where Jones lived to meet the girl'

The Abbey gate was locked and guarded; inside, the entrance way into the ruined galilee porch was marked off by posts and white tape.

'We have photographed and removed the body, but you can see the chalk outline of how it was found. There, in the right hand corner, beyond the tomb. Just look at how the arms are outstretched. You cannot pick out any footprints, most of the area is stone flagged and there are probably traces of dozens of feet but something may show up from the films. You can see into the Abbey grounds through the railings, there isn't much to see.'

He led his companion to the side of the ruins and then took him through the town to interview Kathy Bourne.

THE SOOTHSAYER

'The ruins of reddish brown sandstone, hewn from the
quarry at Dryburgh, are so overgrown with foliage that
everywhere you behold the usurpation of nature over art.'
The Ordnance Gazetteer of Scotland, 1903.

I

'Daith!' she screeched at them, as they gathered outside
the custodian's lodge at Dryburgh. 'Daith!'

'Don't pay ony attention to her,' said the man, coming
out. 'She's a bit touched.' He made a gesture towards his
head with a forefinger. 'She's aye here, skraiking awa', but
quite harmless, and a paid-up life member so I hae to let
her in.'

The woman stood, birdlike, on the well tended grass.
She wore a long, black dress with a gilt chain round her
neck from which hung a heavy cross. Incongruously, they
could see a pair of muddy wellington boots below. Straggly
grey hair fought its way free from a braided snood to
enclose a lined face. The whole effect might have seemed
sombre and inanimate but for the brightness of the eyes
and the vigour of her speech.

The Americans emerged slowly from the shop and halted. Harry Webb at the rear whispered to the custodian.
'Who is she?'

'She's a wumman called Jeannie Redpath, but they call
her Mad Meg. There's an old Border tale about a muckle
mou-ed, that's to say, big mouthed, lassie called Meg, and
as Jeannie has the gift of the gab, they've given her the
same name.'

The woman, in the manner of a trained lecturer, waited
until the party was complete, content to hold their attention
by dancing round in a circle, more than ever like a sparrow
foraging.

In the car park outside, Major McAlistair halted and

stepped out. It was always for him a special pleasure to arrive at Dryburgh. The path to the entrance was straight; the flower beds aligned on each side; the green, well cut grass stretched out below the cedars of Lebanon which shaded an orderly range of gravestones with clear cut lines and legible inscriptions. Beyond them were the Abbey ruins of soft red sandstone, sad in their incompleteness and yet distinct in the pattern of their remaining buildings. He felt that he was inspecting a competent regiment even if there were gaps in the ranks. The custodian, too, had served in the same regiment and greeted him in the proper manner as a visiting senior officer.

He heard the sound of voices and turned to see two cyclists free-wheeling down the hill behind him. He recognised the couple whom he had seen in Jedburgh, and heard their sharp English voices.

'It was worth it, Roger, wasn't it? It was a frightful slog up the hill, but that run down was terrific. And what a wonderful place.'

Roger, conspicuous in his red bobbled hat, heaved himself off the bicycle somewhat stiffly and they rested their machines against the hedge. The Major moved briskly ahead of them, muttering to himself.

'I think that's the little man we saw in Jedburgh Abbey,' said Roger. But Daphne was not listening. All else was quiet in the small wooded valley. She stood enraptured by the peace of the place. Even the coach parked nearby did not distract her from an instant enjoyment of the scene.

The mid-morning sun was high and warm, the road dusty in its dryness, and the roadside verges rich in yellow buttercups. Errant bees hummed among the flowers against the warm walls. Somewhere a blackbird sang and rooks made their heavy passage overhead.

' "Toys for your delight, of birdsong in the morning," ' he quoted laughing at his wife. 'Come on, we have to look at more mundane things, like ruins.'

'Sir Walter Scott's buried here,' she said 'so you shouldn't quote Stevenson at me.'

They, too, took the stone paved path that led to the custodian's cabin.

Their way was blocked by a cluster of visitors, the small, dapper man, conspicuous in his well-cut tweeds, shifted uneasily away from them but all three of them were halted by the American party on the track.

'Those were the people at Jedburgh,' Daphne whispered to her husband.

'Roun an roun till a' is couth
Rhymer gar his kin speak sooth,
By his gift from Eildon's queen
I see oor world with ither een.'

The black figure crooned and jigged through a circle until she saw she held the group's attention.

'Ye've come to the place of daith,' she said. 'This hoos of God is set in a fair place. Enter it with penitent souls and mindful of those who hae come afore you and lie in the yird..'

'True Thomas said:
"When airmies hear the sweet bells ca'
Doun comes the Abbey's haley wa."'

'And the English King that was ganging his way hame down Leaderwater heard the tolling and turned his sodgers to brak the hoos and kill the monks.'

'Not for the last time either, when English Henry was bent on marrying off his son, that sickly laddie, to oor Mary, did he not send his airmies agin to destroy the place. The rough wooing they ca' it. It's aye them from over the Border.'

The Major nodded vigorously.

'An if ye're here on a winters evening when there's nane else about and jist the soun of the rinning water and maybe the doos in the auld trees, you fancy you see the ghaists of the friars in the garth and hear them singing in the kirk, and my kinswoman that lived twenty years in the ruins, times you make her oot greeting in her wae.'

'Meg, you are holding up the party, they have a University man waiting to talk to them.' The custodian interrupted, pointing towards the Abbey that could be seen through the trees. John Brearley steered his flock towards it where Ian McShea in his black wind cheater and red kilt waited impatiently. Today was architecture day; with the well laid out buildings and their smaller, easily understood scale he was able to give full rein to a detailed description, unlike in Jedburgh or Kelso.

He beckoned to them to stand in the middle of the church.

'This Abbey was dedicated to Saint Mary and founded by Hugh de Morville in 1150.'

'And dinna leave out that the cemetery was consecrated the same year on St Martin's Day that no bogles might haunt it.' Meg chirped up from the side.

'Yes, yes,' said McShea, somewhat put out. 'The monks, the Premonstratensians to give them their proper name, came from Northumberland. They wore a black cassock covered by a white woollen cope, hence the name of the White Canons. For those of you who like to know the origin of words, their name came to St Norbert, a meadow pointed out, Pré Monstré, from a vision.'

'In addition to their daily choral services conducted where we stand, their great work was the instruction of the people in their faith. At their height there were over a thousand of their Abbeys across Northern Europe.'

'This church, where we stand, is some 200 feet long, cruciform, that is to say cross shaped, with short transepts, and there would have been a small pyramid shaped, wooden tower over the intersection.

'You will see it in that plan, provided by Real Tours,' put in Brearley, and there was a rustle of paper.

'At the east end, the building had a square apse for the presbytery, at the west end, much of which is still standing, was the main ceremonial entrance which you can see is curved. Above it would have soared a five light, mullioned window, and above that in turn a round rose window in the gable end of the pitched roof.'

'Because the Abbey was built over a considerable period and subsequently repaired, the style of the architecture has varied and is usually termed transitional between the Romanesque and the Pointed. The handsome doorway is an example of the Romanesque.'

'On either side of us, standing in the nave would have been side aisles, and you can see the short arms of the transepts, on the right, the south transept still contains the fine, five light window, and below it the night stair which the monks used to come down from their dormitory.'

'To the left we have a more substantial part remaining. In this north transept we have the burial places of two well-known people.'

Meg danced round to take up a more prominent position as McShea directed the gaze of his audience to the stone tombs.

'First, perhaps the best known Borderer of all time, whose name you will all be familiar with, Sir Walter Scott.'

'Oor Wattie,' said Meg, sadly, half to herself, and then more loudly. 'Think o'it, the black carriage and the black horses with their black plumes nodding, coming doon the brae and a' the fowk gaithered for the funeral.'

McShea glared at her, but she already held the group in fascination.

He continued. 'Also buried here is Field Marshall Lord Haig, the British military leader from the first world war, who caused the death of so many of the British labouring classes. The bayonet is an instrument with a working man at either end.' He allowed himself to insert. The Major shook his head in vehement disagreement.

This was the moment Meg had been waiting for.

She flung her arms into the air and cried in animation.

'True Thomas said;

"Betide, betide, whate'er betide,

There shall aye be a Haig in Bemersyde." '

McShea made the effort to bring back the Americans' interest to him.

'Post-war, the nation bought the house of Bemersyde for the Field Marshall. It stands on the hill above us.' 'Can't you get rid of that woman?' He added in not altogether sotto voce to Brearley. But the manager of Real Tours could see that Meg was just the genuine article as far as his Americans were concerned. When architectural detail palled, they could rest their eyes on Meg's jigging.

McShea directed them to look south. 'In almost every monastery, the practice was to build the monks' quarters as an extension of the south transept. We have seen the corner which holds the night stair that led from the dormitories and the Abbot's room on the first floor. On the far side was the stream. You can imagine how important it was to have a supply of running water both for washing and for the lavatories which have the slightly comic name of rere-dorters.'

'I call 'em something else,' cried Meg, but while the audience waited in a mixture of interest and alarm, she was restrained by Brearley.

'I guess,' said Mrs Oldberger, 'we could all offer alternatives,' and the girls giggled in the background.

'We shall see at Melrose,' went on McShea, determinedly, 'where the stream ran to the north that all the monastic building had to be set on that side.'

'Below these first floor living quarters are the vestry, outside which was the east processional door into the church and which also contained the library, and the parlour where conversation was allowed. You will all notice the connection with the French parler.'

There was an enthusiastic murmur of assent.

'At a lower level is the chapter house, the daily meeting place for the community, here noted for its barrel vaulted roof and sedilia, the stone seats of the monks still intact.'

'And of course that feature which we regard as the essence of a religious house and has given as name to its very existence, the cloister, the square surrounded by a covered walk. Here we can imagine the canons pacing in meditation and from which led off the busy offices and stores of an active commercial enterprise.'

'This cloister here is a small one, set well below the level of the church. The building on the south side was the refectory, or dining hall, and at the corner between it and the chapter house is the warming room. There is also a narrow passage or slype at the south-west corner of the cloister'

McShea gave them a short history of the usual episodes

of destruction, which Meg punctuated with her own comments. 'It was aye the English kings and their sodgers,' she interjected.

He usually liked to point out the neglect displayed by the subsequent owners of the church lands, but he sensed that Meg would defend those that had cherished Dryburgh.

He contented himself with adding that for the ordinary labouring peasants, an unused building provided a ready supply of that rare commodity, dressed stone. 'There will be few old houses in these parts which will not have an Abbey stone in its construction.'

He led the party up the night stair to the monks' quarters.

'I commend to you this view where you can see how well the buildings nestle in this small piece of flat land.'

Aye,' screeched Meg, raising her small figure on a convenient rubble wall. 'Aye, it's a braw haugh.'

'What's that?' whispered Roger to his wife but before she could express her ignorance, the Major at her elbow replied curtly. 'A piece of flat land by the river'

'Finally,' said McShea, replacing his notes in the brief case Brearley held out to him, 'the graveyard among the trees has some interesting tomb stones and is still in use.'

'And they say the founder's buried beneath the chapter house floor, markit by two circles.' Meg was not prepared to give him the last word. 'I can see him there in my mind's ee.'

She teetered on the low rubble wall that formed the edge of the roofless dormitories, the group of visitors giving her little room to dance her circles of incantation, For a moment she swayed as if to fall. Harry Webb stretched out a restraining hand to catch her by a fold in the black dress, and the others turned anxiously to assist or peer down to the cloister below them.

Her feet dislodged some loose masonry, which thudded to the ground beneath.. At that moment Jim Thornell, who had been enjoying his morning smoke in the chapter house, emerged to stub it out. He looked up indignantly at the stone buildings above him.

'Watch what ye're bloody doing,' he shouted up at them. There was a line of faces, all staring down at him but for one it appeared as a moment of recognition. Thornell seemed to be staring back directly.

Meg resisted the helpful hands that sought to bring to the safety of the dormitory floor. She had begun to lose herself in her other world.

'Yestreen I dreamed a doleful dream,
Of daith beside the Tweed's fair stream.'

For a moment there was a silence and a stillness. This utterance was more vivid than her historical interjections into the lecturer's discourse. Molly said to her aunt who was still looking down at Thornell.

'Ain't that just like something from Macbeth. We're doing it just now with sixth year. She's just like one of the witches, the weird sisters.'

'Now isn't that just right,' said Mrs Oldberger, 'I knew that she reminded me of something.

'She's a bit spooky,' said Daphne to her husband and they heard the Major at their side muttering. 'Damned careless, damaging property like that.'

Harry Webb at last managed to pull Meg down. McShea made a final effort to retrieve his audience as their attention returned from the cloister beneath them.

'I have to leave you now. After lunch you will be able to browse among the ruins. Despite what this, er, this lady has said, Dryburgh is a delightful and peaceful place, typifying the monastic layout. You will be able to imagine what a mediaeval Abbey was like when in active use. We shall meet again in Melrose.'

'When shall we three meet again?' said Daphne, still carried away by Meg's intensity.

'In thunder, lightning or in rain?' completed her husband. 'Come on, let's explore.'

As the hum of conversation replaced the brief moment of silence, John Brearley made himself heard. 'Real Tours,' he said, 'have arranged lunch for you at the hotel, and we shall have the whole afternoon to explore the Abbey. Could we meet at the gate in ten minutes?'

'Let's join them,' said Roger. 'I think that I shall enjoy ruins more on a full stomach, and we can fix up our bed for the night.'

The group split up: the older members chose to follow the path the short distance to the river, while the keener and younger straggled down the processional steps onto the cloister green to explore. Daphne and Roger watched them briefly from the church. It was only afterwards that the exact details of the individual movements in this dispersion came to be seen as crucially important.

Eventually the whole company made its way back past the custodian's office, some to walk the short distance to the handsome, red sandstone hotel, which they could see across the lawns, while the more elderly climbed on board the coach. Daphne and Roger checked to see if they could come in again on the same ticket, retrieved their bicycles and followed the Americans. The Major, not altogether pleased to have his day's routine shared, left his car and walked briskly up the drive, leaving Meg and Thornell in possession of the Abbey grounds.

"He's good, that lecturer. You feel he really knows what he's talking about,' said Dwight Graham, as they settled at the small tables for a bar lunch. I began to get a sense of the atmosphere of these old Abbeys.'

'I kinda like that mad woman,' said Mrs Bryant who made it her duty to mix among the party. ' She's the one who brings the place to life, even if she's hung up about death. The way she speaks in old Scotch is just right.'

'Bit spooky,' said her husband. 'All right in the sunshine, but I'd rather not be around in the dusk.'

They could look across the lawn towards the Abbey grounds but the black figure was out of sight.

'Do you think John lays it on for us?' said Webb, rather cynically. 'She's almost too good to be true.'

'You ought to say "too gude to be sooth", oughtn't you?' said Mrs Bryant. 'After all they talk about soothsayers, don't they?'

'It was lucky those stones didn't hit that gardener fellow or we should have had another death on our hands. That

Jedburgh bloke was enough for me.' said Dwight, reflecting at the same time on his previous tour.

Roger and Daphne sat apart from the tourists in a corner. Daphne said that they ought to allow the visiting Americans to enjoy the view.

They had begun to identify the different members of the group. There were the elderly couples moving slowly to their seats and fussing over what was offered, then there was the large domineering woman rather officiously trying to direct the four younger ones. One of these, Molly they heard her named, resembled the grand dame. 'They look alike, same walk,' whispered Daphne, peeping surreptitiously above her menu.

She looked at the two obviously single men, one rather heavily built and sad looking. 'Just lost his wife, I bet,' she said.

'What do you make of the other?' asked Roger, sipping his beer and looking away. She paused to make up her mind on what to order. 'Haddock and chips,' and 'I don't know, his face isn't very touristy,' she replied.

'Yes,' said Roger, 'it's a bit too sharp, like a gun dog about to lift its paw and point at game.'

As if to reinforce his comment, he caught Webb's eye, and they both turned their glances away.

'There's an awful lot of women,' Daphne managed before she was served. 'The two young couples must feel rather pleased with themselves'.

The older women wore frocks and beads and placed their cameras on the tables while their men folk went to the bar. The younger ones were in trouser suits, vying against each other in cut and colour. The middle group, 'widows or divorcées,' decided Daphne to herself, had a slightly resigned appearance, forcing themselves to bright smiles as the two younger men offered them drinks. The four younger women definitely made themselves a group on their own while their bulky doyenne fussed around. They could hear her saying to her look alike.

'Do you really think, Molly, you should be having Martini midday?'

'They don't look a very happy lot, do they, Roger?' They could see the man in the blazer, clearly their tour guide, busily bent on tending them, attempting animation. One of the elderly ladies wanted sauce and had not got it, and another had sauce and did not want it.

'Jack Spratt,' said Daphne between mouthfuls.

'Ought to be easy to sort out,' said her husband. 'There are twenty one of them,' he added. 'I wonder who the odd one out is.'

There was a brief lull as the party ate. 'Do you mind,' squawked one at the table of the younger women, taking offence at another reaching across her for the salt, 'Just ask.'

Daphne could see a kick under the table.

'For heaven's sake,' said their older companion, but the tall blonde girl continued shrilly. 'Beth didn't need to stretch out like a school girl.'

One of the older men at the next table who had finished eating, took out his camera to provide distraction and for a moment there were flashes, and bustle as others followed suit with their camcorders.

'I hope,' said Roger sardonically 'that they only capture the happier moments in sound.

The small, dapper figure in tweeds, sitting by himself, wiped his mouth carefully, rose and went to pay his bill.

'What do you make of him? He doesn't belong to the party.'

'No way,' said Daphne. 'He's local, home product.'

Her husband laughed. 'You should study regimental ties. Tells you at once the background. Good Scottish Regiment. I should think that the fellow took or was given early retirement. Probably a Major, there's a lot of them around. God knows what he's doing here. Perhaps pushed out of the house by his wife while she spring-cleans or perhaps he's shadowing these Americans. A good many of his type are used by the intelligence services. It's rather curious that he should have been at Jedburgh as well.'

'I don't think that he has a wife,' she said, 'he has a button missing from the sleeve of his jacket.'

Roger with a smile looked at his.

They made their way to reception to arrange accommodation for themselves and their bicycles.

'Did you come from Kelso?' the girl asked. They nodded.

'They have found a man's body in the Abbey there. The police say they are treating the death as suspicious and have set up an enquiry unit. It's all on the local news.'

'We were there yesterday, in the Abbey,' said Roger. 'That's very, very, odd.'

He caught his wife's eye. 'And Jedburgh,' she said.

The tour operator in his distinctive blazer was also at the counter, settling his account. He briskly wrote out the cheque, took a receipt and made curt thanks. He had clearly heard what had been said and, hurriedly closing his brief case, he hastened back to his flock.

The group had to wait together for readmission to the Abbey: Roger and Daphne delayed their progress out of natural courtesy blended with curiosity. The Major, if that was what he was, also remained at the back, trapping wind-blown litter with his stick and carefully depositing it in the bin. So it was that the whole party approached the ruins together. Something dark on the ground might just have caught their eye, but for the most part their interest was on the higher outline of the buildings. They paused to study the artist's pictorial reconstruction of the Abbey as it might have been and straggled past the tombs of the famous.

It was then that the foremost saw, black and spread-eagled on the grass, face downwards, at the place of the high altar, the unmistakable shape of Mad Meg.

II

Inspector McConachie and Sergeant Evans had called briefly on Kathy and her mother, both white faced in grief. The women had learnt earlier of Spike's death and were prepared for the arrival of further police.

'We dinna understaund it at a,' Mrs Bourne had said.

'Spike was a good lad, and there's nane would have ony-thing against him.'

Kathy, behind a soiled handkerchief, was almost speechless but would from time to time between sobs let out broken cries. 'Jeez, he was a fine mon, well-kent in the toon, an what'll we do noo?'

The two policemen contrived to look round the small house. It was two up and two down with the bathroom over the kitchen at the back, and a small garden at the rear. It was orderly enough and nothing appeared to demand further investigation.

On their return to the caravan at Kelso Abbey, they learnt that the Hawick police had managed to track down Mrs Thornell.

'Aye,' she said, 'Jim was in Kelso yesterday, and will be at Dryburgh today. Ye can catch him here tonight about six o'clock. He's never late hame from Dryburgh. He doesn't like the hotel bar, there. He hasn't done anything wrang, has he?'

Telephone calls had also revealed the presence in Kelso of the American tourists who had been previously been at Jedburgh.

McConachie was acutely aware that two sensational deaths of this kind in the normally quiet Borders demanded action. He wanted to show to the Edinburgh sergeant that the Hawick force were something to be reckoned with.

'We'll try Dryburgh, Taff,' he said. 'If Thornell was here all yesterday, he may have seen something and if can meet up with any of the tourists, so much the better. The site team will pick up anything here.'

In the car he continued. 'Two deaths, two abbeys, both the bodies laid out, spread like a cross, it's no' canny.'

'Do you think, Mac, we have to deal with a religious maniac? We don't want to find another stiff at this Abbey, do we?'

'The medics still say that they have no reason to think that Moron's death, the fellow in Jed, was anything other than natural, unless he died of fright after being chased by the rugby boys.'

He turned sharply off the highway to take the road to Dryburgh. 'What did you think about the girl, Taff?'

'I thought, Mac, that she knew something, she didn't want to tell us. She hid a mite too much behind the hankie. We may have to go back with a search warrant.'

'I think that if they have anything to hide, they'll have got rid of it by now, and they'll let us in again without any bother.'

The Inspector drew up in the park. They could both see the Real Tours coach in the adjacent space.

The custodian greeted them cheerfully. 'There's some visitors, just back in. Mostly American. You wouldn't be after them, would you?' he said, but on seeing their serious looks, checked his humour.

'There's been a murder in Kelso, yesterday, and we want to find Thornell who was working there and we understand he was due here today. Is he around?'

'Aye, he'll be here. He generally brings a sandwich for his piece. He's nae gone oot, though I haven't heard the mower going, now that I come to mind it. All these visitors were here this morning, they had lunch in the hotel and they are just back now having another look round.'

The two police officers, following the path to the ruins, could see a small crowd ahead of them. They immediately sensed something wrong, almost something electric in the air, there were shouts and cries, signs of consternation. They quickened their pace, pushed through a bunch of women, standing back to let their menfolk proceed them.

At the end of the church, a woman in a black dress sprang to her feet and danced round in a circle.

'Roun an roun till a' is couth,
Rhymer gar his kin speak sooth.
Lay yir ear to haley grund,
Whar the ancient banes are fund,
Them that lie within the yird,
Aye offer Rhymer's kin the weird.'

As the police officers stared round in amazement, it was not so much at the curious figure, relishing their attention, as at the reactions of the spectators. They were clearly in a high degree of agitation. The man, conspicuous in his blazer, seemed for the moment at a loss for words and some of the women bordered on hysteria. An elderly woman was slapping a younger one's face. There were muffled shrieks and sobs. Two of the elderly men were red faced in anger.

'This is too much,' said one.

Major McAlistair set off to fetch the custodian, but became suddenly aware of the presence of the uniformed policeman.

'One moment,' said McConachie, 'would you all just wait.'

He singled out Brearley. 'I take it, sir, that you are the leader of this group.'

Brearley, brought back to earth, nodded. 'Yes,' he said, almost automatically, 'Real Tours.'

'Yes, we saw your coach outside.'

Brearley nodded again.

'Did you know that a man was found dead in Kelso Abbey this morning?'

By this time John Brearley had caught up with himself again. How was all this going to affect his tour?

'Yes, I learnt it from the hotel at lunchtime but I have not yet told my Americans. You will appreciate, officer, how careful we have to be with foreign tourists.'

'Aye, just so.' said McConachie. 'You were all in Kelso yesterday, weren't you?'

'Yes, but I am quite sure that none of my group would have been involved.'

'Mebbe so, but would you mind if I had a word with them, just the same? Are all these people on your tour?'

Brearley pointed out the three exceptions.

'Can I ask you if you were in Kelso yesterday?'

'Yes,' said Roger, indicating his wife, 'we were,' and he watched with interest to see the Major nodding. He looked round for Meg but she, perhaps recognising that she no longer commanded an audience, had vanished.

'I think you had better gather around while I talk. I'll ask my sergeant to take names and addresses as we go along.'

Not to be outfaced, Brearley raised his voice. 'Folks,' he said, 'this police officer would like to address you.'

The Inspector felt that it was not fitting to speak in an official capacity within the confines of the Abbey walls. He took his audience to the grass at the side and cleared his throat.

'Ladies and gentlemen,' he started a little hesitantly, it did not sound quite right. 'I have to tell you that a man was found dead this morning in Kelso Abbey. We understand that everyone here was at the Abbey yesterday and we are seeking help with our enquiries.' That sounded better.

'We have set up an investigation room at the scene of the incident where we shall be interviewing anyone who went to the Abbey from yesterday afternoon onwards and who might have noticed anything unusual. This is, of course, a routine enquiry and I do not wish to interrupt your visit to the Borders,' he caught Brearley's eye, 'but you will appreciate that we have a duty to investigate an unnatural death.'

The full significance of what he was saying began to sink into his audience. Two deaths and the antics of Mad Meg left the women, once full of utterance, now grey-faced and speechless..

'I think, officer,' said Dwight Graham Jnr, rather ponderously, 'You can count on our full co-operation.'

The men nodded, Mrs Oldberger glared at her girls.

'O.K. by us,' said Jane Marshall who stood in front of them like a gander protecting geese. The others, a little belatedly, gave assent.

'I have a list of my party,' said Brearley. He recalled having said this before, 'and we are all staying at the hotel whose address is there as well.'

'We are at the hotel here,' said Roger, giving their names. The Major stepped forward. 'Major Alistair McAlistair.'

Roger listened unobtrusively as the others checked themselves against the Real Tours list. He could now identify the stout, dominant woman as Mrs Oldberger, her relation of some kind, Molly, the young couple, Bryants and

Mays, and the two single men, the spokesman Dwight someone and Webb who did not seem to quite fit in.

'We could perhaps borrow the gate keeper's office,' suggested Evans. 'We can pick up Thornell as he comes through.'

'Now, ladies and gentlemen,' said the Inspector more confidently, 'I suggest that you should each come one by one to see us at the office over there and tell us when you were in Kelso Abbey yesterday and anything you might have noticed. It should not take very long and I say again how grateful the Borders police are for any assistance you can offer. Meanwhile I am sure you would like to continue your inspection of Dryburgh.'

'Folks,' added Brearley, back in charge, 'we will delay the departure of the coach for half an hour. We must not allow this, this untoward incident, to spoil your day here.'

It was a vain hope, the shadow of death hung over the spirits of the party, some more than others. They talked desultorily among themselves, took their turn in the office, with little to offer, and returned to the coach. The Major pushed himself into the queue, anxious to drive home.

Daphne and Roger remained in the deserted ruins. They walked down to the river to enjoy the sound of running water and the view of the rich green canopy of the woodlands.

'What an extraordinary sequence of events!' said Roger as they made their way towards the church. 'You urge me to a peaceful Borders holiday because you say I always lead you to trouble and we find ourselves in this caper.'

'We aren't really in it,' said Daphne. 'Just observers.'

He laughed, and, seeing the last of the Americans vanishing into the office at the gate, he led the way to their police interview.

'We met before, Mr Stone.' The Inspector greeted him, 'but I don't think I have ever met your wife.'

'This is Inspector McConachie, my dear, with whom I once worked.'

'At another Abbey, I recall, but an English one. It was after that I was sent up here. But we mustn't waste time, perhaps we'll find time for a dram before you go south again. Are you still in the same line of business?

Roger nodded. 'Yes, Mac, but this trip is purely holiday, we're on bicycles.'

'Rather you than me.' McConachie showed signs of weariness.

He took them through what was clearly now a standard line of questioning about their previous day while the sergeant took notes. It was established that they had stayed at The Feathers.

'It was the barman who was killed.'

'How?' asked Roger.

'He was shot in the head,' said McConachie, 'but we are not at the moment releasing that piece of information. So keep that to yourselves.'

'Who's he?' asked Evans as the couple left and headed for the hotel.'

'He's a senior officer in the Intelligence Services and our paths have crossed before. He's a good lad, but typically English. Doesn't say much, looks glaikit, but then when he does speak, you find he's noticed everything.'

The custodian, who had been hovering in the shop, appeared as the Stones departed. 'That's the lot, then. Meg's gone, whiles she takes the path by the river, although I tell her it's no right. But no sign of Jim. Perhaps he's had trouble with the mower because I haven't heard it since dinner.'

'Yes,' said Evans, checking the Real Tours list. 'We have seen them all.

'It's not like Jim to be late.' The custodian looked at his watch. 'He's very precise, comes on time and goes off on his motor bike promptly at half past five. Not like him at all to be late. He keeps the machine behind the shop to stop kids fiddling with it. It's still there.'

'Where's the shed for the mower?' asked Evans.

'I'll show you. It's behind the main gateway into the cloisters'

He locked the shop carefully and led the way across the lawns. On the far side beyond where the stream once flowed, they could see where the mowing had stopped and the mower had been left. It was switched off.

'Petrol's turned off too,' said Evans. They shouted but there was no answer.

They spread out to search the buildings. The custodian made his way through the corner passage and in its darkness stumbled on a foot. The body lay stretched out on the stone floor. For a moment he groped with his hands in horror on the dead man's overalls and then recovered to call out. 'He's here – in the slype.' Realising that the police would not know what that meant, he shouted again, 'here, in the passage.'

His cry drew the two policemen who made their way cautiously down the steps into the dark and narrow tunnel with the sunlit lawns barely visible at each end..

'He's here, must have fallen down the steps.'

Evans pulled out a small pocket torch to reveal the gardener lying face downward with arms outstretched and a wound oozing blood at the back of his head.

'Dead?' Evans looked questioningly at his superior, although he knew the answer.

'Dead,' said the Inspector. 'Dead, and not by falling down stairs.'

III

It was to be an evening of intense enquiry for many and inquest for some. Inquest, not in the legal sense because there is not such a thing under Scottish law, but in the old sense of in-quest, personal self-scrutiny.

But it began peacefully enough for Roger and Daphne. Back in the comfort of their hotel bedroom, Daphne took a bath, followed by her husband, and turned back the bed.

'We are on holiday,' she said. He smiled and stopped dressing until the unnatural wail of a siren checked him.

'Good God, what an earth's that in this place. It can't be McConachie announcing his departure.'

He parted the curtains. It was not yet dark but a mist

had come down the valley. He could just make out vehicles and an ambulance in the car park, a flurry of movement in the ruins, uniformed police, men in overalls carrying lights.

'Something's happened in the Abbey, Daphne, come and look.'

They stood, naked, watching the movements.

'They're heading for the cloisters. I think that's McConachie still there.'

I hope that it's not Meg.' Daphne sighed. 'I suppose we should get dressed.'

'Yes,' he said. 'I expect the Inspector will call.'

With the other hotel guests, they resumed watching over their preprandial drinks in the front lounge

'They say that someone's been found dead in the Abbey, a local's just come in and saw a body being carried into an ambulance. Blood everywhere.' said the barman with licenced exaggeration.

It was not the Inspector who came, but a young constable who advanced up the drive in a business-like fashion to reach the reception desk. The manager hurried to meet him and took over from the girl.

'There's been a fatality in the ruins,' said the officer, clearly excited. 'The Inspector asks that no-one leaves the hotel to-morrow until he's seen them. If anyone has to go, he requests that they contact him at the Kelso police station before hand.'

The manager hastened to pass the message on. It was not quite the publicity he liked for his hotel but it probably would do no harm. 'We had better type it out, Mary, and put a copy in each room,' he said. 'And check tomorrow's bookings.'

Like Brearley he was a realist.

Back at the tour hotel, Brearley, ignorant of the latest discovery at Dryburgh Abbey, conferred rapidly with his colleague, Macdonald, explaining what the police had revealed about events at Kelso. It was too public a place for other than a well- acted and guarded conversation

'We must carry on as if nothing extraordinary has happened, and play down the disturbance to the day,'

Macdonald said to him as they stood near the entrance. They both turned to smile wanly at Mrs Oldberger who sailed past with her large person and voluminous bag, protectively leading her niece through the vestibule and upstairs.

'The show must go on. We can talk later. Meanwhile for God's sake, J, look cheerful and cheer them up.'

'I hope, ladies, that the police have not upset you.' He spoke with concern to another group making their way to the staircase.

'No, indeed, Angus,' replied Mrs Sorenson, 'they sure added a bit of life to the visit to the old ruins.' Then she wondered if that was the right expression.

'I need a good stiff drink,' said Mrs Schumacher bringing up the rear.

'Real Tours will lay on something special for you tonight.' Brearley rallied to his task.

He spoke again quietly to Macdonald.

'To start it all off we had this mad woman spouting bloody poetry at us and then playing dead in the church, high bloody altar and all. Gus, it gave me the creeps.'

'We enjoyed our day, John,' said Mary May, wending her way in, 'despite the sad news from Kelso. Did you lay on that poetess specially for us?' Brearley managed a thin smile without acknowledging full responsibility. 'All part of the service,' he said.

At last they were able to take their leave and the Land Rover to reach the privacy of their own hostelry. They sat down over their drinks anxiously, their uneasy partnership under strain.

Brearley was confident enough chatting up the tourists but he was now confronted by a new situation which set him on edge. He broke the silence.

'Jones left the cash all right. I picked it up from the Abbey, went back to the hotel and checked it. The boss said that I was too tight to go back with the stuff. I said that the gardener fellow was hanging around. I don't think he saw me and honest, Gus, I did not set eyes on Jones.'

'They say in Kelso that he was shot,' said Macdonald,

looking at Brearley warily and recalling his partner's army background.

'You know bloody well I don't carry a gun,' said Brearley angrily. 'Anyway you were there as well.'

'I never went near the flaming Abbey, and I came over to Dryburgh this afternoon to warn you and then saw the fuzz were there so cleared off pronto. The whole thing's a mess.'

'It was your idea to use the Abbeys in the first place.'

'It worked before, Jones put the money in the hole and then we replaced it with the stuff. No-one saw anyone,' retorted Macdonald angrily, 'until you get pissed and foul it up.'

They relapsed into morose thought, each wondering if the other was telling the truth.

'We shall have to halt operations,' said Macdonald, assuming command which was his natural role, 'Any panic from you and we are both in the soup, and,' he added carefully, 'I never went into Kelso Abbey. I have witnesses to prove that I never went further than The Feathers. Telephone McShea and tell him what has happened. He must come down on schedule to lecture at Melrose, but a clean run. We can take no further chances. The cops are bound to be around. I'll deal with Sam in Galashiels.'

Back at the hotel the men of the tour party stood in a discursive group at the bar.

'In all my touring, and I tell you that's quite a lot,' the senior husband said, as he waited for his martini, 'in all my touring, I've never known anything like it. Here we are mixed up with two deaths.'

'It makes me recall,' said Dwight, 'two cases I had back home. They found a body in the New Presbyterian church one day, and then the very next evening the police found another at the back of the Roman Catholic Cathedral. Both Episcopalians. Turned out there wasn't anything connecting the two, and it was nothing to do with religion.'

'Sex, I expect,' said young Bryant. 'Always is.'

'Speak for yourself,' said May, and spluttered in his drink as he joined in the laughter. 'Anyway, I don't think anyone would fancy that stiff we saw at Jedburgh. He had holes in his socks:' He added inconsequentially.

'Do you think,' went on the older husband, 'that we should send some flowers or something, to the funerals, just to. show that we are kind of concerned, not just uncaring tourists?'.

I think,' said Dwight, 'we should wait until we learn a little more about the deceased. They might, for all we know turn out to be wanted criminals.'

'Caught by the bounty hunters?' May offered again.

'Seriously,' said Dwight, 'do you think we ought to suggest to John that we shorten the tour?'

'No way,' said Harry Webb, who stood on the fringes of the group. 'We have all paid handsomely for the trip, why should a couple of coincidental deaths put us off?' It was clearly the opinion of them all, as they turned to join the ladies in the drawing room.

As the first of the older married women came down the stairs, they could hear raised voices above them. It was first of all the indignant pitch of the tones that halted them.

Molly appeared.

'What is it this time?' asked the elderly Mrs Schumacher.

'It's Ruth. She says that Beth took her yellow scarf without asking on the trip today and hasn't brought it back. Beth first said she didn't and then admitted she did so Ruth called her a liar and a thief.'

'It'll probably turn up in the coach,' said Mrs Schumacher soothingly.

'More likely that mad Dryburgh woman picked it up and went off with it.' Jane Marshall emerged through the fire door. 'She'll have taken it home to weave a spell upon its owner. For heaven's sake.' She stood waiting on the landing.

There was just a hint of triumph in her voice as if she realised that the girls were really fighting over her.

'Come on down, girls,' said Mrs Oldberger, sweeping all before her. 'We have had quite enough trouble today without you three stirring it up.'

The whole company assembled in the drawing room, drawn once more together by the day's events. Collectively, they felt more able to cope with the unusual turmoil at Dryburgh. Brearley and Macdonald came back from their lodgings to move solicitously among the old and more jocularly with the young.

Elma Sorenson, her round face and slightly pop eyes adding weight to her utterance, said it for them all. 'It isn't so much the two deaths that get me. These things happen. It was that spooky, weird woman stretched out in the church, acting dead. Do you think she knew what had happened in Kelso?'

'And in Jedburgh?' put in Mrs Schumacher. 'Just like we saw.'

'And all that about "daith",' Mrs Bryant was not going to remain out of things, 'it gave me the creeps.'

'I think that you have to allow a little for the Scottish fascination with death. Meg just lets herself to get carried away when she finds a willing audience.' Brearley sought to calm them down. There was tension enough within the group.

'Isn't that right, Gus?'

The Texan Scot picked up his cue. 'Aye,' he replied. 'She's typical of the old Borders folk who like to carry on the tradition of Sir Walter recalling local folk history, dressing it up a bit, perhaps.'

Dwight took Brearley to one side. 'Do you think we should go on, John?' He asked. He had begun to have a premonition that this was another tour that he would never complete.

'Of course, Mr Graham. You wouldn't want the coincidence of the two deaths to put us off. Our Real Tours motto is that the show must go on.'

Warmed and encouraged by their evening drinks and communal reinforcement, they, or most of them, began to put the day's events in perspective. John Brearley sensed the rising morale.

'Wine on Real Tours at dinner, folks,' he said, 'and, tomorrow the peel towers. Smailholm is a real treat. We have special permission to Lord Steel's place, Aikwood.'

'Gee,' said Mrs Schumacher, 'Aikwood, ain't that just the cutest name.'

'What's a peel tower?' asked Mrs Sorenson, not afraid to show she had failed to study her brochure.

'It's one of these baby castles, not yet grown up to become the real thing,' said Bryant, 'where everyone in the valleys took refuge in the hill refuge when the English raiders came.'

'You know,'said Ruth;-

'"The mountain sheep are sweeter,
But the valley sheep are fatter:
We therefore deem it meeter
To carry off the latter."'

She felt she, too, had to get a word in somehow.

'That's not right, Ruth. Those were Welsh sheep. I majored in English Lit, so I ought to know. Anyway I think they had cattle in those days,' said Beth, maliciously

'Now then, girls,' said Mrs Oldberger, allowing a smile of anticipation to lighten her gloomy face at the thought of an encounter with a lord.

But the day was not finished for them or their plans. At nine o'clock reception called Brearley to the phone. He had remained with the party to sustain their humour.

'Is that Mr John Brearley, Manager of Real Tours?'

Brearley nursed a sinking feeling in his stomach.

'It is Inspector McConachie here. Now I have to tell you that a man was found dead in the ruins at Dryburgh Abbey after your departure this evening. We do not consider that his death can be due to natural causes and are mounting a full investigation. You will appreciate that coming on top of the incident in Kelso, we shall have to interview you and your party again.'

Before Brearley could expostulate, he continued.

'I am, of course, sensitive to the susceptibilities of your Americans, and I suggest that I come over tomorrow morning and see them each individually. I will arrange with the hotel to provide a room. Would you arrange your day accordingly.'

'Would, not can,' noted Brearley.

'Would you not reveal this information to your group until breakfast. I am anxious that there should be little time for prepared accounts.'

'Very good, Inspector.' Brearley accepted the inevitable. In any case he could foresee that the tour might very well have to go on because the police would be unwilling to allow the party to disperse. There was still five days to go. At least he would not have to make any refunds but that was the least of his worries.

He bade goodnight to those still at table and joined his partner at their separate lodging.

IV

Major Alistair Peter McAlistair stopped at The Feathers in Kelso on his road home. The day had been out of kilter so that he allowed himself another diversion from his routine. Besides, he was curious to know what the rumours were in the town.

When he eventually reached the haven of his hillside cottage, he brooded over his second evening drink. His solitude did not help his mood. It had been an ill day; he had not been able to follow his usual routine of inspection and had been forced from the scrutiny of stones and inscriptions with which he had become increasingly preoccupied, some might say obsessed.

At The Feathers they had said that Jones had been shot. He looked thoughtfully at his gun. It had come with him out of the army and he had no firearms certificate so the police would not necessarily come fussing to his door. But still, perhaps, he should be rid of it. It had served its purpose.

The police must be very puzzled by two deaths, he thought. What were they likely to do? Would it interfere with his next Abbey visit, Melrose, which was due in two days time? There was so much to be done in identifying the tombstones, and the fascination of the returned casket holding the heart of Robert the Bruce. And then it was such a magnificent setting for the dead. Jedburgh was too lofty and open, and there were few graves in the small cemetery. Kelso was too confined, Dryburgh was too peaceful. Yes, Melrose, with its great skeletal walls and windows, its great sweep of grass was a proper place for death, despite what that mad woman had said about Dryburgh. And Melrose Abbey was also on the Tweed.

The Americans had confused his day but he forgave them, they were not, after all, English.

V

Meg had made her way home on foot. One sight of the police and she was off. It wasn't as if she had done anything wrong so much as they represented the formal order of a world she had long rejected. And, 'forby,' she would have added as she often did, 'that McConachie, my ain first cousin, hae no spoken a word to me since Bessie arrived, a bairn out of wedlock, but a real love child, and that was saxteen years syne.'

She sped down to the river's edge, skirted the grounds of the hotel and took the footbridge across the Tweed. From there she could take the familiar and muddy footpaths to her cottage on the slopes of the hill. She felt safe as the three peaks of the Eildons and their woodlands received her back.

The small house had been given by the duke to her father when he had retired as a shepherd, Herd's Cottage it was known as locally although it had an older name. It was not much more than three rooms, bedroom, sitting room and kitchen, and the bathroom the Council had helped add on when Bessie was born.

A tumble down stone wall surrounded it but barely kept the rabbits out of the rude patch of garden. One bit where she tended some herbs showed signs of care, the rest of the front patch was given to potatoes and greens. At the back were the woodshed and the old outside lavatory set in uncut grass, and two posts carrying the line for the washing. The woodlands, that had taken over the hillside when the sheep were removed, hung above the rear wall and seemed to invade with a thicket of elders and current bushes.

For Meg it was home and always had been. She looked to see smoke from the chimney and knew her daughter was back from school. The bus dropped her off in Newtown as there was only a farm track up the hill.

Bessie was a tall, thinner edition of her mother. She had not ever known her father so she would not have been able to tell what features she might have inherited from him. She had her mother's sharp nose and set mouth with a rounder face, naturally more youthful, but already with a sense of adult responsibility which made her maturely attractive.

They did not immediately greet each other. Silence and a recognition of the pattern of the day was their manner of communication. Meg took off her boots at the back door, went into the bedroom to change her dress, and, re-clad, carried the cross through to hang on its hook in the kitchen.

Although there was an electric cooker, another gift from the Council, it stood unused against the wall, and it was over the old kitchen range that Bessie was stooping to stir the soup when her mother entered.

'So are you wanting to eat early?'

Bessie nodded. 'Aye,' she said. 'There's a disco in Earlston and Bob said he'd pick me up at half past seven.'

Meg was silent. Very often at the end of the day at Dryburgh, visitors would quietly offer her something for her utterances, and, although she did not readily admit to herself that she was a paid performer, she accepted the money gratefully. 'It's for Bessie,' she would say to herself, and she did not trouble to tell the Broo which was her other source of livelihood.

She looked disconsolately at her daughter who caught her glance.

'Did you nae get onything the day, mither?'

'No, The fowks were no unco gieing.' She was not

prepared to go into explanations. 'There was something wrang with them. But I can manage twa punds from the coal money.'

She crossed to the dresser to fetch out a tin from which she counted out the notes.

'That'll get you in, and you maun lean on Bob for the drink.'

By the time they had eaten and the motor bicyclist had rumbled off, the sun had passed round the Eildons, leaving Herd's Cottage in shadow. Meg brought in coal from the shed, drew up one of the two elderly armchairs to the stove, opened its door, and poured herself another cup of tea. The black cat recognising the evening's sequence, jumped from the dresser to the back of the chair, stretching out above the occupant.

It was the time of day Meg liked. She could see the evening sun lighting up all the familiar fields and farms stretching to the south as far as the great rounded mass of the Cheviots, and feel completely part of them. The earth was her flesh and its unspoken voice her song.

She reached out for the book, Thomas the Rhymour and his Rhymes, and settled over its pages. She did not really read the text in detail, but allowed her mind to pick on a word or line. Then she half-closed her eyes to stare into the fire or allowed them to blur at the cross.

She saw again the picture of Thomas of Erchildoune asleep under the Eildon Tree, she saw his spirit rise to greet the Queen of the Fairies and heard her say'

'If you will speak or tales tell
Thomas, you shall never mak' lee.'

Meg rocked herself in the chair in front of the fire and crooned,

'When seven years were come and gone,
The sun blinked fair on pool and stream,
And Thomas lay on Huntlie bank,
Like one awakened from a dream.'

For a moment she, too, was treading the heather and grass on the steep slopes, caught in a web of fancy. She could see in her imagination the sombre ruins of Melrose

Abbey at the hillfoot, its dark, misshapen tower, its lonely mullions, and scatter of tombstones, half lit by the moon. She retreated into the latent depths of her mind for the words she sought.

She glimpsed the lines on the page.

"For a' the bluid that's shed on earth

Rins through the springs o' that countrie"

At Dryburgh she had sensed the presence of death. She did not control what she uttered. What she said was like the old ministers' sermons, words from the belly inspired both by God and the congregation, and there had been something ill about hers today. She had known it when some discomfiting feeling assailed her as those visitors had come through the gate, a feeling reinforced when she had seen Thornell look up to those on the dormitory roof. In her mind's eye she had seen blood.

She sighed again, the world was intruding into her dreamlands: she could find no inspiration. The coal fire had fallen low. She made herself another cup of tea and settled down to await Bessie's return, while the black, contented cat purred above her head.

VI

If the scenes in the hotels and hills were quiet and restrained, they were not in the police headquarters. The Chief Constable had spoken to the Divisional Commander.

He was short. 'Can you handle this?'

'Yes, sir. McConachie is exceptionally experienced, as you know, from working in the south.'

'You understand that these three deaths in these circumstances are going to be headlines from John o' Groats to Land's End, not to mention the U.S.A. You should separate the investigation from the public relations, appoint a press liaison officer to deal with the media. You will have to keep the Abbeys closed as long as necessary, but not too long or we shall have the Tourist Boards yelping. How much information have you given out?'

'McConachie has asked that we do not reveal the cause of the deaths. We still think the first was natural but, of course, in the light of the subsequent murders, we have to reconsider.'

'If I know the Borders,' said the Chief Constable bluntly, 'you can't keep much secret. By the time doctors and nurses and passers-by have had their say, the world'll know what happened and probably have a fair idea of who was responsible.'

'You have Sergeant Evans with you. If you need further help, let me know. Meanwhile keep me informed,' he added.

The Divisional Commander sighed. It did not look as if the golf course would see much of him. He rang McConachie to pass on his superior's vote of confidence in him.

'For God's sake, Mac, come up with someone quickly. We don't want a religious maniac serial killer loose amongst us.'

Inspector Ian McConachie set his mobile phone down carefully on the table. He sat in the gatekeeper's lodge at Dryburgh, which he had taken over for the investigation, the only police caravan being in use at Kelso. Outside the full process of search was under way, the routine line of policemen beating across the Abbey grounds, the photographers and their batch of floodlights.

The doctor came importantly in. A local man called out for the emergency, 'He's dead, of course. I am not an expert in these matters but I think shot in the back of the head.'

'Can you give an estimate of the time of death?' The policeman looked intently at the young man.

'I think,' he said again, 'more than six hours ago, rigor mortis is well set in. I have made notes for your man that should help him.'

The policemen looked at their watches.

'It's just on eight o'clock now,' said Evans. 'Thornell must have been dead when we arrived.'

The doctor handed over the notes and took his leave.

'I can't do anything more for you here,' he said, 'I best

get back where I can deal with the living.'

Inspector McConachie looked thoughtfully across to Evans and lit his pipe.

'You're lucky, Mac,' said the sergeant, 'they won't let me smoke in my office.'

McConachie ignored him.

I think,' he said, 'that there's nothing you can do here, Taff, Suppose you go back to Kelso. Hawick's cleared your attachment to us. You had better ring your wife and say you are staying down here. Fix up a bed and then go round to the Bournes with one of our constables tomorrow morning and have a closer look round. Kelso will spend their time checking the visitors to the Abbey.'

'I shall have to complete what can be done here. We have the curious situation that we have interviewed everyone who was here today but I shall have to see them all again tomorrow, first thing, at their hotel, and Major McAlistair.' He paused. No, they had not interviewed everyone. He had forgotten his cousin Jeannie. He would have to seek her out in the morning as well.

'I think that we can eliminate the Stones, but in something like this, then again, perhaps we can't.'

Evans stubbed out his cigarette. 'Very good, sir. Can't say I can see much sign of drugs down here, more of a town thing.'

The stretcher party made its way along the path to the waiting ambulance and Evans followed them to take a lift with the escorting police car back to Kelso.

The Inspector went over in his mind what had been set in train. Much would have to be left to the following day and daylight. He selected from the shelves of leaflets, one that contained a map of the Abbey ruins and the grounds. He could see that it was not impossible for some unknown person to have gained access from either side over the low boundary fences and walls, and indeed Jeannie must have left without passing the lodge.

He considered the individuals he had interviewed. By that time, it was almost certain that Thornell was dead. Had he really been talking to a killer so shortly after the killing?

He had gained nothing from the conversations other than they had each at one time been in Kelso Abbey the previous day and that they did not seem entirely the usual exuberant bunch of American tourists. He had not taken to Brearley, but then the man had been naturally protective of his tour. He would have to see his partner as well. Then there was that funny, little Major. All he had wanted to do was rabbit on about the tombstones.

Forensic would have to come up with their more accurate estimate of the time of death, that was going to be critical, and what would be the clinching evidence that the killings were linked, the identification of the bullets.

It would all take time. He lit his pipe again, holding the match in the air until it went out. Had he time? Three deaths in three days.

'We have found the bullet, sir, in the wall of where the body was.' The young constable came in excitedly, holding up a cellophane bag. McConachie placed it carefully in his brief case. 'Well done.' he said. 'You know this area, don't you?'

'Yes, sir, I live in St Boswells.'

'You had better be prepared to spend the night here, I'll have a camp-bed and blankets sent down for you and I'll clear with the custodian that you can use his office. You do not have to stay awake all night, just check from time to time that no-one comes into the Abbey grounds.'

The police prepared to depart. The custodian who had remained conscientiously to the end, uncertain of what was required from him in circumstances dictated by the constabulary, handed over his keys, and carefully placed at the entrance a large notice, stating 'Abbey Closed.'

Somewhere in the night, the remnants of a yellow scarf were finely shredded to be flushed away for ever.

DEVIOUS WITNESSES

Where fair Tweed flows round holy Melrose
And Eildon slopes to the plain.
The Eve of St. John: Sir Walter Scott

I

The Inspector was up early the following morning. He had checked at Kelso on his way home and telephoned the forensic laboratories in Edinburgh, but neither had anything to report. He had taken his large frame wearily to bed at his home in Midlem when his wife had barely stirred.

He was on the phone again first thing when she called out that his breakfast was ready.

'You were late last night,' she said, which was the nearest she ever went to asking about police matters. He nodded, and turned on the radio for the Borders News at five minutes to eight.

'A man has been found dead in Kelso Abbey in suspicious circumstances. The police have set up an investigation centre at the site and are appealing for information. The victim has been identified as Elwyn Jones of 23 Niedpath Terrace.'

'Inspector Gray said this morning:'

The officer came on live.

'We are appealing to any members of the public who were in the Abbey or its vicinities on Tuesday last to make contact with our officers in the caravan, even if they do not think that they noticed anything unusual. They will help us to form a pattern of the comings and goings in the area. Police investigations are actively continuing.'

'Do you think, Inspector,' asked the news reader, 'that this death has anything to do with that of the man found in Jedburgh? After all, two deaths in two of our Abbeys are a curious coincidence?'

'We have no reason to suppose that there is any connection between the two.' The officer appointed to handle the media, was short, economic with the truth, as he knew of the third death, but had been instructed to withhold news of it.

'The Tweed Commissioners, ... ' the radio went on. McConachie turned it off.

'That's it, my dear,' he said, and in unwonted expansion to his wife, 'and, I'm afraid by lunchtime if you tune in then, you will hear of a third death, this time at Dryburgh, but don't say anything about it until you hear it on the radio. It won't be just the Borders news either.'

Meg glanced anxiously at her husband. He did not usually talk about his work. He was near retirement and the Borders appointment had been as he put it 'last thing before being put out to grass.'

He caught his wife's eye. 'Don't worry, lass, they have put that fellow to deal with all the press, and just left me to get on with the job. That's probably the easier bit.'

'But, Ian,' she said, 'we've no just the three old abbeys, there's a fourth.'

As McConachie drove towards the hotel to interview the Americans, he pondered his wife's remark. Was he really dealing with a serial killer carrying on a private crusade against Abbey visitors? It seemed a pretty daft idea. On the other hand if something happened at Melrose, he would look pretty stupid himself. He drew up in a lay by. He could not be seen using a mobile phone while driving. He checked with Hawick.

'Yes,' said the Divisional Commander, 'we have made sure that Melrose will station a man in the grounds, inconspicuously, and uniformed police outside. It will comfort the visitors. Jedburgh's open, of course, but Kelso and Dryburgh will remain shut for the time being until you give us the all clear.'

McConachie met Detective Constable Goddard, who had been duly sent to assist him, in the foyer of the hotel. Brearley and Macdonald were talking to those of their tour who had already come down to breakfast. They sat at the restaurant tables in silence with shocked faces. A third death in the very place that they had been, and perhaps at the very time that they had been there, struck home.

The hotel manager had set aside the conference room for police use, and the Inspector asked Brearley to assemble his tour in the lounge when they came down from where he could call them for individual interview.

This time he did not feel a need to be so tactful. After all one of them might well be a murderer.

He arranged that when any one had been questioned, each would not return to the lounge but remain separate, in the conference waiting room. He told his assistant to telephone forensic to see if the police surgeon in Edinburgh could come up with a more accurate time for Thornell's death.

Constable Goddard came back to say that he could not get through. McConachie found a telephone in the conference room and picked it up impatiently. He had to know if the shooting had taken place during the group's morning visit or in the afternoon.

'Mac,' said the pathologist. 'You're being a bit swift. I have barely had time to read your local G.P.'s notes. Did you have a warm day, yesterday? Where was the body lying?'

'It was a warm day but the body was in a cold place, a stone passage they call a slype at the Abbey.'

'That complicates matters, body temperature will have fallen more quickly. Anyway we are still working on your other holy killing. We shall be just as quick as we can but right now I cannot give you any definite answers. I can just tell you one thing, your Dryburgh body, he seems to have the tiniest fragment of cloth, probably yellow, at the entrance wound. The man wasn't wearing a cap, was he?' McConachie made a note to find out. 'But,' the doctor added 'I shan't be visiting any of your Abbeys in a hurry.' He laughed and hung up. Those not unacquainted with death were allowed their humour, thought McConachie, and imagined him restoring a mask to his face, returning white coated, to his gory work.

Meanwhile he had to work on the two possibilities.

He turned to the task in hand, deciding to see Brearley first. The manager outlined the pattern of the two days as planned for his group, how the visit to Kelso Abbey was not organised but left to the individual, while that to Dryburgh was co-ordinated. A lecturer came from the university to give a detailed account of the Abbey ruins.'

'Name,' said the Inspector brusquely. He had not hitherto realised that there was yet another person, connected with the tour on the site.

'McShea, Ian McShea,' said Brearley. 'He's a senior lecturer in the adult education department. Most days while we are in the Borders, he comes with us to give specialist talks on whatever we are seeing.'

'Have you told him what has happened?'

'Yes, I telephoned last night.' Brearley glanced uncertainly at his interrogator. 'I had to let him know in case any of our future plans were thrown out by this, this ...' He waved his hands.

McConachie eyed him, inwardly kicking himself for not ferreting this out before.

'When did McShea leave Dryburgh?'

'He finished his talk on the roof, the dormitory building that is, and then left for Edinburgh. He always has to get back by lunchtime.'

'Did you see him go?'

Brearley shook his head. 'I was busy seeing my people off the roof and explaining to them the arrangements for lunch at the hotel. But his car had gone when we did go across to the hotel.'

As far as he could remember, he went on in answer to other questions, 'after the talk there was about quarter of an hour before we went for lunch. Some decided to leave the ruined buildings until the afternoon and walked down to the river, while others started to explore immediately. I can't tell you offhand who went where but I can think and try to give you a list later.'

'What about the afternoon?'

He described how they returned to find the black figure

stretched out in the church. He thought that everyone had been collected together in the one place and had had no time to disperse.

'Are you sure?'

There was a pause. 'No,' he said. 'We were all looking at that mad woman.'

'Lastly, Mr Brearley, is there anything else you think it would be helpful to tell us.'

He shook his head. 'Can I ask you, Inspector, if we can go on as planned with the tour? We still have a four days to go. I have quite a lot of money committed to it and some of the party are talking of quitting.'

'From our point of view, the police that is, I should not want any of your party to depart immediately so that it should suit us both for your tour to continue as planned. Kindly let me know your daily schedule. And I think it would be helpful if you could write down as much as you know about where the different members of your group come from and how they join the tour.'

'Perhaps you could ask another person to come up, might as well go in alphabetical order.'

McConachie lit his pipe, ignoring the strict injunction against smoking on the conference room wall. He would for once take advantage of his uniform. It struck him again to be a little curious to be grilling a lot of United States citizens about the deaths of two very local Borders men.

John Bryant came in and the Inspector waved him to a chair. He had arranged the furniture so that he and the witness sat in upright but comfortable chairs with the light coming over his shoulder, while Goddard sat at the table to take notes..

'Mr Bryant, ' he said, 'you will have learnt by now that there has been a second death. Yesterday I went over with you your movements in Kelso so I don't need to go over all the business of full name, address, age and occupation'.

Bryant smiled. 'I guess not,' he said.

'I have now to ask you about yesterday at Dryburgh. The gardener was killed sometime between when you all saw him from the roof and when his body was discovered in the late afternoon. I need to ask each of you what your movements were during those two occasions you were all in the Abbey grounds.'

The young man nodded. 'I'll try and do anything to help you, captain.'

Goddard rose to switch on the overhead projector to throw an enlarged plan of the Abbey and its surrounds onto the screen with which the conference room was conveniently provided

'Well,' said Bryant, 'you'll know, I guess, that in the morning we all met up at the church to listen to that university guy and then went up onto the roof where that funny, black woman kept interrupting him. She knocked some loose stones over the edge. I didn't see the fella underneath but I heard him holler. After the lecture, we all trooped down the stair ready to go to lunch.'

McConachie listened attentively, warming towards his witness. Bryant had close- cropped hair, horn-rimmed spectacles, and a rounded face that gave him an owlish and observant appearance. Intelligent and honest, the policeman thought.

'Mr Bryant, before you all went to lunch where did you go. Perhaps you could show me on the map.'

'The party split up a bit, some went straight down to the river. 'He closed his eyes in recalling the scene. 'Yeah, I think the oldies, as we call them, carried on down the path, while our lot decided to explore the old buildings right away.'

'Our lot?'

'That's Mike and Mary May, the four girls, Jane, Beth, Ruth and Molly, and Margaret Lake, she's never sure which group she belongs to. Dwight, Dwight Graham, and Harry Webb, and my wife, Leslie, of course.'

'Our lot all started, I think at the reconstruction, you know that picture of what the place used to look like, and we had just decided where we were going when that little fellow with the moustache, not in our group...'

'You mean Major McAlistair, was he there, too?'

'I don't know his name but he always sees to be around.

Well, he stopped Les and me and said, "Don't miss this," and he pointed to a stone in the ground where some workmen had scratched the lines for an old game. "Nine Men's Morris", I think he called it. "Perhaps you still play it across the herring pond", he said. He seemed a bit funny, too.'

McConachie let that pass. He would have to investigate the Major's funniness later.

'Oh yes, and those two, the couple with the bicycles, they were there too, interested in the scratches. By that time we all split up and poked about in the different buildings in the cloister. Les said she did not want to go into that chapterhouse until later. It's a gloomy looking hole and she did not like the man she had seen there. Then we saw other people heading for the gate so we went down the steps by the warming room and cut across the grass to join them at the lodge.'

He could not remember the individual movements of the others of what he called 'our lot'. In the afternoon he had stood in the church watching the 'funny woman' and then almost immediately had been interviewed by McConachie and the sergeant. After that he and his wife felt that they had had enough and they retired to the coach.

In turn Leslie Bryant confirmed her husband's account of the day. The only observation that she could add was that, as she had been nearer the edge of the roof, she had seen the man, whose name she had learnt was Thornell, emerging from the room below. She had been struck and rather frightened by the way he had stared up at them. It was as if he suddenly recognised someone.

Dwight Graham Jnr, as he like to be described, came next. He sat down heavily in the proffered chair.

'You have quite a problem on your hands, Inspector.' He had taken the trouble to get the rank right. 'As a lawyer, I can recognise a difficult case when I see one. I said to John we ought to pack up this tour right away and get out of your way.'

'Yes, indeed, Mr Graham,' said McConachie, not making it clear which statement he was agreeing with. 'You will appreciate that we should like you all to remain at hand until we have solved our two killings. After all some of you may even be required as witnesses.' He did not added, ' or as accused'.

He went over the same ground and Graham's account tallied with Bryant's. Yes, before lunch he had explored the ruins, he had looked into the chapterhouse but seen no-one there. No, after lunch he had not re-entered the cloister but remained at the church watching Meg until interviewed at the gatehouse and then rejoined the coach.

When the Inspector thanked him and asked him to send the next person up, Graham half rose and then resumed his seat.

'Might I ask you something, Inspector if I am not being too presumptuous?' He studied the Inspector's face.

Taking McConachie's look as assent, he continued. 'Would you tell me how these two men were killed?'

McConachie deliberated with himself. After all his witness was a responsible lawyer.

'Yes,' he said, 'I think that I can safely tell you, Mr Graham, but I should like your undertaking not to pass it on. They were both shot.'

'Indeed,' said the attorney, 'then I had better tell you which of our party carries a gun.'

He leant forward earnestly from his chair. 'Harry Webb.'

The Inspector questioned him closely and thanked him again to close the interview. He decided to continue with the alphabetical order although he realised Webb would be the last. With each successive witness he went over the same ground, establishing a little more detail of the pattern of movement by Bryant's party, which he would have to study later. Meanwhile he needed to work through them quickly.

Webb came in and sat down confidently in the chair.

'Mr Webb, this is Constable Goddard who is taking notes.' McConachie began, to establish the presence of a third party. He let his eyes pass across the man's jacket to where Graham alleged there was a shoulder holster. Webb's long, rather grey face, seemed for a moment almost to anticipate the question.

'Mr Webb, I understand you carry a gun.'

The man's expression did not alter.

'Well, Inspector,' he replied in a stronger southern drawl than the other Americans used. 'Well, I did reckon it was time I came clean with you.'

His hand reached into the inside of his coat pocket in a movement which might have caused alarm in his home town, and brought out a wallet from which he took a card. He passed it over.

It carried a photograph, signature and the legend, 'United States Federal Bureau of Narcotics.'

'Let me explain,' he said. 'We have been interested for some time in that man, Angus Macdonald, who is suspected of drug trafficking. I don't have to tell you, Inspector, how seriously we regard dealing in drugs in the States. We have for a long time regarded his tourist activities as a cover so I was instructed to become one of the group he signed up for this tour.'

'Why did you not tell me this yesterday? You gave as your occupation, insurance salesman.'

'I did not want to blow my cover unless I had to or unless I had gathered enough evidence against Macdonald. If we had had a long session at Dryburgh, everyone would have wondered why.'

'And you have a gun?'

'Always have my gat,' He tapped his chest.

'How did you bring it into this country?'

'Special clearance from your drug squad at Scotland Yard.' He produced another official document from his wallet

Why the hell did those at the centre not keep those in the field informed, McConachie thought to himself.

'Mr Webb,' he said in as level a tone as he could muster, 'we shall have to check this. It would really have been much easier if we had been informed of all this in advance.'

He reached for the telephone and spoke rapidly to Hawick. 'They'll ring back,' he said. 'Mr Webb, I have no reason to doubt your documentation and clearly it would

be helpful if we can co-operate once your status is confirmed. I think we should stop now so that our interview is
no longer than with the others.' He parted from Webb as
politely as he could and went downstairs to get hold of
Brearley.

'Would you tell your party that I am sorry to have had
to delay their day but I am sure they will appreciate the reasons. Your tour must go on and no-one should be allowed
to depart without clearance from us. Please keep the group
together. Where are you going today?'

'We are due at the peel towers, Smailholm, and
Aikwood. Tomorrow, Melrose Abbey.'

'I have stressed to those in the tour, mostly the older
women, that there is no reason to be alarmed, the two victims were local, but some of your group may be key witnesses. Oh, and can you ask Mr Macdonald to see me. He
seems to have been left off the list.'

McConachie clumped up the stairs. His wife told him
not to use lifts, exercise keeps you fit, she said. Back in the
conference room, Goddard handed him the phone. 'Hawick
confirm Webb's bona fide. 'The D.C.'s just as angry as you
are, sir, but he wants a word.'

'London says Webb's genuine, and has clearance to
keep a gun. God knows why we are not kept informed.
Meanwhile I had the American consul in Edinburgh on the
line. She's had complaints that the American tourists are
not being allowed to get on with their trip. Their 'consti-
tootional' rights are being interfered with.'

'I have just released them for today's sight seeing, and
asked that the tour continue.'

'Good.' The Divisional Commander did not waste
words or his subordinate's time. As McConachie put down
the phone, Goddard ushered Macdonald into the room.

II

Sergeant William Evans had duly found himself a snug
billet for the night. A police officer's widow kept a bed and

breakfast in Kelso and could always find a bed for a copper on late night duty. He set off next morning to report to the caravan by the Abbey to find out what the investigation had revealed.

'We are checking and cross checking all the evening's visitors,' said the officer in charge, 'but we shall have to wait until the Inspector returns to reconcile what we have with his accounts obtained from that American group. Meantime we've had a further hint that Jones was involved with drugs. I think that you should take young Ginger here and call on the Bournes again. He'll take the dog.'

The red headed constable went off enthusiastically to collect the animal from his van. It looked like a cross between a dachshund and a Border terrier, one ear cocked and the other down, with a short, rough-haired, tawny coat.

'Doesn't look much, sergeant,' said the constable, 'but a first class nose. We had best walk him there so that he can lift his leg on the way and not in Mrs Bourne's front room. He gets a bit excited. Answers to Mop.'

They crossed the old graveyard to avoid the busy town streets and made their way to Neidpath Terrace.

Mrs Bourne first made some protest at this second police intrusion into her home but she realised that it was better to have them inside than for all the neighbours to see them at the door.

'It's just routine, you know, Misses,' said Evans. 'We want to make sure that we did not miss anything last time, and you will want to help to bring Spike's killer to justice, won't you?'

'What's the dog for?' Kathy standing, twisting her handkerchief with her fingers, eventually found words.

Evans turned directly towards her. 'We have had information that suggests Spike was involved with drugs. Do you think that is possible?'

'No, he wasn't,' she said and Mrs Bourne broke in to say defiantly. 'Spike wouldn't do onything like that. He was a good lad.' And she clutched her handkerchief again.

'You won't mind then if we have a look round.' For Evans the denials were familiar and these were not convincing.

'Should you no have a warrant or something?' Kathy protested.

'Ms Bourne,' said Evans, rather formally, 'if your mother was to ask us to leave, we could, of course, obtain one. But it would suggest to us that you had something to hide which may or may not be the case. But remember that Spike may have concealed things here which neither of you know about.'

It was a well-rehearsed line. The two women gave a reluctant consent and sat down unhappily on the sofa in the front room. They listened as the police went upstairs and heard them moving from room to room, urging the dog to seek.

'Smells like the proverbial tart's parlour,' said Evans in the couple's bedroom.

'And the bathroom stinks of bleach,' said the dog handler. 'Mop's nae got much of a chance.'

The two men came downstairs to complete their search, running the dog through the kitchen and opening the cupboards. At one point Mop pointed excitedly at a packet in a shelf corner, and the constable called Evans over so that the two of them could witness the discovery. But it was only an elderly packet of fruit lozenges.

They asked the women to shift from the front room while they let the dog loose there and then took it out in the small back garden where there were signs of a recent bonfire.

'Are you allowed a bonfire in the town, Mrs Bourne?' asked Evans.

'Aye, 'she said, ' as lang as it nae a bother for the neighbours. While's I ridd up the patch and burn the bit twigs and garden rubbish.' She seemed more placid.

'There's nothing here,' said Evans, as they went out, 'so you did not need to be worried.'

There was a blue Mini parked at the doorway. 'Is that your car?' asked Evans as they left.

'It's Kathy's,' she said, closing the door firmly behind them.

'I just feel, boyo,' said the sergeant to his companion as they walked back to the Abbey, 'that there has been stuff there. In my line of business, you get a hunch about people. I sometimes think I have a better nose than dogs.'

They reported back to the caravan. Already the news hounds were there, toting their cameras round the perimeter of the ruins to obtain as clear shots as were possible of the inside. Evans made his way into the caravan ignoring their questions.

'I've told them,' said the local sergeant, 'that they will be given a statement at half past twelve at the police station and that we have nothing to say here. They'll get the announcement of Thornell's death at Dryburgh and then all hell will be let loose. The fellow from the Reporter is already onto it, God knows how, but we should have finished searching the grounds by now.' He looked at his watch.

III

In Hawick, Shelagh Thornell was in dire distress. The day before, when the police had come round as she came in from her morning shopping, she had said.

'Is there anything wrang?'

'No, no, Mrs Thornell,' the policeman had replied. 'We just want to find where Jim is working the day to ask him some questions.'

She did not say that when her husband had come in late the previous evening, he had seemed ill at ease. She had put it down to his drinking. Then last night when he had not come back for his tea, she had braced herself for another return of a churlish, bad tempered man. When the doorbell had rung, she had opened it to see the station sergeant, McLaren, a relative on her mother's side.

She stood, miserable in her expectation with her mouth open.

'Can I come in, Shelagh?' he said.

'Is it, is it Jim?' she stammered.

'Aye,' he said, 'there's been an accident at Dryburgh.'

'Is he deid?' she asked, lifting here eyes to his.

'I am afraid so, Shelagh. I can't give you any details, I just got the message on the phone to tell you. I'll come mysel' first thing tomorrow when I know exactly what happened.'

He put his arm gently round her. 'Now, sit down and I'll make a cup of tea for you.'

'Na, na,' she said, 'I can manage that.'

She busied herself in a familiar routine, glad to find something for her hands to do. He followed her through to the kitchen.

'Is your daughter still in Hawick?' he asked. 'Can you get her to come round?'

'Aye, but she's got twa bairns.'

'You had better give her a ring. I expect your son-in-law can manage the kids for the night.'

Mrs Thornell poured out the tea and sat inertly on the couch, nursing the cup.

'I'll tell you what,' said the sergeant, 'you mind we live only a few doors down from you. I'll get my wife to come in until you've managed to get hold of your daughter. You don't want to be on your ain at a time like this. Can I use the phone?'

It was not long before his wife appeared, it was a duty she had done before. At the sight of her, Shelagh Thornell burst into a flood of tears.

'Would you tell her,' he whispered to his wife, 'that I shall come back in the morning.'

He took the phone call first thing the following day.

'You had better question her,' McConachie instructed him. 'Take another officer with you and try to have the daughter present.' Mclaren reported that his wife had said Shelagh Thornell seemed more composed when she left, then returned to the Thornell house to ring the front door bell once more..

'May we come in, Shelagh?'

She led them to the front room, comfortable with its lace curtains and unused look. Her daughter was on the phone in the corner.

'He says he can manage the bairns, Mum, so I can stay the day.' She looked up apprehensively at the two police officers.

'I am glad you can stay,' Sergeant McLaren spoke. 'We have to ask your mother some questions.'

'What happened to Dad? Can we see him?'

They sat down awkwardly.

'I cannot say more at this moment in time, my dear, than that he was murdered.' The women looked sharply at him.

'But you said that it was an accident?'

'Yes, I know, Mrs Thornell,' Sergeant McLaren felt he had to keep this conversation formal, 'sometimes it is better to put things that way when we do not know exactly what happened.' He glanced at the clock on the piano. He would be able to explain more fully before he left.

'Can you tell us about your husband's work?'

'When he was laid off at the mill, they told him that he had to accept onything offered. He dinna liked to be idle, him that was a skilled mill hand all his days, and I didna want him sitting aboot at hame, sae he took this job of cleaning up the Abbey grounds. Jed, Kelso, Dryburgh and Melrose and then a day spare for onything extra that turned up in the week.' She dried a tear on her face.

It all eventually came out. Yes, there seemed recently more money, she had thought it was the horses, his bad temper had seemed to turn to secrecy, and she thought that maybe he was delivering something round the town of an evening.

'And was there anything unusual about his behaviour on Tuesday evening?'

'He was late back, which he often was from Kelso, so I didna expect him early.'

Pressed, she admitted that she found him more surly than usual which she attributed to drink. 'I was aye feart he'd lose his licence and then no be able to work at a'.'

IV

Inspector McConachie sat back in his chair in the hotel conference room. He had not obtained anything new from Macdonald. He had not liked the fellow at all. About as trustworthy as a weasel, he thought, too glib. But of them all, according to him, he had not gone into Kelso Abbey although he had been in the vicinity, nor had he appeared on the scene at Dryburgh.

Then there was Mr Harry S. Webb, seemed a bit odd that there he was with a gun, yet his credentials seemed in order. He had let the man go on the peel tower trip so as not to prejudice his position with the group, but he would have to find out the whole story from him when they met later in the evening. He told Brown to pass the details of Webb's pistol to forensic, who already had the bullet from Dryburgh.

It was becoming complicated. He had to do things in the right order. The troops could cover all the routine ground. He telephoned the police caravan in Kelso to learn from Evans that nothing had been found at the Bournes, nor had any bullet been found in the Abbey there.

'Nothing new from here,' said the Sergeant, 'but the press are off like Rhonda Valley greyhounds to Dryburgh.'

'You were right about the drugs link, Taff, one of these Americans is an agent of the U.S. Federal Bureau of Narcotics. I have arranged to meet him this evening when the tour comes back. It would be useful if you could join us. I am off to see the Major, and if I have time, Jeannie, you know the one they call Mad Meg, I'll try and pick you up at six in Kelso.'

Taking Constable Goddard with him, McConachie set off for the remote village in the Cheviots. It was the sort of peaceful landscape, more sheep than humans, into which the Inspector had expected to settle without undue disturbance. Now, he thought to himself, although with little immediate apprehension, within this gentle world of farm-land and ancient buildings, he was engaged in tracking down a killer.

He sent Goddard into the Post Office to ask the whereabouts of the Major's house, and was directed to the top of
the hill, almost across the border. They found him at home.
He received them rather brusquely, leading them into the
sitting room with a large bay window facing the rising
ground of the green hills. On the arm chairs and sofa a
number of plans were laid out, which the Inspector could
see were of the Abbeys and their graveyards.

Major McAlistair cleared them to one side so that his
visitors could sit down.

'I am sorry to interrupt you. Major, but we needed to
ask you a few more questions,' the Inspector began.

'You mean about Kelso? I thought that I had given you
an account of everything I knew.'

'Yes, you did. It is not about Kelso, it's about Dryburgh.'

"What about Dryburgh?' The Major stared fiercely at
him. He seemed to bridle at yet another interference into
his stamping grounds.

'Have you not heard that a man, Thornell, was found
dead at Dryburgh after you and the others left yesterday
evening?'

'No.' The Major showed no surprise. 'It was not in the
paper, and I do not listen to the news until the evening.' He
paused as if to let the information sink in. 'That makes
three.'

It was the Inspector's turn to remain impassive.

'Yes,' he said, 'so you will understand that we need to
find all we can about everyone's movements in the grounds
at the Abbey yesterday.'

The Major was a very clear-headed witness. 'I like to
keep an eye on these visitors. I once caught some English
tourists chipping at the stonework for souvenirs. I told
them their ancestors had done quite enough damage in the
past.' He confirmed the pattern of the visitors' traversing of
the ruins and lawns, which Goddard took down carefully.

'You go to these Abbeys regularly, don't you Major?'
asked the Inspector as he was standing up to leave.

'Yes,' he replied. 'I have made it my duty to seek the
improvement of their graveyards. Never been done. The

English destroyed the Abbeys, and now all these English that the heritage bodies employ don't do a thing about them. They simply don't understand that we Scots feel strongly about our dead. I used to work for the War Graves Commission where we did take care of them.'

He stopped. 'That Thornell, is he the gardener fellow who worked in the Abbey grounds? I knew him as Jim.'

McConachie nodded.

'Shot, you say?'

Again the Inspector nodded, although if he had said it, he had not intended to.

There was another pause. McAlistair was pondering.

He said at last. 'You know, I am just remembering it. As I was leaving the Abbey grounds for lunch, I wanted to be ahead of the crowd, I think I heard a shot, bit muffled. I looked around because I expected to see pigeons taking off from the woods, but there weren't any.'

Goddard took out his notes and added this new information in the appropriate columns of his notes.

'Would you be sure, Major? This could be critically important.'

'Yes, I am,' said McAlistair shortly.

When he turned to go, McConachie turned to thank him.

'By the way,' he said, 'do you have a gun?'

The Major did not reply immediately. He fussed over the curtain that screened the front door.

The Inspector was about to repeat the question, when the answer came.

'Shotgun and certificate.'

Before the police left the village, McConachie stopped the car again at the Post Office.

'You might just go in again, Gordon, make an excuse to buy a paper, and see if you get any local background to the man. He did not seem to have a wife.'

The constable re-emerged. 'The old wifie was quite chatty. I explained that we were doing a routine check on shotgun certificates and she blethered on. His wife died last year, he had a dog which was injured in a car accident and she says the Major had to shoot the animal. Bit of a loner, he writes regularly to his children in the south. In fact, she says, everything he does is very regular. She was a bit surprised last night when he came back late.'

'Well done,' said the Inspector. 'Food for thought there. Now for a very different cup of tea.' The constable allowed himself a dutiful smile.

McConachie decided to drop Goddard off at Kelso. 'Tell Sergeant Evans I'll be back to pick him up in about an hour.'

He did not think that his cousin would be seriously involved in the murders, she would talk, if she would talk at all, better to him on his own.

He took the car through Newtown St. Boswells, stopped at the foot of the hill track and climbed up to the cottage. He could see Jeannie working in the garden, lifting potatoes with a graip. She saw him coming but went on with her work.

'Evening, Jeannie,' he said.

'Is it you, then, Ian?' she said, carrying the shaw to one side to shake off the crop, which she gathered carefully into an old wicker basket.

She stood for a moment looking at him, both hand resting on the fork handle, and then, picking up the basket, hurried round to the back of the house to reappear at the front door.

'You'd best come in,' she said, 'but be sure to tak the dirt off your feet aforehand.'

He dutifully scuffed his shoes on the mat, doffed his uniform cap, tucked it under his arm and followed her into the kitchen.

'Bessie's awa' oot,' she said, 'so you'll nae see her, but it'll no be her you've come to see. You've had saxteen years.' She glanced fiercely at him as she put the kettle back on the heat of the range.

McConachie sat down gingerly on the elderly armchair she pointed to. He looked round the kitchen that was like the one he was brought up in. It was a friendly room with no pretensions other than to sustain life: its simple furnishings comprised the old cast iron cooker, a stack of wood and a scuttle of coal, a handsome oak dresser with hooks for the cups and cupboards for the plates, a few tins for the necessities of tea and sugar, and no doubt the spare cash. The worn deal table was smooth with the years of use and scrubbing, and the photographs on the slate mantel were brown in their simple frames. For a moment he compared it to his own sitting room, glossy and centrally heated, full of the right furniture keeping up with the Jones.

'Aye,' he said, 'it's been a lang time, Jeannie.'

'Well,' she said, as she poured out the tea, 'I dinna jalouse that ye've come here, all dressed up like that, to blether about what's lang past.'

He became a policeman again.

'You were at Dryburgh Abbey yesterday?'

'Aye,' she said, 'until I saw you lot coming.'

He let it pass. 'Have you heard what has happened?'

She said: 'Bessie came back from school with tales of two dead, murdered, she said, the yin in Kelso and the other at Dryburgh, but I dinna ken onything aboot them.'

'But you were in Dryburgh, what were you doing?'

'I'm a paid up member of yon heritage people so I can go there when I like, can I no?' She bristled at this interference.'

He sought to mollify her. 'I'm no saying that you shouldn't have been there, but was there any particular reason for going there yesterday?'

'While's I feel ca'ed to go to yin place or anither. Yesterday I just wanted to go and speak to ony folk at the Abbey who wad heed me. I gie them the wirds True Thomas gies me.'

She began to rock herself in her chair as if to fall into a trance.

He hastened to continue.

'Look, he said. 'Jim Thornell, you must know him, was killed, shot in the passageway below the cloister at Dryburgh yesterday. Were you there all day, did you see him?'

She turned towards him, for a moment her eyes seemed

to be focused beyond, but they cleared.

'Aye, I saw him, he stood below us, cam into the sunlicht and then went back into the shadow. He shouted at us and looked at yin.'

'What do you mean, Jeanie, "looked at one"? Try to remember who was standing beside you. Was it one of them that caught Thornell's glance?'

'Bluid,' she said, drawing her knees up in her hands and swaying from side to side. 'I saw bluid,' she said.

The Inspector checked on the time. He had one last attempt to bring his witness to respond to his question but she had escaped into her own world.

'Did you see Thornell again during the day?'

Jeannie made no answer. She crooned to herself and he could only half make out the words she spoke.

'Melrose tower stands ta' against the sky.'

'Jeannie, are you going to Melrose tomorrow?' he found himself asking.

It was no use. He would have to come back or perhaps some other officer would have to be sent, to try and extract a more coherent account of Mad Meg's day. If only they could establish if Thornell was killed before or after lunch. He took his leave, frustrated and cross with himself, having thought that he would have been successful with his relative. She was dafter than he had imagined.

He looked at his watch again. He had time to seek out the Stones at the Dryburgh Hotel; he preferred in any case to keep his dealings with Roger to himself. He returned to his car and took the road north across the Tweed to make his way through the woods to the hotel by the Abbey where he found the couple enjoying an evening drink in the lounge..

Roger greeted him. 'We rather thought that we might see you, Mac. We are about to take off for Melrose. Can I get you some refreshment?'

He shook his head.

Daphne asked. 'Do you want to speak to my husband in private, Inspector?'

'No,' he smiled. 'Not on this occasion. I really need to

ask you about the sequence of events at Dryburgh. You'll know by now that we found the gardener, Jim Thornell, shot in the grounds after you left last night.'

They confirmed to him what he already knew. After the announcement of lunch, they had remained by the tombs, talking to the man they now knew as the Major, until he had left to follow the group through the cloister. He had said to them that he wanted to reach the hotel before the crowd. Daphne thought that the older members of the party had gone down to the river and then come directly back without re-entering the ruins. They themselves had followed them to the gate.

McConachie relaxed briefly; he felt that he had known Roger long enough to trust him.

'You'll have heard, Roger, that there seems to be a connection between these murders and drugs?'

Roger nodded. 'Yes,' he said. 'I had the idea that you wouldn't have a drug problem up here, but they tell me that this was a vain hope. Nowhere seems clear of it.'

'Too true,' said the Inspector grimly. He paused.

'Am I right, Roger, that your people are now working with Scotland Yard in dealing with drug traffickers?'

'Yes, Mac. It's not my particular line, but I have colleagues who are closely involved.'

'Could I ask you to do something for me? One of this American party has produced documentation claiming to be an agent of the Federal Bureau of Narcotics. Rather late in the day, Scotland Yard has confirmed his credentials. Could you get me a confidential report on the man from your office? He carries a gun and I don't like him.' He looked up uncertainly to se if his personal animosity was considered irrational.

'If he's the man we're thinking of,' Daphne allowed herself to remark, 'we share your view. We watched them having lunch yesterday. He certainly does not fit in with the others. In fact,' she went on rather inconsequentially, 'we think that they are a not a very happy party.'

'Certainly,' said Roger. The Inspector took out his notebook, wrote down the name, Harry S. Webb, followed by such details as he thought suitably descriptive, and handed over the sheet. 'I have added the Hawick station number which will also reach me on my mobile.'

'Very grateful for anything you can find out. It is pretty upsetting to have this sprung on you in the middle of a murder investigation, and something of a coincidence. You'll appreciate I must move on. Good-bye, Mrs Stone, I hope that we can have a more social meeting before you go south again.'

When he had left, Roger took a long draught of his beer.

'Yes,' he smiled at his wife, 'yes. I know we are on holiday, and I am not going to get involved.' But he did get up and go to the telephone.

V

When the Inspector returned to the caravan at Kelso, it was to find Evans with the Kelso sergeant, sitting in silence. He sensed that the two men did not get on. Perhaps there was local resentment against the Welshman from Edinburgh. He let the Kelso policeman speak first.

The Sergeant handed him a sheaf of papers. 'These are the tabulated movements in and out of Abbey for Tuesday evening, sir. Edinburgh forensic has given an estimated time of death between eight thirty and ten thirty p.m. which does not help much. I have taken statements from those witnesses whom I thought relevant. I can't say I see anyone conspicuously suspect. Evans, here, took the dog to the Bourne's house, that's where Jones lived with the girl, Kathy, but found nothing.' He looked a little acidly at Evans.

The Welsh sergeant felt he had to defend himself.

'I think,' he said, 'with due respect, sir, that they had had time to conceal anything they needed to. I still think this is a drugs case.'

'Maybe, maybe,' said the Scot, 'we're getting a bit of feedback in the town, nothing very definite, that Jones was distributing stuff, but I have another bit of information which is important, Kathy seems to have been carrying on with Thornell. She has a car, a blue Mini, and on Tuesdays, whenever Thornell was in Kelso, she picked him up while Spike was at work, and they would go off together.' He looked up at the Inspector for approval.

'How did you find this out, sergeant?'

'We first had an anonymous phone call, shortly after the announcement at lunchtime, and I sent a man to check the story out with neighbours in the terrace. They didn't like to clype,' - he shot a quick glance at Evans to see if he would fail to understand - 'but eventually several were prepared to confirm what we had been told.'

The Inspector looked thoughtfully at him. They were both thinking the same thing. Murders were so often the outcome of brittle human relationships. Was the entanglement with drugs a different dimension? He would have to see Kathy Bourne himself.

The sergeant interrupted his train of thought.

'Sergeant Evans has been talking to forensic and he had better tell you what they say.'

The Inspector turned to the Welshman. 'Well, sir, fairly simple it is. Both victims were shot, they have the bullet from Dryburgh, 9 mm., probably from a Browning pistol. The wound in Jones's head is compatible with the use of the same weapon. But without the bullet, it is not possible to say categorically that this was so. They give the times of death, Jones 8.30 to 10.30 in the evening, and Thornell 12.30-3.00 p.m. Both shot at close range.'

'That's no bloody use.' McConachie swore to himself.

'Forensic said that to be more accurate they needed to know at what time Thornell last ate. They are sending a preliminary written report.'

The telephone rang and the local sergeant answered it. 'Hawick want you to confirm that the Americans are going to Melrose tomorrow.'

'Tell them that I am on my way to their hotel and will ring from there.'

He added the bundle of papers to those in his brief case. 'We had better go and see, Sergeant Evans, if Mr Harry S. Webb has come back from his sightseeing. I think that what he will have to say will be of special interest to you.'

In the car he went over the ground.

'Now, Taff,' he said, 'consider where we have got to. We have the three Abbeys. Heaven help us if anything happens in Melrose tomorrow, but I don't think that we can stop anyone going there. Hawick have said that there will be a discreet police presence.'

'We have three deaths, forensic are still checking again on the man at Jed. At each Abbey were the American group, the tour managers, Thornell the gardener. Damn, I forgot to ask the Major if he had been at Jedburgh, Mr and Mrs Stone whom I like to think are not involved. In the wings, so to speak, are the lecturer McShea, Kathy Bourne and the one they call Mad Meg. She's my cousin, you know, Jeannie Redpath, but I couldn't get a clear word out of her.'

'The connection between the death at Jed and Kelso is that both bodies had their arms outstretched, like a cross, they say, and possibly drugs. The connection between Jones and Thornell is that they were both shot and Kathy Bourne. What do you make of that?'

'If it was Wales, sir, where we feel passionately about everything, I should have said, cherchez la femme.' He liked to show off a bit of culture. 'But I don't think that we can be wrong about the implication of drugs. There's one thing that's certain. Where there are drugs, there is violence. Now that 9mm. weapon, that is just the pistol the drug runners use, and I don't suppose there are many obtainable in the Borders. Sort of weapon retired soldiers bring back from abroad.'

'Yes, we have them in the police armoury at Hawick, and, incidentally, it is the weapon Webb carries.'

His mind momentarily went back to his interview with McAlistair.

'What did you make of that Major who we interviewed at Dryburgh? I saw him again today.'

'Bit of a crank, sir, I thought. Just wanted to witter on about protecting the ruins and the gravestones, when we were wanting to ask him about the serious matter of the Kelso death. He didn't seem to like the English much, did he?'

'Moran and Jones were English.' McConachie mused aloud, 'but that's hardly a motive for killing them. Anyway Thornell was local, from Hawick.'

'Yes,' said the sergeant, 'I know he lived there but I heard them saying in the caravan that he came from Carlisle.'

They drew up at the hotel.

'The plan is,' the Inspector spoke before they alighted, 'the plan is that we go in ostensibly to find out what the tour's arrangements are for tomorrow and then take off down the road where, if the coast is clear, Webb, as if out for an evening stroll, will join us in the car. He remains anxious not to be seen in any way associated with the police. So for the moment I have agreed to go along with him.'

They found Brearley and Macdonald with the whole party assembled in the hotel lounge. There was the sound of animated conversation and raised voices but silence fell as they entered.

John Brearley turned in obvious relief when he saw them.

'A number of my party want to cut short the tour but I have been explaining to them that we are too mixed up in these deaths to be able just to run off. Perhaps you could say something.' He looked almost helpless.

The Americans regarded the uniformed Inspector anxiously and expectantly, his burly figure affording some comfort. He deliberately put down his brief case officiously on a convenient table and took his time.

'Ladies and gentleman,' he began, and cleared his throat. 'As you know there have been two violent deaths in the two Abbeys you have visited. I leave out the death at Jedburgh, which as far as we know was natural. You will realise that your evidence as witnesses has been of great value to us, and we may need to ask each of you further questions before we can solve these two murders. The victims in each case were shot.' He avoided catching Harry Webb's eye.

'I cannot legally stop anyone returning to the States,

after asking for a sworn statement, but you will understand that when we are at this stage of preliminary enquiry, further questions and answers might be of critical importance.'

'So it would be of great help to us if you all continued on Mr Brearley's tour, which I understand has some time to go to go.'

He glanced at the manager who nodded. 'Four days, Inspector.'

'Now, if some of you are thinking that there is any risk in visiting our local attractions, I can say that the two dead are both local so that I do not think that you need have any reason to imagine any personal danger. In any case we will attach one of our men to your visits.'

There was a low murmur of cross-talk before Dwight Graham rose rather ponderously to his feet.

'I think,' he said, 'we should see this as a matter of dooty to carry on as the Inspector suggests and assist him in catching this killer. If he assures us that we are safe, I would put a formal proposal to you all that we continue with the tour.'

'Ah do think,' said the tubby Mrs Sorenson, 'that it's just right and democratic to have a vote, and I agree with Mr Graham.'

'I should like to second the motion,' said Mr Webb from the far corner of the room.

'Inspector,' it was the rich, booming voice of Mrs Oldberger, 'I am sure your wonderful Scottish police will look after us, but supposing one of us has a family crisis back home, would we be able to go?'

'Yes, indeed, Mrs,....' he fumbled in his mind, as he prided himself on remembering names and the lady was unmistakable, 'Mrs Oldberger,' the lady beamed, 'should anything like that happen, I should be grateful if the person concerned got in touch with us before departing.'

'That sounds all right, doesn't it?' Mr Graham had taken over the chair, 'should we have a show of hands?'

It was not unanimous, some waited to see what their neighbours did, but enough of the young and the menfolk carried the day so that it was not necessary to deal with the niceties of the noes and abstentions. After all, each was free to act independently.

McConachie made his telephone call to Hawick to confirm the following day's programme and elicit the result of the interview with Mrs Thornell before the two policemen left for their rendezvous.

'This is Sergeant Evans, Mr Webb, he's an experienced drugs officer from Edinburgh.' Inspector McConachie introduced him as the American took the front seat in the car parked in a side road.

'Pleased to meet you, Sergeant.' The two men shook hands awkwardly as Webb settled himself.

'It sure is a relief to meet up with you guys. I've been bottled up with that lot for a fortnight, unable to let my hair down and while in my line of business you get used to playing possum, it makes a change to talk. I can't think why our seniors don't clear with you from the start, but I had better go over the ground again. Back home we reckon that Macdonald uses the cover of his tourist agency to run a profitable sideline in drugs. He has made visits to Costa Rica and Venezuela, handy for Columbia, but we have never been able to catch him with any stuff on him. We can tap phones pretty easily in the States but if the guys use code on the internet, it makes it darned difficult.'

'You mean you have suspicions about the man, but no firm evidence against him?' McConachie cut in, slightly irritated by Webb's long-windedness.

'That's about it, Inspector. So I was detailed off to sign up with Real Tours and see if I could come up with something. It is not just the distribution of drugs nowadays, it's the clearing of the cash. We try and make the laundering of the money as difficult as possible, but our banks pride themselves on the confidentiality of their customers' accounts.'

'Macdonald's a heavy gambler, so that if we have ever questioned him about a large sum of money in his possession, he can say that he won it in off the course betting or at the casino. I have stood behind him when he's won and lost heavily.'

'So what have you discovered on this trip?' McConachie was beginning to wonder if the man had not just come over for the ride.

'I can't say that there is anything wrong with the outfit. Brearley runs a good biz. We go to all these different places and he lays it all on splendidly. Should do for the cost of the tour. Still, I can't complain about that, Uncle Sam always looks after me, real generous with expenses, too.'

'Have you come to any conclusions, then, Mr Webb?'

'I just don't know. Sometimes I guess it's all a straight tourist business, and then I get the feeling that there is something going on. That lecturer guy, McShea, he's been around all the time we've been in Scotland, and he and Brearley and Macdonald meet up on the side, and it doesn't seem to me that they need to spend so much time together. They always carry fat brief cases so I managed to put a chalk mark on Brearley's, and I am pretty sure the next day it was the one McShea was touting. Have your people anything on McShea?'

McConachie shook his head but made a mental note.

'We are always interested in the university,' Evans broke in, 'but I know nothing against McShea.'

'What else?' asked the Inspector, he was not prepared to contribute any of his information until he was sure he had exhausted Webb's.

'You mean about the party? Well, they seem the usual lot, a group of oldies, the young marrieds after a bit of your culture, that's the Bryants and Mays, always got their secret bedroom jokes, a few lost divorcées who pretend they understand them, and then the bunch of camp girls, not sure which sex God meant them to be, although I think that young Mollie is straight. Her aunt, Mrs Oldberger, she's a powerful woman, never get much out of her. My pal is Dwight Graham, and he's a bit of a pompous what do you call it, but I have never let on to him. You never quite know if any of them are mixed up with Macdonald's affairs. On a tour you can always make up an excuse or complaint to seek out the manager and talk to him on his own.'

'Only this morning those girls were all onto Brearley

about some yellow scarf that went missing at Dryburgh. I think he said that he would ask you if it had been found.'

Something niggled in the Inspector's mind, somewhere else in the day there had been mention of yellow.

'I think we should tell you, Mr Webb that we have established that Thornell was ferrying heroin from Kelso to Hawick. We are not yet completely certain, but it seems likely that he was obtaining it from Jones, the man shot in Kelso Abbey. This would link the two deaths.'

'Sure thing, Inspector, in my brief drugs and violence run like a horse and carriage.'

'My present job,' McConachie went on, 'is to track down the person responsible for these murders, but all discoveries of trafficking will, of course, be vigorously followed up. This is Evans's, here, special field. From your inside position you should be able to help us with both. If you will keep us informed we shall do the same for you. We are still not sure if we have two problems or one.'

As Harry Webb stepped out of the side road, he met his friend, Dwight, walking on the main road. 'Taking the evening air, Harry?' he asked without expecting an answer. They could both hear the sound of a distant car engine receding into the dusk, as they strolled back together to the hotel.

'Now, Taff,' McConachie turned to the sergeant once they were on the road again. 'It's been a long day. Supposing you come back with me and stay the night, Mrs Mac will look after us, and after a good meal we can go over the ground. You can use my mobile or wait and telephone your wife from home.'

After supper, Evans was still trying to explain to Mrs McConachie why the daffodil was the real Welsh emblem and not the leek, when the Inspector guided him firmly into the small room that served as a study.

'Better here than the station. We shouldn't get interrupted.'

The phone rang, and he left it to his wife.

'Probably the Woman's Rural. Very active in Midlem.'

But she shouted through. 'It's Kelso for you, Ian.'

He picked up the phone.

'We thought that we should let you know, sir, that the woman in the Dryburgh Post Office said that she saw a blue mini parked for a short time at the Abbey yesterday morning. We have not yet had a chance to speak to the Bourne girl.'

The Inspector replaced the phone and passed on the item to the sergeant.

'Let us suppose, Taff, that the same person and the same gun killed in Kelso and Dryburgh, then we can compare the two lists of those who had the opportunity at each Abbey. The trouble is that it is the same group of the Americans that stayed on in Kelso as those who went first to the ruins in Dryburgh after the lecture, although we have also to remember McShea. In addition we have the Major, and now just conceivably Kathy Bourne. The difference in the victims is that Jones came from outside to go for unknown reasons to the Abbey while Thornell was in Dryburgh the whole time.'

'According to the Major, Jones asked him to look after the bar around 6.30, and then came back in again before, according to other witnesses, going out about nine thirty and not returning. The owner came back at ten thirty and was, understandably, pretty upset to find his licenced premises untended.'

'Now, we know that some of the Americans returned early from Kelso to their hotel so we can rule them out. This same lot and Mrs Oldberger went down to the Tweed at Dryburgh before lunch, so that if Thornell was shot then, we have as possibilities, the four girls, our friend Webb, the lawyer Graham, the two young couples, Bryants and Mays, and Brearley. It looks as if McShea had left directly he finished speaking, but we shall have to check that. Then there's the Stones, but as I said, I don't think that they would be involved. Finally we have that Major.'

'And now, sir, I suppose we have to include Kathy Bourne. Could she have got in to the Dryburgh grounds without being noticed?'

'I suppose, Taff, we have to consider her although the

custodian never mentioned anyone else, but it is easy enough for a visitor to bypass his office. So that is something to bear in mind. All these same people including Kathy but not as far as we know McShea, were around in Kelso. The Americans were picked up by Macdonald at the coach park just after ten o'clock., when Brearley took the Land Rover back.'

He referred to his notes. Brearley and Mrs Oldberger spent part of the evening together at the hotel in the square, until she went with her niece to the concert. Graham and Webb started off there with them. Webb later went out with Margaret Lake for what she called a romantic stroll in the moonlight beside the river, and that included the Abbey. Graham said that he became fed up with Brearley's heavy drinking and so he went off on his own. The Bryants and Mays did a round of the pubs, playing darts, "wanting to get a real sense of the Scottish scene, off the tourist beat." They ended up at The Feathers. The four girls certainly did and said they stayed there most of the evening. They all seem to have had too much to drink. Macdonald also had a drink at The Feathers, he brought the coach in early, he said, and had time to kill.'

Evans glanced up at the Inspector to see if the turn of phrase was intentional.

'My theory is, sir, that it is all drug related. Jones was distributing, one of these Americans was supplying, they meet at the Abbey and have a row. Jones is shot. Thornell we know was also in the game. He knows who did it and so he is shot as well. They all say that he seemed to give one of the party a particular look.'

'But why was Jones's body laid out like the Dryburgh one?'

'Can't say, sir. Perhaps he just fell that way.'

'I shall have to see Kathy Bourne to-morrow. As you say, the moment there's a more domestic element in a problem, it all becomes a little clearer. She adds a different dimension, although it does seem odd that, if she was at Dryburgh, no-one seems to have seen her. I shall have time to interview her again first thing in the morning before going to Melrose. Hawick police will cover the grounds at the Abbey. Perhaps it would be better for you to check on McShea in Edinburgh'

'Yes, Mac, I can do that, but I think that we are forgetting something. If anyone is distributing drugs, it means that somewhere they are holding a supply, presumably carried with them, in their rooms, in a hotel lock up, in their vehicles. Should we not get a search warrant?

McConachie took a healthy mouthful from his glance before replying, and then relit his pipe.

'I take your point, Taff,' he replied thoughtfully. 'We have been distracted by the minnows.' He was also aware that Evans had pressed him earlier to have moved more swiftly to search the Bourne's house. 'But I don't think that we have sufficient evidence against any of the group, much though I dislike and distrust the two managers. You can see what an almighty outcry there would be from the Americans if we acted without firm grounds which we simply haven't got. Perhaps Webb will come up with something.'

The Sergeant held his peace. He felt that matters of this kind would have been handled more forcefully in the city but he was content for the moment to enjoy his host's whisky.

'Let us hope nothing happens in Melrose,' he said. They drained their glasses and retired to bed. It had been a long day.

Meanwhile others were contemplating their plans for the morrow. In his Cheviot cottage, Major McAlistair was studying the layout of the Abbey grounds: high on the Eildon hills, Meg stood at her kitchen window, staring at the moon and mouthing the words that consumed her mind: at the tourist's hotel most of the party were in the lounge still arguing about the merits of continuing the tour, a few had retired to uneasy sleep.

Late in the evening at their separate inn, Brearley and Macdonald sat in glum silence with an empty bottle of brandy beween them. There was a third glass beside theirs.

'He's bluffing,' said Macdonald.' He doesn't have anything on us. He says he saw us shifting packages from the coach into the Land Rover but so bloody what. We're completely clean now, and Jones is dead, and Thornell, if he was involved.'

Webb was still one of those up at the hotel. He had decided to move quickly if there was to be any profit in the affair for him. He had watched and then forced himself on the pair in the inn.

'What can we do for you, Mr Webb?' they had said in their managerial capacity, and offered him a drink. It was the sort of occasion that he liked to have the company of his gun. He had said that he knew what they were up to and that he might be persuaded to stay quiet. They had angrily denied it, of course but he said that he had seen them shifting the stuff outside. He had then left them. 'Think about it,' he said.

But he had something else up his sleeve. He asked Margaret Lake, before he went out. 'Look, Margaret,' he said, 'would you do something for me? I'm playing a kind of a game. Could you stay in the lounge and watch the switchboard for half an hour to see if anyone is called to the phone?'

'If I am right,' he said to himself, 'if anyone else is involved, they'll get a ring.'

When he came back, Margaret nodded and whispered a name into his ear. By the time he returned to his room, unslung his holster and took to his bed, his roommate Dwight Graham Jnr, already seemed fast asleep and snoring heavily.

Nearer dawn the lights of a patrolling police car briefly lit up Melrose Abbey as it stood darkly and gauntly awaiting daybreak, the stones of its broken building and graveyard yielding their heat into the chilling, moonlit air.

THE HIGH GALLERIES OF MELROSE

'Where; cloistered round the garden lay;
The pillared arches were over their head,
And beneath their feet were the bones of the dead.'
The Lay of the Last Minstrel: Sir Walter Scott.

I

Sam Thwaites, the elusive Sam whom Macdonald failed to reach by telephone, lived in Galashiels. It was not surprising that messages never reached him as he spent much of the day in the pub where he was known as sad Sam. He had a good enough degree in history from Edinburgh University and qualified as a teacher but somehow his life had never found a useful conclusion.

He taught for many unhappy years where his classes took charge of him until he could take early retirement worn out by the frictions of undisciplined schools. He had retreated to his mother's house in Gala, and after her death had drifted into a round of melancholy drinking and endless smoking. He was not a conspicuous fellow, long straggly grey hair was matched by a long drooping moustache, generally stained with nicotine. Not unnaturally he harboured the bitterness of unfulfilment.

His friend, Stanley told him he needed something stronger than tobacco, so he took to cannabis with the feeling that each puff was a protest against society at large and all those school children who had made life a misery for him. Stanley had said to him one day.

'Look, Sam, I have a line which I have been at for some years, it gives a bit of excitement to life and you make a bit of cash as well. Every now and then, I gets a phone call from this fellow, and I runs up to Melrose Abbey, pick up some stuff.' He gave Sam a wink. 'If you were interested, I'll tell you more.'

'You mean the hard stuff, Stan?'

'You see, Sam, me and my girl are going to get wed and I want to stop. There's no risk, really, but I want to go respectable. You being a history man, you ought to enjoy abbeys and the like. I have it all set up for you. All that happens is you get a phone call and get the times.'

Stanley fixed it with the team. It was all on the phone because he had not ever met with the voice that spoke to him. They went together on a trial run so that Sam could see the place.

'It's dead easy, Sam. Just wait until there's no-one around. You go into the ruins at the far end, by way of the bit that sticks out into the graveyard, they call it a transect or something like that.'

He led the way. 'There,' he said, 'don't look obvious like. You can see that grating door in the wall which is locked to stop anyone going up a little staircase. God knows where it goes. The point is that you can lift it off the hinges, put what you've got in that hollow behind the pillar. So you puts the cash there in the morning and later in the day you pick up the stuff.'

Waiting until there was no-one else in the crossing, he had moved swiftly to the grating and showed Sam how to ease it off its hinges.

From time to time he visited the Abbey to make himself familiar with the ruins, each time finding himself tense and nervous although he was doing nothing wrong.

Some time elapsed before he received the instructions for his first drop when he was due to deposit the cash from Stan, but it was not surprising that the later telephoning rang in an empty house. Sam had continued on his daily social round with a sense of agitation that required extra assuagement. And the pub telly was showing a football match. Had his mother been around she would have heard the news. Stanley, too, might have forewarned him, but Stanley was on his honeymoon. As it was, armed with a sketch pad which he adopted as his cover for repeated visits, Sam set out for Melrose in the morning oblivious of the previous days' events and their ominous connection with his destination.

II

For Robbie Burns, the custodian in the entry office of Melrose Abbey, it was approaching the end of the busy summer season. Every day coaches full of foreign visitors would arrive in the park across the road behind him. He would concern himself with the sale of tickets and brochures, and the hire of portable cassette players describing the Abbey in different languages. From his kiosk he could not see much of the grounds and buildings over which he presided because the window was hung with T-shirts and tea towels suitably decorated, but every morning before he opened up, he stood outside to survey his realm.

If the time of year was right, his eyes could follow the line of the foundations of the nave, set in the neat green turf, through to the gaping hole at the end of the monks' choir, and he could let them rest on the tracery of the great east window lit up by the morning sun. To his left on the north side further lines of the foundations showed to the student the elaborate layout of the monastic living quarters amid the present day lawns. The stream carrying the diverted water from the river Tweed passed under the wall which separated the Abbey grounds from the museum.

He preferred to look to the south where the morning sun, when it rose above the steep slopes of the Eildon Hills, would light up the red sandstone buttresses and transept of the Abbey and the ancient stones of the graveyard. Occasionally he would pause to look at the pictures outside his office giving the history and an artist's reconstruction of the monastery as it might have been, but his imagination had never had the time or inclination to go far. His employers sometimes sent actors down dressed as monks to try to bring the past to life, but he was content to see the place as ruins and look after them.

When he opened his office on the morning, the day after the news of Thornell's death had been reported, he had barely time to unlock the doors before the telephone began to ring. He took a quick look across the grounds, the sight of some uncollected litter an agitating reminder of the missing gardener. His wife had said to him as he left home. 'Rabbie, you mind yourself, three deaths in three Abbeys. It's no canny.'

'Look,' said the man in the Edinburgh Office. 'We have been in touch with the police and they tell us that they will be there all day. Just let them know at once, if anything worries you.'

'Like hell,' he said to himself, 'there will nae be time to start telling the polis onything if someone shoots me.'

However, the police were the first to arrive in the shape of a uniformed local constable accompanied by a plain clothes detective.

'We're keeping an eye on things, Rabbie,' he said. 'You'll ken why. Young Goddard here will wander in the grounds, as a tourist like.' Young Goddard stood rather sheepishly beside him, dressed in a polar-necked pullover, shorts, socks and sandals with a camera slung round his neck.

'There's a van from Edinburgh outside with an armed squad, so they're a' taking it seriously, but I dinna suppose onything'll happen. To my mind it's twa local men that were shot and they say that there's a woman involved. It's aye the wimmen.'

Goddard said nothing. He thought that he knew rather more.

Sam had arrived early. From the car park he watched anxiously as he saw the policeman arrive and was relieved to see him depart. He did not wish to have too many visitors in the abbey grounds but at the same time he preferred not to enter on his own. He waited until a couple arrived on bicycles. They padlocked them to the railings and then made their way to the kiosk. He heard the wife say to the husband.

'The panniers will be safe enough, Roger, won't they?'

And his reassuring reply. Sam followed them in with his bag for drawing materials slung over his shoulder.

As they entered, a coach drew up in the car park and offloaded a group of German tourists who crowded into the ticket office. They pushed in to show their tickets and as usual asked fiercely why the Abbey was a ruin.

'Ve in Germany had our Koln Cathedral bombed by you, and ve hav rebuild it.'

Rabbie was used to this and gave what he called, appropriately, his spiel.

'You see,' he replied, as he checked the tickets, 'you see, English armies burnt it down several times. Edward II sacked it in 1322. The Lord's Body was cast upon the High Altar.' He was never quite certain what that meant but it sounded suitably awesome. 'Richard II destroyed it in 1485 but it was then rebuilt, then the Earl of Hertford finally brought it down in 1545. That was the Rough Wooing,' he would say.

German visitors always found this very difficult. 'Vat you say rough vooing?' He would explain that Henry VIII of England wanted to marry his son Edward to the young Mary of Scotland.

'So vy burn the kirsches?' He was not sure himself.

If he were lucky, when he was pressed for answers, Meg would appear. There were some from the Edinburgh office who did not care for Meg. They said she was both dirty and unhistorical. They objected to her appearance, her copious black garments which were not all that clean and they alleged that her lined bird-like face gave her an aggressive expression that scared visitors. He would reply that she added a touch of history to the place, as if she had been around in the past, and in any case why had they let her in as a life member. There was no answer to that. As the party of Germans began to make their way into the Abbey grounds, he looked up to see Meg arriving, as if on cue.

'Morning, Meg,' he shouted.

With eyes set on her audience, who had begun to fumble with their cassette players, she pushed through the doorway to reach a commanding position on the lawns.

'Look,' said Daphne, 'there's Meg again, we must go back and hear her.'

Her husband, and Sam who was behind them, turned in their tracks. Meg jigged around until she had everyone's attention.

She began to recite.

'Gang to the heid o' the kirk and ye'll hear the monks canting. There's fowk that'll nae stand still to listen. Dinna fash yerselves with buiks and yon machines. Use the een God gae you and see them prayin. Syne there's bluid, ay bluid aboot the Abbey. Ye can hear the cries of dying monks singing out

"Oor tired spirits canna' rise
Without anither sacrifice." '

While she continued, Sam, sensing that she was a useful distraction, moved with feigned aimlessness towards his destination, but was then put off when the couple, who felt they had enough of Meg, followed him. She faltered and stopped as the Germans fidgeted briefly before dispersing purposefully to the serious duty of sight seeing, which even her jigging could not halt.

She watched intently as the kiosk door opened behind them but it was only to admit the stocky figure of the Major, conspicuous in his well cut suit and cloth cap. She was not going to waste her words upon him.

Major McAlistair after a curt nod to the custodian, who had not served in his regiment, moved briskly in his usual circuit of the grounds. He was in a sombre mood. There was something untidy about these three deaths, they represented a disorder he had been able to do little about. At the same time he could see that what had begun at Jedburgh might logically be completed in Melrose. Armed with these thoughts and his walking stick, he strode among the gravestones stabbing at any piece of paper that came his way.

'Roger,' said Daphne, standing in the entrance to the south transept, 'do you see who's here? It's that man with the army tie you recognised.' Out of their sight Sam loitered near the cache.

A few more visitors had entered the kiosk. The last was familiar to the custodian.

'Morning Mr Stayman,' he greeted him. 'I had forgotten you were on today. Which is it the monk or the soldier?'

Stayman was a member of the local dramatic society

who was employed from time to time to dress up and give a suitable recitation to visitors in an attempt to dramatise the past and give life to the old stones of the ruins. He varied his selection of venues in accord with the contents of his act.

He was an elderly fellow whose balding head and circuit of remaining hair readily set off a monkish costume. He took his duties more seriously than his audiences tended to do.

'I shall be Brother Octavius, today, and I think in the clerestory gallery. I find that most effective, and I like to think that my final rendition of the first three verses of the Te Deum laudamus is much appreciated. I hope that your mad woman is not around. She totally ruined my last appearance at the cloister entrance. That is why I thought that I should escape her by using the gallery. Have you the key of the grating?'

Rabbie duly handed the key over. 'You will be careful on the stair, Mr Stayman. You know that we don't allow visitors to use it, and there'll be pigeon droppings in the gallery itself.'

Clutching his handbag containing his monastic garments, Mr Stayman made his way across the lawn to change in the public toilets. He did not think it proper to undress on holy ground.

It was well on in the morning before the Real Tours convoy arrived, coach and Land Rover. In the first place there had been continued disagreement about visiting the Abbey at Melrose at all.

'I don't care what you say,' Mrs Sorenson announced at breakfast, 'me and Niels talked it over all night, it just ain't common sense to go looking at a fourth abbey when each of the previous three have ended up with a dead body. And if it ain't against common sense, I am superstitious enough to say it just don't feel right. So we shan't go.'

It took all John Brearley's tact to persuade the three elderly couples to accompany the rest of the party to the town, pointing out that there was no obligation to enter the Abbey, and they could wait comfortably in the hotel where they would all meet up for lunch.

Although, as Brearley explained to them, McShea was not able to give his usual morning lecture having been detained by university matters in Edinburgh, their start was still delayed by the argument. Brearley, himself, did not wish to reach the rendezvous too early. More particularly as his partner had failed to make contact with Sam. 'And,' as he snarled at Macdonald the night before over their cups, 'you don't even bloody well know what he looks like.' If there was money around, he wanted it. They were committed to the visit, even if the police were around.

'Don't be a fool,' snapped Gus, 'If the fuzz are there, keep clear of that staircase.'

The party straggled cautiously through the gatehouse. 'Real Tours,' Brearley called out without his usual panache, 'Real Tours.' He waved his pass towards Burns who nodded them in to where Meg awaited them. As they looked round, it was almost a relief to see a familiar figure but also one that aroused a sense of foreboding. Dwight Graham Junior busied himself once again with his camera, and others, who had missed the previous opportunities, pulled out theirs.

The warmth of the sun and the presence of other visitors began to offer the Americans a sense of reassurance. They moved away from Meg and fanned out across the grounds. Macdonald had stayed outside while Brearley escorted his customers within, ready to take any opportunity to approach the staircase door. He went back into the kiosk to meet his partner who was ostensibly guarding the vehicles in the park.

They stood together beside the postcard stand while Gus reported that there was a policeman patrolling the street, and what he took to be a full patrol car in the side road.

'Even if I was stopped and searched, Gus,' said Brearley, whose nerve was returning, 'it isn't a crime to carry cash, and you know I don't carry a gun.'

Back in the grounds, he moved casually among his party, finally entering the church by the cloister door. He notice the number of Germans, conspicuous by their dress and earnestness and other visitors, among them a young man feverishly taking photographs as if his life depended on them, but he barely gave a thought to a scruffy artist packing up his work.

Sad Sam had achieved his purpose, murmuring to the custodian that the sun was now too high for him to continue, he passed inconspicuously though the gatehouse and returned home. 'I'll be back later,' he said, 'to finish off.'

Harry Webb led Margaret Lake across the lawns to where Bruce's heart was buried. Hearts seemed more romantic than old altars; he was beginning to warm to Margaret, enjoying the sight of the shape of her breasts through her light summer blouse.

'Why don't you take your jacket off, Harry? Aren't you too hot?'

He shook his head. 'I guess I am kinda used to wearing one,' he said. Besides, he knew that he had to keep his shoulder holster concealed.

While the others abandoned Meg and spread out across the grounds, Mrs Oldberger put her ample arm around the shoulders of her niece, Molly, and drew her away.

'Molly,' she said, 'I think you and I should look around on our own. We've had quite enough of your three school mams. They behave just like children. Lord knows what kind of example they set to their classes. I've had quite enough of them, and I am sure you have, too.'

She marched Molly away among the gravestones.

'I've been thinking, Molly, that we ought to cut our tour short. I don't want to upset Mr Brearley. Could you perhaps check out an airline for tomorrow from Edinburgh, and then come to say that your Mum's been taken sick.'

Molly looked sharply at her aunt, who always seemed the most resolute of the party. She herself had indeed begun to weary of her three companions, and while the drama of the three deaths had not frightened her, she realised that she had no kindred spirit with whom to share her thoughts, and her aunt had seemed distant.

She accepted her aunt's suggestion without demur.

'Now,' said Mrs Oldberger, 'Let's go and see that pig playing the bagpipes that the book says is one of the gargoyles among the buttresses.' And she led the way through the gravestones.

Ruth McKinley and Beth Havers abandoned Meg to follow Jane Marshall who headed for the north wall and the gate to the museum. The triangular relationship had reached a pitch of intensity beyond reason that they each might have understood in other circumstances. Jane Marshall walked with a barely concealed hint of mastery and a complacent look, while the two younger women followed, vying with each other to achieve some sign of special recognition.

Ruth, the tall blonde, reached out to take Jane's hand but her offer was spurned, Beth, struggling with her shorter footsteps, spat out.

'It was my turn to share your room last night, Jane, why don't you play fair.'

Jane strode on. 'I think that we should do the museum first, don't you, Ruth?' and led the way to the gate in the wall.

III

Inspector McConachie began the day in his office. He did not believe that his presence would add to the usefulness of the protective squad at the Abbey. He waited for further confirmations from the police forensic professionals. Yet when they came, they shed little further light on the killings.

The experts considered that the two shootings had been carried out by the same type of pistol but that without the second bullet, they could not be certain. That did not seem to matter to McConnachie, it would have been extraordinary in the circumstances, were two different pistols involved. The surgeons saw no reason to alter their original opinion that the death in Jedburgh was from natural causes. It was possible that the arms had been outstretched sometime after death, while on the corpse from Kelso, the absence of bruising on the forearms suggested that little force had been used to extend them.

They could not come to any more accurate conclusions about Thornell. The stomach contents did not include his midday meal. Indeed McConnachie already knew that as they had found his piece in the motor bicycle panniers. This seemed to indicate that he had been shot before the party had dispersed to the hotel. They also substantiated the details of the fragments of yellow cloth found in the head wound, silk, probably of Japanese manufacture. Forensic thought it likely that the cloth had been used to muffle the sound of the shot.

At any rate in McConachie's mind this cleared the pattern of events. Sergeant Evans would continue on the drugs investigation while he himself would pursue the more pressing problems of the murders. He could not clear McShea from the field although he did not appear to have been at Kelso. The Edinburgh police would interview him. He could not see his cousin, Jeannie, being involved and yet if they could get sense out of her she might be a key witness for the sequence of events at Dryburgh. Before he turned his full attention to the American party and the Real Tours managers, there remained Kathy. He set out for Kelso.

He parked his car beside the blue Mini at Neidpath Terrace and rang the bell. Mrs Bourne opened the door on the chain, then with a relieved look, freed it to open.

'I am sorry, Inspector,' she said. 'We've been that bothered by the newspaper men. We get nae peace at hame and canna go oot.'

'I hope, Mrs Bourne, you told them that you could not say anything and that they should go to the police.'

'Aye,' she said. 'We did just that but they kept trying to get photos. Kathy's in the kitchen.'

She led the way to where her daughter sat over a cup of tea. She appeared even more lifeless than before, barely lifting her eyes towards the visitor. He took a chair opposite her, while Mrs Bourne hovered over the teapot.

'I need to ask you some questions, Kathy. Do you mind

your mother being present?'

'Naw,' she spoke so softly he could barely hear her. 'She kens it a.'

Her mother poured out fresh tea and he accepted the proffered sugar, giving himself the excuse to stir in silence.

'Did Spike find out about you and Jim?' he asked at last.

She looked away and then turned towards him.

'Aye,' she said. 'When he came back that afternoon, the day it happened, he told me that he had returned at lunchtime and seen Jim and me in the car. I think he wanted me to do something in the evening for him, but he was that angry. I said that we weren't married so that what I did in my spare time was my business. Anyway, he carried on at me and said I was mucking up his business, as he had his own dealings with Jim.'

'Did you know what that was, Kathy?' He looked directly at her. She kept her gaze away. 'Naw' she said.

'Come on, Kathy,' he said firmly. 'Do you mean no because you never chose to ask but that you guessed or just no because you did not have anything directly to do with the drugs, but you knew where the money came from them?'

Kathy remained silent.

'Did you see him again?'

She did not answer immediately and then looked up at him.

'Aye,' she said at last, as if she had made up her mind. 'Aye, I went round to the pub, late, to catch him. I just keeked in and saw he wasne there at the bar so I went roon to the back. I saw him in the lamplight, heading for the Abbey. So I followed. I didn't want nae trouble between him and Jim. I could see Jim's motor bicycle in the lane so I kent he was still there. As I reached the Abbey wall, I heard them talking. It wasne angry talk, saft they spoke so I turned back and went hame.'

It rang true to the Inspector. He could see that the woman would not want to intrude into what seemed a peaceful encounter between her two lovers.

'What time was that?'

'I dinna ken,' she said, 'back of ten o'clock, maybe.'

'Did you see anybody else by the Abbey?'

'There were other folk about but I dinna mind them. You see Jim had a key to the gate and he was often late and left to lock up hisself.'

He left the subject of the evening. He could see why she would not have started an alarm when her man had not come home.

'And the next morning, Kathy?'

She hesitated, almost defiantly.

'What about it,' she answered. 'The polis came round and told me what had happened.' She wept again into her handkerchief.

Were they real tears of grief, he asked himself. When she recovered, he asked her bluntly.

'Why did you go to Dryburgh?'

She was reaching for her cup of tea, but she checked the movement and he could see that she was surprised. She had clearly prepared her previous replies. This time she began as if to deny it and then realised that it was no use.

'I, ...I had to find Jim, ' she faltered.

'Go on.'

'You see, I thought that he must have done it. I had heard them together. Whit was I to tell the polis, if they asked me?' She paused in confusion. He sat in silence.

'I went in the car at dinner time. I thought that I'd catch him then. But I didna want to be seen. There were folk there a' ganging to the hotel, and I waited until I could go down in the bushes by the hotel wall, but I never saw him. There was just that mad woman in black so I called to her, but I could get nae sense from her.'

'So you never saw Jim Thornell?'

She shook her head. 'No,' she said. 'I just came hame.'

The Inspector rose to his feet. 'I shall send an officer round to take a statement from you in writing which you will have to sign. It would have been better if you had told us all this earlier.'

Her mother had been sitting silently at the table. He turned to her. 'We shall also have to take a statement from you, Mrs Bourne, to confirm the times of your daughter's movements from here. I want to ask you some further questions.'

'I understand, Mrs Bourne, that your husband was a soldier, that he was discharged from the army some three years ago, came back from Germany and died almost at once.'

'Aye,' she said, 'that's richt, he didna live long efter.'

'Did he bring anything back with him from Germany?'

Mrs Bowie looked mildly surprised. 'He just had an old bag with bits and pieces of his uniform. He used to say that when he got better, he'd need it if he was called back. I couldna bring myself to look at it efter he passed on. I am no even sure where it is noo, someplace in the attic.'

'Could I see it?' he asked. 'Did the Sergeant not go up there?'

She shook her head. 'He never asked aboot it.' She looked at her daughter, who rose reluctantly from the table. 'You'll have to fetch the ladder down.'

McConachie followed her upstairs to the passage outside the bathroom, where she took the hooked rod from the corner and, engaging it in a ring in the ceiling, she brought down the fixed ladder. He held it while she mounted and slowly lowered to him a large military holdall. He waited until she descended and went back to the kitchen. There was not enough room there so he carried it through to the front room.

'Can I see inside?' he asked.

They unrolled it for him. There was the man's field uniform and service dress with the sergeant's stripes, beret, ties and khaki socks. Nothing unusual. He bent forward and rummaged in the corners. His fingers encountered a small firm object.

'It's a pistol bullet,' he said holding it out for the women to see. He shifted the clothing and found some paper, oily to touch. He extracted it and spread it out. It was wrinkled and brown with that slightly transparent look which paper acquires when in contact with grease.

'What was wrapped in this?' He turned to Mrs Bourne.

'I never went into it,' she said. 'I couldne bear to after Jock died. I just left the bag where it was and I am no fit to go up that ladder.'

He turned towards Kathy who did not meet his eye.

'Have you seen this before?' She shook her head.

Neither of the women could or would offer any exclamation.

'May I take the bullet and this paper away?' he asked and took their silence for consent.

It was after the Inspector had left that Mrs Bourne faced up to her daughter and said. 'You knew right enough that Spike went through your Dad's things. What did he find there?'

The Inspector sat in his car pensively and reached for his mobile phone. The Melrose police van reported all quiet. Evans reported from Edinburgh that he had found McShea at the University. Yes, he lectured to the touring party, no, he had not been to Kelso Abbey, yes, he had been to Dryburgh and had left immediately he had given his talk on the roof, no, he had not accompanied he party on the visits to the peel towers, he never did as there was local guidance. Yes, he did usually go to Melrose Abbey to give a lecture, but because of the murders, he had cried off. Yes, he had discussed it with the tour managers.

Evans added that McShea had answered his questions frankly but did seem a little unhappy at a police presence, albeit plain clothes, in the department offices. The sergeant had not felt that could ask any of McShea's colleagues about him. He apparently lectured in political theory for the most part to adult education classes and Evans was extending his investigation towards anyone they could locate who attended them.

McConachie switched off. That seemed to take McShea out of his equation, however much it fitted into Evans's. If, which now seemed certain they were dealing with drug suppliers and there had been drugs at Kelso, where were they now? Could Jim Thornell have taken all the stuff home? Damn it, he had not checked with his own police at Hawick if they had searched Mrs Thornell's house. That was really Evans's problem but it was his parish. He rang Hawick to set them into motion. Then he set out for Melrose.

He took the road north of the river Tweed, past the boundary walls of Floors Castle. On the ridge, the peel tower of Smailholm stood out against the sky. At least, he thought, the Americans managed to visit that without leaving behind yet another corpse. There was not perhaps much room for a discreet murder within its narrow compass, although someone might have been tempted to nudge their neighbour from the vertiginous stone parapets. He rid himself of such macabre thoughts: the tree-lined road was sunlit, the hedges friendly, the fields they enclosed harvested and filled with straw bales. Ahead of him the three peaks of the Eildons, sometimes so dark and sinister when wrapped in cloud, seemed welcoming, green with a hint of the red from the heather, only sombre in their woodlands of fir.

He shrugged off his thoughts of pleasant, pastoral retirement, turned from the bypass into the town square in Melrose and found a space among the tourist coaches in the car park.

IV

In the Abbey grounds, the visitors were still dispersed. Mr Stayman emerged from his make do changing room, clad in the white robe of a Cistercian monk. The curious followed his progress across the lawn towards where the cloister had once stood. He made a conspicuous circuit to attract attention, moving with head bowed as seemed suitable for his role.

Harry Webb, squiring Margaret Lake, gave a shout to the Bryants and Mays who were peering down into the canalised stream. The custodian urged some tourists in his shop to hasten to the Abbey building itself. Returning from the museum, Jane Marshall and her two acolytes saw the converging movements and quickened their pace to join them. Roger and Daphne had wandered among the gravestones and were returning through the door in the south transept when they were abruptly surprised to see an ancient monk fumble beneath his garments to extract a key from the pockets of a modern pair of trousers, unlock a door and vanish.

'Like a ghost,' said Daphne, smiling to her husband.

'I think,' he said, 'it is part of a real life scene, laid on for us visitors.'

They turned into the body of the church, where members of Real Tours were gathered. Those who had seen the monk enter the church looked round for him, others were still letting their eyes take in the architectural details. To those standing by the pulpit screen, the left-hand side was marred by the unsightly wall built among the ruins to form a usable place of worship for the post-Reformation church. But to the right the clerestory gallery with its windows still let in the light.

It was from there that a great groan echoed through the unhappy vault. Mr Stayman had practised it until he knew exactly where to throw his voice to have the greatest affect below him. The motley crowd stirred in astonishment. Young Bryant was the first to see the white robed monk, high above them, and pointed, excitedly, towards him.

For a brief moment, the actor knew that he held his audience. He allowed a pause for those coming in from the sunlight to take their place, he could even see Meg, whom he could imagine discomfited, before beginning.

'Miserere mei, Deus,' but he did not waste his Latin for long, ' have mercy on me, O God, for the great Abbey of Melrose has been sore afflicted. I, Brother Octavius, alone survive. In all its time has it not bestowed great blessing on our people and now it has been cast down by terrible afflictions. Look at its beauteous stones and imagine it filled with the chants of the devout and the prayers of thy servants. Have not the English armies with their rapacious mercenary soldiery committed sacrilege beyond forgiveness? I was kneeling at Lauds when we heard the horses.'

In his narration, Brother Octavius would point to the different parts of the church. He knew from experience that his audience could not stay long like prairie dogs fixed in an upward look. Meg tried to set up a counter distraction towards the High Altar, Beth managed to seize Jane's hand, Harry S.Webb admired Margaret's bust as her blouse tightened with her upward glance, Roger and Daphne listened intently while the audience for the most part enjoyed the re-animation of the ruins. The Major fidgeted, he had heard it before, it re-fuelled the intensity of his hatred of the English. He stood at the end of the choir in the crossing entrance, tapping with his stick in irritation. John Brearley passed him edging towards the south transept, Mrs Oldberger and her niece stood beside him, apparently following the monk's story.

It ended with his final 'Miserere mei' as if addressed to an armed intruder, followed by a prolonged and anguished groan.

His audience were not at first quite sure whether applause was appropriate in what had been a church but, led by the Bryants and Mays, stuttered into a burst of clapping, Mr Stayman made his way gingerly along the gallery and down the narrow staircase.

'Here he is,' shouted Mrs Oldberger, so the crowd gathered around him in the transept. Brearley watched anxiously and was relieved to see that the actor had no time to explore the staircase foot. Indeed he was so surrounded by his congratulatory audience that he omitted to lock the grating behind him. It was always awkward to reach the key in his trouser pocket and he was content to leave it until he had unfrocked himself.

Once again the tourists dispersed. John Brearley cursed to himself as the Major and others loitered in the transept. He could see the staircase door behind which the money should be cached, tantalisingly unsecured. As he stood uncertainly looking out on the graveyard with a purposeless air, Jane Marshall and the two women hovered beside the monk's doorway.

'I bet you won't dare to follow me,' she said, and, pulling the unlocked grating wide open, she set off up the spiral stair. Close to tears, Ruth was aware of Beth's hesitation so she plunged into the dark hastily pursued by her rival.

Major McAlistair heard the muffled voice and the footsteps, and turned sharply on Brearley. 'If they're your lot, you had better call them down, it's damned dangerous in there. Loose stones and no rails.' He glared at the Real Tours manager, conspicuous in his blue blazer.

Brearley did not want the women there, danger or no danger. He shifted himself to the entrance and called out.

He thought that he could see something like a package in the corner but there was no way of extracting it unobserved.

'Come down, you are in danger,' he shouted. But the women had negotiated the stairwell and were emerging onto the gallery. Indeed Jane Marshall was announcing herself to the few remaining in the church, waving downwards while she maliciously watched her admirers edging their way along the uneven passage which was inadequately railed. The tall Ruth who was awkward in her movements stumbled and hugged the stonework desperately. She could just grasp the edges of the clerestory windows. Beth moved more cautiously on all fours, unable to risk looking down.

For a while Jane savoured her triumph before swinging round to return past her subordinates. It was then that Ruth missed her footing again and swayed across the Beth's crouching body. She clutched at the end of the short piece of rail and sprawled half across the recumbent Beth and half into space, one foot scrabbling at the uneven masonry. The screams of the two women redirected the attention of the dispersing crowd, who stood horror struck but powerless below.

'Don't move, don't move,' shouted Webb. 'For God's sake, hold on.'

Beth was trying to extract herself from Ruth's weight but she could not free her arms to reach the body slipping into space. Jane Marshall emerged from the staircase door, any glimmer of smugness immediately effaced when she was confronted by the consternation of those staring upwards. The piercing shrieks drew the attention of the custodian and the constable at the gate who dialled on his mobile telephone. The driver of the van with its armed posse started his engine. McConachie who had just entered the Abbey grounds ran into the building. He did not know how to reach the gallery but he was relieved to recognise the young man in shorts and sandals pushing purposely through the throng, and, as he watched, appearing aloft.

'I can hold her,' he shouted down, clutching Ruth by the arm and jersey.

The Inspector looked quickly around. Most of those beside him were gawping uselessly. Brearley stood in agitation. Then Burns, the custodian, appeared.

'I told that mon, Stayman, the place was no safe.'

'Never mind that, where's your ladder?'

'There's aye yin behind the toilets.'

Bryant, standing nearby, heard the question and set off with Burns to fetch it. Then Burns stopped in his tracks.

'It's kept locked,' he said. 'I'll have to get the key.'

He set off at the double. The three figures tangled in the gallery seemed to have reached some kind of equilibrium although every now and then dribbles of dust and loose stones cascade down to the alarm of the spectators. It annoyed the Major who was already inwardly agitated by the disorder in his beloved Abbey. Mr Stayman returned to be astounded and embarrassed by the scene of confusion. He made his way to lock the grating door until it dawned on him that his failure to secure it was the cause of the impending calamity.

The Inspector by that time had found the access to the gallery. Realising that the incident seemed unrelated to the more serious problems of his investigations, he sent the uniformed constable back to halt his men outside. Then on catching sight of Roger, asked him to stop anyone attempting to follow him and mounted the staircase. He swore as he banged his head as he groped his way, grateful for his police cap. He emerged momentarily dazzled by the sunlight filtering through the clerestory windows, and stretched himself down to add another hand to grip Beth in her precarious position.

'Thanks, sir,' said Goddard, 'should be O.K. now.'

John Brearley hovered. He felt that he ought to be exercising responsible concern but his whole mind was bent in anxiety towards the packet which might or might not lie at the staircase foot. No-one seemed to have noticed anything yet. He tried to find an angle from which he could see into the cache but it was too dark and Roger barred the way. Mrs Oldberger with niece in attendance, also interested herself in the door way, irritated equally by Stayman who stood guiltily beside it with the key in his hand and Jane Marshall who wept hysterically under the crumbled tower.

Molly ran alternately back to see what was happening in the gallery and then to her aunt in the transept. When the ladder arrived from across the lawns, Roger asked Daphne to stand at the entrance to the choir to report the progress of the rescue operation. It was not all that easy: from the somewhat grotesque tangle of limbs, Ruth's two legs had to be guided to a firm footing on a rung, and the rest of her body to a vertical and safe position above it. Beth was ultimately persuaded to follow suit, anything rather than to stand upright above the vault. The two women, shaking and sobbing, confronted each on firm ground at the ladder's foot.

'You did it, you meant it.' Beth spat at Ruth. The Bryants and Mays shepherded them apart and slowly towards the custodian's office.

The company, clustered under the high roof, heaved a collective sigh of relief and each turned to anyone nearby to release their tension. Webb found himself beside the Major.

'Might have been another body,' he said.

McAlistair, upset by the whole disruption to his day, muttered. 'No order, no order,' and stumped off in his irritation. As if to annoy him further, Meg carried away by the excitement began her jigging routine.

'There's aye daith among auld stanes,' she cried, but no-one paid much attention.

For John Brearley there was no relief. He could see no way of approaching the staircase well. At least the package, if it was there, had not been discovered. All attention had been upwards, but the presence of the policemen made it impossible to approach. McConachie came back with Goddard, now clearly identified as a member of the force, and stood with the custodian as Mr Stayman locked the gate and handed back the key.

'You had better report this to your employers,' the Inspector said to Burns. 'You simply cannot allow the public to have access to a place as dangerous as that, and I shall have to inform the station in Hawick.'

He sent Goddard off to an early lunch. 'I'll take a turn round the grounds for half an hour. Don't be longer than that.'

'Thanks, Roger,' he said quietly and then caught Harry S. Webb's eye, but not wishing to be seen in close association with either set off to tour the grounds on his own. The sun shone on a scene, peaceful once more, normal except for Burns and Stayman carrying the ladder back to its repository and bickering among themselves.

Brearley began to guide his flock towards the gate. He raised his voice to announce that Real Tours lunch would be served at twelve thirty in the hotel. Most of the party had already decided that they had had enough for the morning.

'Four Abbeys and nearly four stiffs,' remarked Dwight Graham to Webb as they walked down the nave.

Roger stood looking up at the gallery. He had not seen much of the whole incident. Was it, indeed, but the folly of inquisitive women? Daphne went out into the sunshine, the shadowing building had begun to feel cold. The drama of the rescue had left her tensed up. When she realised that Roger was no longer at her side, she retraced her way back into the transept. As she rounded the corner she met one of the touring party, also close to the jamb of the entranceway. It was of those situations in which each moves instinctively to one side and back again in a momentary impasse.

Daphne felt a need to say something, silly as it seemed. She had a picture in her mind of the last time she had seen the tourist. It had been at Dryburgh.

She stammered out. 'Did you find the owner of that

yellow scarf you picked up?'

At that point, Roger, calling out for her, came out of the choir into the transept. 'We must get a move on, Daph, if we are to get to Blackhouse tower.'

The American hesitated in uncertainty, then turned abruptly to head for the exit without having had time to make reply

VINTAGE CARS BY YARROW WATER

'What's Yarrow but a river bare
That glides the dark hills under?'
Yarrow Unvisited: William Wordsworth

I

Fred gave the bonnet of his Alvis a final polish with special attention to the red triangle at the front. It was the day of the Borders Veteran Car rally for Vintage and Post-Vintage models and, while he knew perfectly well that the dust would accumulate long before he joined the others, at least the discerning eye, and there would be many, would recognise care and affection. They would meet on the Buccleuch Road in Selkirk before heading for Craik Forest.

This gave time for the competitors from east and west to assemble, nursing their vehicles into reluctant starts and guiding them cautiously by highways and byways towards a testing run in the afternoon.

Fred reckoned it was pretty unfair to allow post-war cars to enter when they were mass-produced, but as he frequently remarked there was nothing to compare with the real hand-built machine. He lifted the bonnet again both to check and admire the spotless engine.

By the time he reached the rendezvous, most of the cars were assembled. He drew up behind the one bull-nosed Morris, whose owner, he knew of old. Further along the road he recognised other familiar cars. There was a pre-war Ford Model Y, a Lanchester drophead coupe, an Austin Seven, a Riley Kestrel which made him think sadly of the destruction of the Coventry works in the blitz, then several others with the canvas collapsible hoods like his own, which you never saw nowadays on the roads. Part of history, he said to himself, the times when motor travelling was an expression of freedom and fun.

The drivers, familiar faces and owners, forgathered to agree the route by the Yarrow road before crossing over the intervening hills to come down to the Tushielaw Inn on the Ettrick. Their navigators checked and rechecked the maps of the Forest and adjusted them in their cellophane folders, making the necessary notes of the check-in times for the scheduled points. They each synchronised their watches so that they would be ready to agree times with the marshals at the start.

The driver of the foremost car, set to go, watched idly as the traffic crossed ahead of him on the Yarrow road. He noted a timber lorry which he could see might be an obstruction and a few cars, but they might all turn off towards Peebles, leaving the twisting, valley road to St Mary's Loch free.

As he stood impatiently by his car at the rear of the column, Fred heard the voices of two bicyclists. The sharper, English words drew his attention. There was a man in a red bobble hat and a woman in a blue anorak.

'It's good to see those old mills being brought into use,' Roger was saying to his wife, but her attention had already shifted to the line of parked vehicles.

'Look, Roger,' she said. 'Just look at those splendid old cars. We must stop and see them.'

Her husband, who had settled to a routine of determined pedalling, braked sharply in surprise. They leant their bicycles against the wall.

'Now, that's how we should be travelling,' he said. 'I wonder where they are going.'

He soon engaged Fred in enthusiastic conversation, finding that the convoy would share the same road with them to the inn at Tushielaw. They stayed long enough to admire the different vehicles until Roger persuaded Daphne that they ought to be on their way again. They returned a little reluctantly to their bicycles and as they turned onto the highway gave a friendly wave to the motorists.

These, too, were anxious to resume. There was no definite signal to start, just a comradely consensus that the moment had come, but the owner of the Lanchester could not make his engine fire. Donning his goggles, he fiddled under the bonnet until, triumphant, he held up his thumb to the column as his engine burst into a series of roars and backfires. Then, as they were about to set off, the photographer from the local newspaper waved them to halt.

'Come on, come on,' exclaimed Fred, impatiently. 'We haven't got all day.'

'Got to keep the press happy, you know,' said the owner of the Riley, who had been made responsible for the group's public relations. 'In this day and age, we have to keep everyone sweet. Should have had the local councillor here as well, Fred, shouldn't we? They're never there when they're wanted.'

In the early afternoon sunshine, with hoods down where they could come down, with scarves, helmets, gloves and goggles set to one side, the party at last emerged from the Buccleuch Road to cross the Ettrick bridge.

'Tushielaw, here we come!' said Fred, glad to be off.

II

Inspector McConachie, satisfied that the almost empty Abbey grounds contained no evidence of evildoing, acknowledged the salute of the constable on the road and followed the tour party to the hotel. In a gesture of reassurance he went into the lobby where the group were milling about before settling down to lunch.

He nodded curtly to the two managers who were conferring in the corner, and greeted the elderly who were already seated.

'I do hope, captain,' said Mrs Schumacher, 'that you have found out who did these horrid murders.'

'At least,' said her husband, 'nothing really unfortunate has happened here. We might even venture into the Abbey this evening.'

The Inspector greeted cheerfully the younger women who were waiting with Mrs Oldberger to go into the dining room.

'Have you found out anything, Inspector?' asked Bryant, having checked out on the correct rank. 'It would sure be a great relief to know that none of us were under suspicion.'

McConachie shook his head, making a non-committal reply.

'Captain,' asked the tall blond, 'have you by any chance found my yellow scarf which got lost at Dryburgh?' She did not add, not by me but by Beth.

'No,' he said. 'But I had better take your name.'

'Ruth McKinley,'

'Yes, of course. I should have remembered it.' He noted it down. 'What was it made of?' And he pretended not to be too interested.

'Silk,' she said. 'Best Japanese silk, my momma gave it me.'

He checked with Brearley that the party was still complete before returning to his car to telephone headquarters at Hawick. He learnt that the police had, with Mrs Thornell's permission, searched her house and found a quantity of drugs concealed in the garden shed. The evidence was mounting, Evans reported from Edinburgh that he had traced a mature student who, under some pressure over a past record, alleged that he had obtained heroin from McShea.

'We could pull Brearley and Macdonald in and question them,' the Superintendant suggested. "What do you think, Mac?'

McConachie hesitated in thought. 'Let's wait,' he said. 'We can certainly see the links in the chain, but I am not sure we have the whole picture. I am still not clear about the murders. We know traffickers resort readily to violence. But I saw Kathy Bourne this morning. They had her father's army bag in the attic whose contents lead me to suppose that there had been a revolver at one time packed in it. Let's haud our hand, meantime. Nothing has happened here this morning but we shall have to keep the armed squad at least until the American party has left the town. They are lunching at the hotel and quite possibly will go back to the Abbey in the afternoon.'

'Right,' said the Superintendent, 'but for Christ's sake keep your tabs on the party, we've had every newspaper, God knows how many members of Parliaments and Councils, not to mention that woman United States Consul from Edinburgh, on the phone. I don't know how the press failed to appear at Melrose this morning. You were lucky.'

His voice dropped as he became more serious again. 'I have had from Scotland Yard, a bit of a funny about that man, Webb. You know that we now have MI5 working with us on drugs. Well, they have come back to say that their contacts with the CIA have suggested, just suggested, no proof, that he plays a double game, running with the hare and hounds.'

So it was that when Inspector McConachie took his sandwich and refreshment at a smaller inn than that patronised by Real Tours, he had food for thought. It was his one daily indulgence. He would say to his colleagues. 'You people relax in the golf club, I take a midday snack in a pub and keep in touch with the other parts you don't reach.' Not that he drank beer in uniform that would have been a sin against the police Holy Ghost.

He considered what his superior had said. Should he take more precipitate action, arrest the tour managers, search their rooms and vehicles, interrogate the members of the party more fiercely? He wondered for a moment if they would plead that amendment which Americans always seemed to be pleading in their own country that allowed them to shut up. None of these actions seemed likely to uncover the killer. The only man actually found with drugs, Thornell, was dead.

He reflected on the morning. Nothing seemed to have happened except for the bizarre interlude with the women. He could not see anything sinister in that. He looked sadly at the list of guest ales, as he enjoyed his masochistic squash.

Then his attention was suddenly arrested by a conversation in the adjacent room. It was unmistakably an American woman's voice asking about two bicyclists.

He listened more intently.

'Aye,' he heard the landlord say. 'Aye, they were here but they have moved on.' McConachie could not catch the next few words, but then the landlord shouted to his wife and he heard her reply. 'Tushielaw, they said.'

As McConachie looked without regret at the little left in his glass, he surmised that it must be Roger and his wife, who were asked for. While he finished his drink, to his surprise he heard a further enquiry. This time it was a man's voice. He had listened to it long enough in the hotel and in the car. It was Webb's strong Texan tones. This time the landlord knew the answer and no sooner had he replied than the door slammed.. By the time the Inspector reached the roadside, Webb, if indeed it was he, had vanished among the other pedestrians.

The Inspector made his way swiftly to the larger hotel to stand conspicuously in the doorway in his uniform. He ignored the owner's offer of assistance but caught the eye of young Goddard who was dutifully and reasonably inconspicuously propping up the bar. He was almost taken aback by his superior's abruptness.

'Who's gone?'

'Sir?'

'Which of the party has left?'

Goddard recovered. 'One of the women went out, the large one.' He couldn't remember the name but did not like to admit it.

'Mrs Oldberger?'

'That's it, sir, I remember now.' Two pints of beer had not helped his clarity of thought. 'She went out across the market place. Perhaps back to the Abbey.'

'Who else?'

'She was followed by that tough looking man.' This time names had completely vanished.

'Do you mean Webb, the agent with the gun?'

Goddard nodded weakly, he could see his chances of promotion fading.

McConachie headed for the dining room, disguising the

need he felt for haste. He picked out the blue-blazered Brearley and, with scant courtesy, drew him from the table.

'Where is Mrs Oldberger?'

It was the manager's turn to react to the Inspector's fierceness.

'I don't know,' he said at length.

'Where's she gone?'

The man's face showed confusion. 'I don't know,' he said. 'She asked if she could borrow the Land Rover.'

McConachie felt he wanted to shake the man to provide an answer. He had reasons from the past to have a sense of alarm whenever Roger became involved in events.

'Where's Webb?'

'How the hell should I know?' Brearley retorted, finally riled into anger. 'Probably spewing his guts up in the bogs for all I know.' He glared defiantly at his interrogator.

'Where do you park the Land Rover and what's its registration number?'

Brearley called to his partner.

'We can't wait for that.' McConachie propelled the manager out of the hotel and across the square to the car park.

'Is it there?' he demanded.

Brearley shook his head. 'No,' he replied, 'it was beside the coach.'

McConachie shouted to Goddard to stay with the tourists and to telephone Hawick that he was heading for Tushielaw. There was something desperately wrong when Mrs Oldberger and Webb broke ranks.

As he made for his car, there was a shout from behind.

'Inspector!' It was Graham, 'Inspector, I think that I ought to tell you some more.'

He drew level. McConachie reluctantly stopped to listen.

'Yes,' went on Graham, rather out of breath. 'I don't know what you have made of our friend Webb since I told you about his gun.' He looked somewhat aggrieved. McConachie realised that he had not explained what had been reported to him.

He was about to offer some sort of apology, but the

American was too eager to convey his information.

'I've watched him two nights. I pretend to be asleep while he slips down the road to the place those two managers stop at, that's Brearley and Macdonald.' He put in as if the policeman might not have known. 'I can follow him with my night glasses. Useful things, you know. I thought that maybe he was spying on the two, and the first night they may have spotted him. Last night they took the Land Rover out and I saw him in the headlights. Later, I came to the conclusion he must have gone into their place. Inspector, I thought you ought to know about this.'

More and more McConachie thought that he ought to be following Webb. Impatiently he thanked Graham without further comment or explanation. Leaving the man obviously disgruntled, he hastened to his car to take the Tushielaw road.

III

As the traffic thinned out on the Yarrow road, Roger and Daphne could ride two abreast and chat.

'At least no body at Melrose,' she said, 'I was beginning to wonder if the Roger factor of never having a peaceful holiday was working again.'

'No fear of that and now we're shot of them all,' he laughed. 'But talking of bodies we are have just passed one of the nastiest killing fields in Scotland where the Covenanters massacred the men of Montrose's army, and all their women and children at the Battle of Philiphaugh in 1645, on the banks of these rivers. Lang's book says there's a place beside Newark Castle called Slain Men's Lea where they butchered all the prisoners.

Daphne shivered.

'Are you all right?' he asked.

'It must be someone walking over my grave. It is rather sad that such a green and pleasant land has seen so much violence.'

The road snaked through the woods so that the sun

flickered at them as it found its passage among the trees; the ground on one side rose steeply above them and on the other fell abruptly to the hidden river.

In Selkirk, behind them, the participants in the Rally were revving their engines in impatience as the photographer took his time and his pictures. In turn behind these, Mrs Oldberger had parked the Land Rover in a lay-by to study the map, while in the side streets of the town, Harry S. Webb sought a taxi and McConachie was disengaging himself from Graham.

As Mrs Oldberger resumed her pursuit, she checked her handbag again feeling the gun inside it. She recalled how Webb had lifted it off the ground for her at the hotel, almost obviously weighing it in his hands, but that, too, did not matter now. She took the road to Selkirk, then the lower road bypassing the town, following the route the Rally had taken.

Fred and his friends were some way ahead. He with his navigator, Tim, were at the rear in the Alvis, tail-end Charlie they called it. He had a mobile phone so that they could keep contact with the Ford at the front, similarly equipped. Every now and then they would receive a message about on-coming traffic. At one point near the bridge over the Yarrow at Broadmeadows, the timber lorry was reported as halted and blocking the road. The convoy converged and stopped.

It was only a brief delay. The road emerged from the constraints of the narrow glen and the woodlands into more open country but still between the steep slopes of the hills. The river meandered below them, the road twisting in sympathy to make passing a difficulty. The Lanchester gave trouble again, spluttering to a jerky standstill. It was Tim's turn to halt the leading vehicles.

When they were underway again, Tim looked back to see a Land Rover speeding behind them obviously wanting to overtake. It swung out dangerously to be confronted by an approaching car which forced it back to their rear.

'Bloody silly woman,' said Tim, swivelling round to watch her. 'Bloody silly woman in Land Rover wanting to pass.' He spoke into his mobile.

'Roger,' said the Ford, 'We can space out but there's no straight for miles.'

The curving and undulating road with its concealed bends and dips was not going to daunt Mrs Oldberger. She swung her vehicle at speed past the Alvis, and, completely single of purpose, prepared to overtake each of the veterans in turn. She might well have succeeded, had not a tractor emerged from a field to her right as she accelerated to pass the vehicle at the head of the column. Swinging over sharply to the left to avoid it, the rear of the Land Rover crumpled the off sidemudguard of the Ford and forced it brutally against the roadside wall. The driver managed to halt his car and sat momentarily in stunned shock and horror.

Mrs Oldberger surged on. The owner of the Ford forced his side door open with difficulty and stood beside the damaged wing, slowly dissolving into tears.

He stared fixedly down the road after the vanished Land Rover.

'And she didn't bloody well even stop.'

His navigator picked up the mobile phone that had fallen from his hand at the impact.

Harry S. Webb in his taxi had contrived to keep the Land Rover in sight until it had begun its dangerous interweaving of the convoy, but as the veteran cars now drew into the side, he found his way clear. He urged his driver on until at a final bend, the road was again blocked, this time by a tractor, the damaged Ford and a group of agitated drivers.

'What the hell's the matter?' he leant forward to ask the driver.

No-one at first paid any attention to them but at last, one of the group standing in the road, motioned his companions to one side. The taxi driver engaged gear to move on.

'Check what's happened.' Webb could not make out what the Scots voices explained.

'They say that a woman driving a Land Rover struck the Ford and didn't stop.'

BLOOD AT BLACKHOUSE TOWER

'For bluid lies mingled in the dew in the dowie dens of
Yarrow'
The Dowie Dens of Yarrow: Henry Scott Riddell.

I

Those who turn off from the few main roads in the
Borders stray into a land of rolling uplands with long,
secret valleys, which cradle the lines of old drove roads and
the trails of bygone forays and cattle reiving. Until the
kingdoms of Scotland and England were united, this was a
country that knew little of royal rule, governed only by the
whims of family chiefs from their peel towers, squat
strongholds set at strategic points.

Blackhouse Tower was the fortified home of the
Douglases, built on the banks of the small stream that
carries their name at the meeting place of two glens.

'Even here,' as Roger remarked to Daphne, 'you cannot
escape the violence of the past. My book says that a lover
eloped with a girl, and when her seven brothers pursued
them, he killed them one by one. There are said to be seven
stones round the tower marking their graves.'

'I can't see them,' said his wife as they rested their
bicycles against the fence. 'There seem to be rather a lot of
stones. They probably each represent a body!'

The tower stood high above them against the sky.

'Peel tower, peel same as paling,' said Roger who liked
looking things up. 'It usually has a vaulted lower floor for
storage and a ladder or a narrow spiral staircase to reach
the upper storeys. They say that this staircase twists to the
left so that fellows defending could poke down with their
weapons held in the right hand. I read once that the Kers
who were all left handed built their staircases the other
way, must have helped their right handed attackers as

well.'

They studied the tower which seemed forlorn and dilapidated.

'Doesn't look very safe,' said Roger, pointing to a warning notice.

Daphne turned to look back on the hill track by which they had come. The Douglas burn wound down through rough boggy pasture, interrupted by wooden rails suspended over the water to divide the grazing. Above the small patches of level ground, the hills rose unevenly with tussocky grass, bracken and then finally patches of purple heather. Cattle and sheep were scattered contentedly across the landscape in astonishing number. Beyond the tower further valleys stretched into the distance. Only on the far contours of the hills were there any trees.

'Pretty bleak,' said Roger. 'It was all part of the Ettrick Forest where all the baddies lived until King James strung them up. They could have had a high old time rustling all these beasts.'

'We had better enjoy the view while we can,' said Daphne, studying the sky.

Some of the warmth had gone from the summer air. There was still partial sunshine, but the light seemed to have been filtered out, leaving a golden tinge to the landscape. Fleetingly it was welcoming and attractive, but as Daphne felt the touch of a chilling wind on her cheek, a damp mist began to settle about them.

They hauled their bicycles into the lee of the building past the notice displaying the warning of danger and took themselves to the stairwell. While the corners stones and stairs were of dressed stone much of the stonework of the wall linings had pulled out leaving loose debris underfoot.

'These warning notices are always an exaggeration,' muttered Roger as they groped upward in the dark. 'Owners have to protect themselves for insurance.'

'Oh damn.' He banged his head on the low curved ceiling as they arrived at the first floor. There was little of it left. They could see the indentations in the wall where the beams would have been inset and some of the vaulted roof of the storage chamber beneath them still remained. There was a hole in the centre.

'That's where the occupants could haul up supplies from below,' Roger pointed out to his wife

They could climb little further on the stair that petered out after a few more fragile steps. Twisting ivy branches contrived to hold the stones in place which its larger roots threatened to dislodge from below. Through the leaves the pair peered out over the crumbling wall.

There was now little to see. The mist, thickened by a steady drizzle, shrouded the whole landscape; of the pleasing hills and vales and their grazing animals nothing could be seen, and for a moment nothing could be heard beyond the low hiss of the falling rain around them.

Roger thought he could recognise the sound of traffic on the main road a mile away but then the noise grew louder before fading again. Shortly it increased once more and was coming clearly closer.

They stayed in the shelter of the staircase watching as the vehicle approached with its lights on.

'Looks like a taxi,' said Roger, 'I don't think it will be an angry owner come to catch us trespassing.' But they remained silent and concealed.

A man got out. He stood, glancing around, and then must have caught sight of the bicycles. He advanced towards the tower.

'It's that American, you know, the one with the restless manner,' whispered Daphne, not quite sure why she was keeping her voice down.

They kept quiet as the man walked round the ruin, vanishing from their sight, to reappear when he completed his circumference. He examined the roadway.

'He's keeping his hand inside his raincoat,' said Daphne. Roger nodded uneasily.

There was an abrupt intrusion of loud voices, but it was only the taxi driver fiddling with his radio and somehow reassuring. Roger and Daphne felt free to come down naturally from their vantage point with a clattering of loose stones.

The American swung around and reached into his pocket.

II

On the main road, Mrs Oldberger drove on. She had taken the Tushielaw road where it branched off at the hotel. She was beginning to realise that she should have caught up with the bicyclists. She had seen them in the distance ahead of those old cars and they could not have gone far. She noticed a man with his dog at the road side, and drew up sharply to accost him.

It took time to make sense of what he said.

'Aye,' he said, 'it's a braw day, but it'll nae last. I'm thinking, mebbe it's the haar settling in.'

He began to realise that the driver had not stopped to ask about the weather.

'Are you lost?' he asked, recognising that her speech was not local.

In the end she managed to ascertain that no bicyclists had passed him. 'Mebbe, your friends went on to St, Mary's Loch, speir at the hotel,' was his parting advice, barely uttered before she jerked the car round and set off back to the junction.

As she came back to the hotel, she saw to her dismay the fleet of veteran cars gathering in the yard. The drivers were huddled together looking back down the road, a group of them were already walking back to where the Ford rested sadly against the wall. She sat in frustrated fury as a bus with two cars following prevented her from moving. No-one paid any attention, just another four wheeled drive vehicle, they would have thought, until she took the left hand turn towards St Mary's Loch. Then one of the drivers spotted her.

'It's her, it's that bloody woman again. Look, look!'

She was dimly aware of the faces turned towards her and the surge of anger behind her, but by that time she was well down the road and speeding past the bus. Once again she halted some distance on to discover that the cyclists had not been sighted.

She turned back. Her mind moved as relentlessly as her driving. At each of the few farm roads, she drew up to scrutinise the surface. Bicycles don't vanish, she said to herself. At the only tarmacked junction she was fortunate enough to find a farm hand closing a gate.

'Twa cyclists, you say. Aye, they turned up the Douglas burn by yon farm.'

While an angry rally driver was reporting to the Hawick police from the hotel that a dangerously driven vehicle with a mad woman at the wheel was heading for Moffat, the Land Rover had turned onto the Douglas Water road. Mrs Oldberger took the uneven track grimly. The settling mist limited her range of vision as she looked on both sides where the route might diverge. She had no wish to stop again until she was out of sight of the traffic. She switched on the headlights so that she was able on the softer ground to pick out tyre marks where they emerged from the frequent puddles. There were car tyre marks as well but these had no significance for her. As the surface of the rough and winding road turned to rock at the hill edge, there were no diversions and she accelerated.

III

Harry S.Webb brought out his Federal Bureau of Narcotics card and handed it to Roger.

'Look,' he said, 'that's to establish my identity. I don't know you by name, but I have seen you both at those old Abbeys we've been taken to. Your police know all about me. They know what I know and believe that the two that run the tourist party are mixed up with drug dealing. Now today one of the party, Mrs Oldberger, quit the hotel and set out to find you. I felt her handbag and I reckon she carries a gun.'

'So I added two and two together, and maybe made five, but by my book it's four.'

Roger scrutinised the card, half-listening to the fast speaking American and fumbling to dry his blurring spectacles.

'Steady on, Mr, ... Mr Webb, what makes you so sure that this woman is pursuing us? Why should she?'

'I can only say that it's mighty odd when a woman breaks away from the group, asks after two strangers, borrows a car, packs a gun and follows them, I get jumpy. Specially when we've had two shootings already. God knows why you, but that's not the point.'

Daphne listened anxiously, studying Webb's face and then looking back to her husband.

'Shouldn't we go to the police?' she asked.

Roger also contemplated the American thoughtfully. He seemed genuine enough and certainly they had both thought him odd man out in the tourist group. This did not necessarily make what he had said to be true. On the other hand anyone mad enough to take a taxi up a hill track in a remote Scottish valley, must have some good reason for his actions.

'Where is this woman now?' he asked.

Webb appreciated the question. He was dealing with a realist.

'She overshot where you turned off, but that does not mean that she will have gone far. She will have realised that you could only be a short distance ahead of her. She will probably turn back and ask.'

They stood in silence for a moment, awkwardly, aware of the damp mist around them. The American spoke again.

'It may not make sense to you, but there are two dead already, and if that woman is a killer, she won't stop now. She spells danger as I read it.'

Daphne felt the situation was unreal. Here was a comparative stranger, come half way up a mountain in a soaking drizzle, trying to tell them that a mad woman had set out to kill them. She was used to Roger's capacity to involve himself in some funny situations but here they were on holiday.

'But why?' she burst out.

Roger spoke more brusquely. He had to accept the man's warnings.

'What do you suggest?'

There was again a lull as they heard the noise of a car engine.

'Is it on the road?' Daphne said nervously.

Webb tapped his holster in reassurance.

'I have my gat,' he said.

They listened again intently. The sound of the engine was still distant, rising and falling as if muted by the shoulders of intervening hill slopes.

'Could be a shepherd,' said Roger, 'but he is not likely to come out in this weather.'

Webb without waiting on the couple's compliance swung round to the taxi driver.

'Get your cab off the road behind the tower.'

The man, his attention still bent on tuning his radio, looked at the American with astonishment. He had only agreed to take the hill track after extra payment, and now he was suddenly asked to drive onto the soft ground.

'You're acting bloody daft, mister,' he said. 'A'm no driving my taxi into that bog.'

The sound of the approaching vehicle grew louder, unmistakably on the hill track.

Webb could wait no longer. He pulled out his gun and showed it.

'This ain't a joke, there's a murderer in that car that's coming. We've got to be out of sight. Now move.'

He shouted to Roger and Daphne. 'Bring your bicycles to the back of the tower.'

Under the unexpected duress, the taxi driver revved his engine to slither squelching across the saturated grass, the tyres gripping uncertainly among mud and loose stones.

Daphne, now acutely on edge, looked again to her husband who led her to the bicycles half sheltered by the tower. They joined the American and the taxi driver at the rear of the ruin.

The driver kept repeating. 'You'll have to pay me bloody extra and for ony hurt done. There's a spring gone for sure, and a'm telling you now, that I'll have the police on you for threatening me.' He kept one eye on the gun.

'Shut up!' said Webb. 'Look, Stone, there's just a chance she drives on past this place, the road does go on, doesn't it?' Roger nodded. 'If she does, we get out. You'll have to leave the bicycles and come with me in the cab.'

It all seemed increasingly mad to Daphne. They were being conducted into realms of fantasy by this unknown American, brandishing a gun. But her husband put his hand on her shoulder to calm her and his glance told her that he accepted the man's actions.

'Get in the car with Webb,' he said. 'I'll watch from the staircase, and if the car is driven by a man, it will be a shepherd, if it is a woman, we'll know that something's wrong. If she stops or continues, I'll have time to rejoin you, and we make a run for it.'

He caught Webb's eye, the American nodded. Roger scrambled over the fallen stones and ivy to reach the staircase to climb to their previous viewpoint.

The noise of the engine grew steadily louder. When it rounded the spur of the hill some half a mile away, Roger saw the blurred headlights as pinpoints through the thick murk that still reduced visibility to a hundred yards. On the curves of the road, the lights swung eerily to either side, gradually revealing the details of earth and stone and grass.

As he strained his eyes, - his long sight was still good, he thought to himself - a reflection from the wet rocks showed up the driver. It was a woman. It was for him an utterly convincing fact, confirming the man's account.

He checked back on his line of retreat. He would not have much time if she stopped at the tower, and he saw no reason to confront her.

Crouching down, he peered through the ivy leaves as the Land Rover took shape and colour. It bumped and lurched on the harsh stones of the track that turned sharply to reach the puddled mud in front of him. He could see now the woman at the wheel and recognised her as one of the American party, the dominant one always bossing the younger ones.

She brought the vehicle to a halt, looked round carefully and at one moment he thought the intensity of her stare was piercing his cover. But she did not stop the engine. Apparently satisfied that there was no-one there, she accelerated abruptly and resumed her way, splashing through the burn where it crossed the road.

Roger moved cautiously down the crumbling stair as quickly as he could to cross to the car.

'She's gone on,' he spoke to Webb. He could see the tense faces of his wife and the driver, who had fallen reluctantly silent. Webb took it in his stride. His leathery face showed relief.

'Let's go,' he said.

Even as he spoke, they could see the Land Rover halted further up the valley and hear the noise of the engine in manoeuvre.

The taxi driver needed little encouragement to take off. He was with a madman and all he wanted was to head for home and the security of an inhabited town.

'For Christ's sake, keep your revs down,' shouted Webb as the man's foot plunged on the accelerator.

Their wheels skidded and churned in the soft ground before hitting the firmer surface, taking them with a jerk onto the built up road. As the driver took to it with a mixture of panic and caution, Roger was able to look back through the rear window. The mist had become more variable. He saw the Land Rover halted at the tower and the woman dismount. She must surely be aware of a departing car, at half a mile's distance, but she seemed to study the ground for a moment before making a rapid circuit of the building.

'She'll have seen our bicycles,' he reported to Webb in the front seat by the driver. 'She'll know we were there.'

'Yeah,' said the American, 'but we're a jump ahead.'

Roger watched as the Land Rover took off in a cloud of spray, bracing himself against the frame of the cab and his wife, as the driver tried to avoid potholes or swung crazily round the bends in the road.

'She's gaining on us,' he said.

'There's only a short distance, now, to the main road,' the taxi driver was beginning to have hope of salvation, perhaps in similar desperation his forbears had once driven stolen cattle away from their pursuers. His lapse of attention led to the disaster. As his right wheel slipped on the hill edge, he over-corrected, and the left wheel struck a protruding boulder, crumpling the wing and bursting the tyre. With a strident metallic clatter, the vehicle settled in a hollow clear of the track, and stopped with the engine roaring.

The driver sat, stupefied. Webb, dazed, yet reached over to switch off the engine. His door was jammed. He wrestled at it with his gun in one hand. Daphne and Roger disentangled themselves in the rear seat.

'Come on, honey,' he said, throwing the off side door open. 'We must get out of here. Webb can look after himself. If we are the targets, it's time to go.'

Seizing Daphne by the hand, he pulled her up the short bank of scree and led her at a trot over a broad bank of tussocky grass. There was no immediate cover, the mist which might have concealed their escape had lifted. Roger did not speak until they had established a safe distance from the track.

When they halted, panting, to look back, it was to see the Land Rover slowing down beside the damaged cab and then drive on.

'She saw us up here, Daphne, I am sure she saw us. God knows why she is chasing us, but once she saw us, she had no interest in anyone else. But if what we remember is right, she is not physically capable of chasing us over this sort of country.'

Daphne was too breathless to reply: she could only nod her head. While he had her silent, he grinned at her and said. 'I don't think you can blame me for this escapade, can you.' Although he did not know it, he was right.

'We had better keep to the hills until we can reach the main road at a point where there are no side tracks and where we can pick out the Land Rover, if it's lurking. Then we'll find a telephone.'

They listened. What might have been the sound of the Land Rover seemed to be receding, becoming confused with the rumble of traffic on the Selkirk road. They resumed their jog trot towards the rounded summit of the hill amid curls of low cloud and wisps of damp mist that came and went around them, for the meantime safe.

From time to time Daphne gasped in alarm as a sheep scrambled out of its shelter in a hollow, and once a hare started from her feet, looking for a moment as large as a deer. At one moment they heard what sounded like shots behind them, which halted them in alarm

'That woman will never get herself up these slopes,' said Roger. Daphne was prepared to be reassured, but the sequence of the day's events had been too frightening to allay her deep-seated panic. The sky and the fields across the Yarrow momentarily revealed themselves to give the couple their bearings as they contoured round the hill. They could see beneath them a farmhouse with its steadings and, at this side of it, the stone walls of a stell, a circular sheep shelter. There seemed to be no sign of the Land Rover although they could hear the occasional noise of a tractor and motor traffic.

The mist lifted uncertainly and sporadically.

'I'll go across to the hill edge to see if I can make contact with Webb. He has a gun, and while I don't think that we need protection, I'd be happier to know where he is before we take to the road. Can you manage down to that circle of stones and wait for me there?'

Part of Daphne wanted to scream, 'Don't leave me,' but she contained herself, accepting her husband's instruction.

'I can get down there, Roger,' she said, 'but are you sure it's safe?'

'If you see any sign of the woman, stay on the hill.'

He vanished over the ridge leaving her, resting on a boulder. Her trainers, good for bicycling had become saturated and squelched, her hair straggled out from under her beret, as wet as it was, and she suddenly felt very tired. However, she rose reluctantly to her feet, and, peering anxiously around, began to make a cautious descent.

The going was treacherous with abrupt shelves where the sheep had sought shelter beside their tracks that continued along the slope. She slid from one to the other, zigzagging downwards. It had been easier climbing uphill. Occasionally she glimpsed the fields below but too often the visibility was limited. She kept looking hopefully around to see her husband but although the brow of the hill was clear, there was no sign of him or anyone else. She wondered whether Webb was still with the cab.

She scrambled over a crumbling stone dyke and then, as the ground levelled, met a wire fence. She could see the shapes of cattle within the field and, on the far side, could make out the walls of the sheep shelter. Behind it was the blur of farm buildings.

She pushed herself through the wires of the fence avoiding the barbed wire. The noise drew the attention of the bullocks which turned in curiosity towards her, shuffling their feet.

'O God,' she thought, 'there mustn't be a bull.'

Half turning to keep an eye on the cattle, she followed the fence to make her way to the stell. Then with wild delight she spied just above the stone wall, her husband's red bobble hat. He had reached the farm before her. She had no time or wish to remember that he had not been wearing it on the hill and that it had been left with the bicycles.

IV

Roger, too, had found the descent back to the cab awkward going. He went warily although he was pretty sure the woman and the Land Rover had quit the hill road but she could have returned on foot on the flat ground. As he reached the track, a figure emerged from the murk. It was the cab driver, cursing and swearing into the air at the expense of his progress. He started back on seeing Roger.

'Have you got the polis? Ma car's a write-off, and that wumman came back. I wisna going to bide with that mon with the gun for another moment. I ran off, and, I can tell you, when I heard shots I ran faster, but I dinna ken which way. Have you got the polis?'

'Is he still there?' Roger asked, stemming the flow with difficulty.

'Have you got the polis?' The driver went on, almost incoherently.

Roger repeated the question and still obtained no answer. He took the man by the shoulders and shook him.

'Is the woman still there?'

'No, no. She drove past me. I had to jump for ma life.'

'Where's Webb, the man with the gun who hired you?'

'I dinna care whaur that madman is. He'll hae to pay.'

The thought of his damaged taxi brought the driver angrily back to reality.

'Aye, he said he'd wait to see if you two came back.'

'Right' said Roger, 'You go and find a telephone and ring the police, and I'll find Webb. If you get lost again, follow the stream down to the Yarrow.'

The driver continued his half running, half walking progress towards the main road, while Roger turned up the track to where they had crashed.

He found the car but it was empty. He pulled the driver's door open to make sure there was no-one alive or dead inside. He called out, but there was no reply. The mist was creeping down again into the valley bottom. He could only just see the slope of the hill that had been their escape route. He still felt uneasy. Surely the driver would have been right in saying the Land Rover had gone past him?

Did he believe what Webb had told him at the tower or was it Webb the woman was pursuing? Where was the man now?

He walked cautiously round the car, making it the fixed centre point of his search, gradually extending the circle, until its limit took him to the stream's edge. He stood wondering whether to cross, then became aware of the ditch trickling beside him into the mainstream, and as he took the water more fully into his vision, he realised that it was tinged with red. For a moment he accepted it as the colour of gravel: only slowly did it come to him that this was geologically wrong. The ditch angled behind him. He leapt across the corner to discover Webb's body sprawled against the side, partly immersed in the trickle into which his blood seeped.

Roger bent over the body which stirred in response. He was not dead.

With a 'Thank God for that' under his breath, Roger hauled Webb carefully into an upright position. The injured man groaned, and it was almost as if his hand made a reflex action for his shoulder. Roger's foot splashing in the ditch bottom kicked against something hard and metallic. Propping Webb up with one hand, he fished the pistol out with the other.

Webb's eyes opened, recognised his rescuer.

'She came back.'

He closed his eyes again, leaving Roger time to examine him to see where he was shot. The blood was staining the shoulder of his jacket and he had a gash on the temple. Webb himself groped with his uninjured arm to seek out the damage.

'I remember firing when she turned a gun on me.' He remembered rather more which he was not prepared to reveal; that Mrs Oldberger had refused to consider his price for silence. She had come back and found him cautiously waiting. He had quickly backed away when he understood that she was not prepared to negotiate. He had almost moved out of sight when she had fired, knocking him against a boulder and into the ditch. Even now, partly stunned and weakened by the loss of blood, he was not going to give anything unnecessarily away.

Rather slowly he struggled to his feet, and then slumped down again.

'Steady on, man,' said Roger. 'First of all, we had better get some kind of padding on what looks like a chest wound.'

Fairly rapidly the two men contrived a dressing to staunch the blood, whereupon, Webb who was showing remarkable resilience, rose shakily to his feet again.

'I reckon,' he said, 'with your help, Mr Stone, I could make the road.'

V

On the narrow grass verge, Tom Malachi and Bob laboured to make the Ford roadworthy. The mudguard and running board had been buckled, the bar of the bumper bent out of shape, and the wire-spoked wheel distorted unuseably while the tyre had burst. His colleagues, having parked their cars in the hotel yard, came back down the road in angry sympathy.

After the first flood of tears, Tom's feelings had settled into fierce but practical fury.

'You a' maun gang on to Craik, just gie us ony tools ye hae which might help us. Bob and I will see whit we can do and mebbe limp back to the garage in Selkirk.'

The drivers had contributed what they could, Fred was able to tell Tom that they had reported what had happened to the Hawick police.

'A fat lot of guid that'll do.' said the owner grimly as he collected the tools. 'Hae ony of you a hacksaw?'

As the convoy of veterans set out on the road to Tushielaw and Craik, the two men concentrated on their work of repair.

The impact of the Land Rover on the offside of the Ford had been slight as Tom had sought to avoid the in-turning vehicle but the damage to the nearside as it struck the wall was crippling.

They could force up the continuous strip of metal that formed the running board and mudguard, and lash it clear of the wheel. But the bumper had been forced back against the wheel, jamming the bolts that secured it to the front of the chassis. In the end they had to hacksaw the bumper ends off to get to the warped wheel.

Here, too, there was difficulty with the badly distorted hub cap, but after using hammer and chisel to drive it free, they were able to inspect the axle end beneath,

They worked in a familiar silence for a time but occasionally Bob was aware that the older man was muttering.

After his retirement from the local government roads team, Tom's life had been simple, dedicated to its two elements. As an elder of the kirk, he took his Sunday duties seriously, while his love and care of his car, almost as passionate, filled the other days of the week. Bob had never heard Tom swear. He wondered what he was saying after this provocation.

He listened as they wrestled with the obstinate hubcap.

'... all the malesouns and waresouns that ever gat wardlie creatur sen the beynnyng of the warlde to this hour mot licht upon her. The maledictioun of God, that lichtit apon Lucifer and all his fallowis, that strak thaim frae the hie hevin to the deip hell mot licht apon her.'

Tom broke off.

'Git the spare, Bob, off the back and we can see how it fits.'

To their delight, it sat in place despite some distortion around its mounting, and the mutilated hub cap secured it. They tidied up round the car, gathered the tools into the back and prepared for the great moment.

Tom still muttered away with occasional sideway instructions. 'You'll hae to get in from my door.'

They sat tense together for a moment until Tom reached forward to pull the starter, the engine spluttered and then fired. He pressed the foot pedal and it roared.

'Let's see if we can move.' Gingerly he let in the gear and turned onto the road. There was some clatter from stray metal but they were mobile.

'We'll take a short rin up past the hotel just to see a's richt before making for hame' Tom said briefly, interrupting his recitation.

Once assured of progress, Bob felt he could ask Tom what he was saying all the time.

'Weil,' he said, 'It's no perhaps just proper for me that's an elder of the kirk to wish ony folk ill, but I thought that in the circumstances, I could repeat the Archbishop of Glasgow's Monition of Cursing against the Border Reivers and direct it agin yon woman. I was made to learn bits of it as a boy and it kind o' sticks in my mind and comes oot on occasions like this. I never quite like to say it, you ken, because it's Catholic.'

'I dinna ken it a' but it ends like this "... until they forbear their oppin synniys forisaidis and rise from this terribill cursing, and mak satisfaction and pennance."'

'Amen, amen,' said Bob piously, 'and I jist hope the polis come and catch her. She may be ony place by noo.'

They stopped at a piece of hard standing off the road by the foot of the loch.

'The engine's rinning fine,' said Tom, ' but there's a bit clatter. We'll check everything, you do the lashings and I'll look at the wheel.'

Diligently they made certain that all loose metal was secure.

'That should tak us to Selkirk.' For a moment he was pleased with their repair, then remembering the act of destruction of his pride and joy, he had to wipe a tear from his face, leaving a smudge of oil.

As they returned down the road towards the hotel, they saw a Land Rover emerging from a hill road, heading in the same direction.

'It'll no be her, again.'

To their astonishment, as the light silhouetted the driver, it was unmistakably the woman. The Archbishop's Monition, which still jingled in his mind, was banished as he watched fiercely. They were not going fast enough to overtake and they were well behind when she turned off the road into the farm. Even in the mist, there was no doubt it was her.

'She canna do us any mair hurt if she's stopped,' said Bob. 'Shall we gang in efter her and get her particulars?'

They halted at the side first of all. They could see the house and steading. It took them time to make out the Land Rover, but a gust of wind cleared the air for long enough to see it stationary by the hay barn. There was no sign of movement.

They parked carefully so that there was no excuse or chance of a repeat collision.

'Tom, dinna try and stop her if she charges oot. Like as not she's a murderous creature.'

VI

Daphne's heart had lifted with the mist when she saw the red bobble hat. The cattle snuffled and collected behind her while she crossed the field towards the grey walls of the stell. She had heard the sounds of traffic from the road. Roger and that American must have succeeded in restarting the cab and reached the road before her.

Roger,' she called out, as the stones loomed out of the haar. A figure stood up within, red hat on the head, but it was not her husband. Mrs Oldberger stood with the gun concealed. She needed Daphne within the stell, without the protective stonework.

'There's a gap there,' she pointed out. The cattle scuffled behind Daphne. She did not want to go near the woman. She hesitated, she could duck down and run. She wanted to know why.

'Who are you?' she managed to say.

'Come inside and I'll explain everything,' said the other. She had a strangely compelling manner. With the cattle kept snorting and shifting behind her, Daphne edged towards the narrow opening in the wall.

Mrs Oldberger was not going to waste time on explanations, Brought up in a world where every household had guns, and guns were for use, she was not prepared to leave a witness who had seen her pick up the yellow scarf alive. Molly had booked the escape flight from the airport, all that remained was the elimination of the woman. She waited for Daphne to emerge through the gap.

'Hey, womman.' The shout was an utterly unexpected intervention between the would-be killer and her intended victim. The gun went off but both had had moved. Tom and Bob stared in alarm and uncertainty, speechless. The cattle until then at Daphne's heels turned to stampede away across their field.

Daphne seemed to recover first, her nerves keyed by tension: in anger and shock she cried out.

'She tried to shoot me, that woman tried to shoot me!' and remained in cover behind the wall.

But that woman, despite her bulky figure had moved more quickly. Ignoring the shouts of the men, she reached the Land Rover, started the engine and took to the road for Selkirk.

In the silence that followed, Daphne burst into tears.

For Mrs Oldberger, purpose had changed. She drove as remorselessly with only escape now dominant in her mind. Her drug running schemes had now crumbled, her last vicious and mindless determination to destroy the English woman who had seemed the only real witness against her had been frustrated, the only thing left was escape. She was single minded in everything she did.

She considered clinically her progress and potential interception. Behind, there was the certainty that the men at the farm would reach a telephone. If they had come in that vintage vehicle she had seen in the driveway, they were unlikely and unable to pursue. The others had seen her heading west, so that their information would mislead. At home there might have been screaming sirens and screeching tyres, here she felt reactions might have been more leisurely. As if in keeping with her thoughts, a police car nosed gently round the corner, its occupants paying little heed to the four- wheeled drive vehicle proceeding in the opposite direction.

She rehearsed in her mind carefully each stage. Money was going to be important, she would not wish to use her name when she paid for the tickets, in case there was an alert against her. In any case she saw no need to leave the cash concealed in the Abbey. Molly awaited a telephone call for a rendezvous and would have the hire car in readiness. She had been told to recover the passports from the managers on the pretext of wanting to cash travellers' cheques.

She drove more carefully, the last thing she wished to face now was another and more conspicuous crash. She had to remind herself, when she reacted instinctively, that the rule of the road was to the left. There was a bus moving briskly down the valley which halted where she could pass it. Further on there were other people clearly waiting for it.

She slowed up to see the destination at the front. It was Melrose.

It seemed for her providential. If by now there was a search for a Land Rover, it was time to abandon it. She would continue as close to the Tweed Valley as she dared. In any case she would if necessary hijack another car.

She needed an obvious bus halt and nearby an uninhabited and screened track leading off the road. She chose with care, and as she stepped down in the concealment of the woods, she saw the police car returning towards Selkirk.

She put a scarf round her head, donned dark glasses and only approached the bus shelter as it rounded the corner to draw up.

'Melrose,' she said, holding up a five pound note.

The driver said something like 'B.G.H.?'

She looked confused.

'Borders General Hospital?' he tried again.

'No, no, the town, the Abbey.'

He gave her a ticket and engaged gear as she took a seat immediately behind him.

VII

Inspector McConachie had had a bad afternoon. He had taken the direct route by the Ettrick valley and found no-one. He had called at the inn at Tushielaw. Yes, the Stones were expected but had not yet appeared. When he crossed by the hill road to St Mary's Loch, he encountered the convoy of veterans. They strung out awkwardly along the road and he had to both locate both a parking place and prevail on them to stop.

His car was not marked but at the sight of his uniform, the drivers swiftly voiced their complaint and told him what had happened. That woman, they said had never stopped but headed on for Moffat. It did not make much sense to the Inspector if Mrs Oldberger was pursuing Roger and Daphne, but the couple might, of course, have decided to lunch at St. Mary's Loch.

When he checked at the hotel there, he drew another blank. He rang again on his mobile phone but headquarters only confirmed the earlier report that the Land Rover was heading west.

To his relief as he retraced his path past the foot of the loch, he saw Roger and the American, Webb, emerging onto the road in front of him.

Explanations were brief. McConachie, leaving Roger to tend Webb, reached for his phone. Now that the Land Rovers whereabouts were known, they should be able to trap it. It could not have gone further west or he would have met it on the loch road, it might have turned off at the hotel to follow the veterans to Tushielaw, but far more likely she would head for Melrose. He managed to make contact with the police car down the valley, the sergeant reported that they had seen nothing.

'We're stopping every four wheeled drive vehicle,' said the sergeant, 'but there's nae yin wi' a woman driver, sir.'

Roger put his hand anxiously on the Inspector's shoulder. 'Mac,' he said, 'we should move, we still don't know where Daphne is.'

McConachie responded quickly, he helped Roger to ease the wounded man into the back seat and to move in beside him, before driving off at speed. They had gone little distance before another group was visible at the roadside. To his delight, Roger could see his wife with two men. He could see from the way she stood that she was agitated. Barely had the car halted than he leapt out to embrace her.

'Thank God, you're all right, Daphne, I was worried sick.'

She managed a smile but he could feel her continued trembling. Then they all began to speak at once, and as abruptly stopped.

McConachie turned to the older man whom he recognised.

'Mr Malachi, quickly, man, tell us what happened.'

When the old driver recounted what they had seen and reached the point of the gun going off, the Inspector reacted grimly. It was now amply evident that they were dealing with a killer. He reached again for his car phone to alert the armed squad.

'Make it clear,' he added, 'no-one should approach the woman. Members of the public should inform the police if they sight her.'

Tom and Bob elected to stay with their Ford, in no hurry to follow the Inspector's car as Daphne took the front seat while Roger propped up Webb at the back.

'Unless she's turned off to Tushielaw or another side road, we have her trapped between here and the Selkirk police car. But,' he continued, glancing at Daphne's alarmed face, 'we'll no go near her, Mrs Stone.'

They sped past the Gordon Arms Hotel at the road junction and through the scattered houses that represented Yarrow Feus, Yarrow and Yarrowford, until they met the police car parked at the Bowhill turn off, and drew up along side.

'She's no passed this way, sir,' shouted the sergeant from his window.

'How long have you been here?'

The sergeant, a careful man, looked at his watch.

'Twelve minutes,' he said. 'We came back, having found no trace of the vehicle on the Moffat road, made for Selkirk until your instructions reached us. There's been a bit of traffic and we stopped all the four wheeled drive ones as we were not sure if Land Rover meant the particular make or not.'

'You have the message now, loud and clear, sergeant, that this woman is armed and dangerous. Not to be approached. If you think you sight her, do not attempt to approach. Let her pass and phone in. She's had a shot at Mrs Stone here.' He added to give weight to his instruction.

He tried to construct a timetable in his mind. Could the Land Rover have slipped though to the Peebles road or turned off on one of the few valley side roads? It did not seem likely.

The huntress had now become the hunted. Yet Mrs Oldberger , her mind set only on escape, sat confidently on her bus seat, concerned only with a modicum of concealment. She had met too many obstacles in her life to consider defeat. She had not been overly daunted by the slow reactions of the Scottish police, they did not seem to move with anything like the pace of those she had often outwitted at home. She had identified Webb from the outset as a stooge. Nor was she prepared to exercise herself over the future of her minions, Brearley and Macdonald.

Molly alone mattered to her. When she reached Melrose she would phone from a call box and her niece could evade that silly, young plain clothes man in the bar, to slip out and join her.

She composed herself in the seat behind the driver, half-listening to the conversation around her from her fellow passengers. She could understand little of it.

'There was a smash up the valley,' she heard one remark.

'Aye,' said another. 'Jock told me that yin of those auld cars was rin into. Tam Malchi's and he's fair upset aboot it. Stood greeting like a bairn in the middle of the road. The polis have been by and back again. That was them waiting at the Bowhill turn off.'

The coach seemed to take ages to reach the edges of Galashiels before turning at the roundabout to speed to the hospital. By then the talk had turned to medical matters.

'He's doing fine,' the woman behind Mrs Oldberger spoke, 'but they wilna let him smoke his pipe, an' that's no very guid for his temper.'

'Are you visiting someone?' She leant forward to ask Mrs Oldberger.

Slightly startled, Mrs Oldberger shook her head.

'No, no,' she replied. 'I'm heading for the city, for Melrose.'

'Dinna gang near the Abbey, Missus,' said the man, 'there's been some carry-on in these Abbeys, I can tell you. My cousin who's a bobby in Hawick, he tells me a' the polis have been armed and are looking for a killer.'

'You don't say,' Mrs Oldberger managed, but by that time no-one was listening as they all pushed past her in the aisle to alight at the hospital entrance.

Inspector McConachie waited with Roger and Daphne in his car. When the ambulance arrived to remove Webb, he took the driver to one side.

'I haven't an officer to send with you, but I should be grateful if the hospital would not discharge this man without letting me know.'

He made contact again with the police communication centre at Hawick which was collating the information from the officers in the field. At the Bowhill turn off the sergeant and the constable would continue to check all vehicles as they passed. One police car had taken the hill road to the Ettrick valley, where it was clear that no Land Rover, and in particular that one, had overtaken the convoy of veterans, nor had any been sighted from the Ashkirk and Hawick direction where there were roadworks and traffic lights.

'We had better go back up the valley, Roger, and look at the side roads,' the Inspector said. 'The sergeant can carry on here.'

He turned the car to retrace their way slowly, examining each side track. Roger was the first to see the Land Rover through the trees, A shaft of sunlight struck the windscreen. McConachie stopped on the roadside. Leaving Daphne in the car, the Inspector with Roger approached the concealed vehicle with extreme caution. Eventually he called out. The pigeons rose in alarm from the trees and a rabbit scurried into the undergrowth. There was obviously no human there but they still circled the Rover warily; they could see the distinct sign of scraping on the rear, near side.

'That'll be it,' he said to Roger. They stood, scanning the woodlands for paths and tracks, possible lines of escape. When they returned to the car to telephone, it was Daphne who pointed to the bus shelter.

Buses are so much of the routine of life, that they escape notice. Like the Father Brown story, as Roger later remarked, where witnesses swore no-one had passed, but they had failed to observe the postman. By the time the police boarded the bus at Melrose, it was empty, the driver had gone home and his relief could provide no information.

It was late afternoon by the time McConachie drove

them back to the town.

'Look, Roger,' he had said, ' I don't think that you and your wife should continue on your own until we have this woman locked up. We don't know why she's gunning for you. I had better offer you police protection in a hotel. I'll send a truck to fetch your bicycles and belongings. We'll lodge Daphne in safety and you can come on with me.'

Roger agreed readily: he did not wish to miss out on the hunt. It was not just that he liked hunts but he felt he had now a very personal interest in someone who had tried to kill his wife.

'We still don't know why.' He looked at his wife who had fallen into uneasy sleep beside him. She woke up at the sound of her name. 'I want to go with you,' she said. 'If Roger's going on, I won't feel safe without him.'

They drove together into Melrose.

VIII

Back at the hotel, Detective Constable Goddard was still taking his duties seriously at the bar. It was centrally placed so that he could observe the comings and goings of the Americans. Several of them used the telephone so that it was hardly surprising or a failure in his surveillance that he did not notice Molly in the booth. At about the same time, the weather was lifting, a few shafts of desultory sunshine encouraged Brearley to make one more effort to animate his clients.

'One more visit to the Abbey, folks, ' he said, 'it's a beautiful sight in the evening light. Real Tours admission covers you all day.'

Goddard had noticed him in earnest conversation with Macdonald in the course of the afternoon, but they had been careful to allow any audible conversation to be on safe topics. There was only now acrimony between the partners, they had no idea where Mrs Oldberger has gone, Macdonald wanted to cut and run while they could. He could feel the net closing on them.

'That's a copper at the bar,' he kept saying, 'they're on to us.'

It was Brearley, now keeping his cool, who kept saying. 'Hold on, they haven't anything on us. If you run, they'll know we're doing something. Anyway I want that cash from the Abbey. Let's get the party across there again.'

The break in the clouds encouraged them towards the Abbey gate.

In her Eildon cottage, Meg had enjoyed the sun above the mists. She sensed now a stirring within her. It was not a call to the woods and trees, nor a summons to walk on the heather to feel the wind on her face, she felt drawn back to the Abbey, an urge to utter warnings of death.

She had eaten her light midday meal and waited until her daughter had returned from school before setting out. The sun seemed to lighten her path down the hill in contrast to the dark foreboding in her heart. The mist was lifting as she reached the ridge above the town from which she could look down on the ruins of the church below. Like ants on their nest, small figures seemed to be converging on her destination.

Major Alistair Peter McAlistair, too, felt a deep malaise. His disquiet stemmed from the forces of disorder that seemed to threaten what he called his Abbeys. The sequence of untoward events that had begun in Jedburgh and followed him to Kelso and Dryburgh demanded a cul-mination in Melrose. For him, although he might not have fully recognised it, there had to be an ultimate logical completion.

He had loitered in the town for the day, uncertain in the absence of his routines until he decided to return to the Abbey when the evening sun once again lit it up..

It gave Sam Thwaites a rational cover to return from Galashiels to set up his easel among the gravestones. He wanted to retrieve the 'stuff' with an increasing awareness of his own personal need.

At the entry kiosk, the custodian, thankful that the flow of visitors had ceased, began to check the day's takings in his till and prepared to close the shop. He had still to make a final tour to inspect the grounds. As he glanced out to see the brightness restored to the stones and grass, at the same time he realised that further visitors were approaching. The door of his gatehouse was pushed open

THE BELL STAIR

'Who spilleth life, shall forfeit life'
The Eve of St. John: Sir Walter Scott.

I

Mrs Oldberger conferred with her niece on the road. She was not going to alarm her with a recital of the day's events. It was enough to convince her that departure had to be swift.

'Molly, you just wait here with the car, I just want to say a last goodbye to that old church.'

Slightly puzzled by her aunt's manner, Molly complied and Mrs Oldberger pushed into the entrance.

'Real Tours,' she uttered defiantly and sailed on without waiting to acknowledge the man's nod of consent.

She could see the artist at work among the gravestones set in the damp grass, glistening with the moisture of the vanishing mist, but she took no heed of him. The westering sun lit up the facade of the ruins, warming the red sandstone of the seats of the old cloister, of the pulpitum set at the front of the truncated nave, of the flying buttresses, and of the line of family tombs in the flanking wall. The stark tracery and the slender mullions of the great window at the east end were brilliantly outlined against the sky. For all this fragmented beauty she had no time or interest, her one aim was the hidden money and immediate getaway.

She heard voices behind her. For the moment, the speakers were hidden by the trees edging the road, then she was relieved to see that they were strangers alighting from a coach in the park. She looked round quickly as she entered under the roof of the Reformation church. There seemed no-one else in the grounds. But to her dismay as she reached the transept, she heard footsteps and the little man with the moustache and walking stick appeared from the cloister door behind her. He glanced at her, seemed to hesitate, not quite sure whether he should speak or not. The Major knew he had seen her before, and was not sure whether this constituted an introduction.

As he vanished, she was aware of another sound, a voice chanting. She remembered that mad Scottish woman saying you could hear the old monks singing from their choir. She shivered in apprehension for a moment and told herself not to be silly. Then Meg came in from the graveyard droning and murmuring.

Mrs Oldberger pretended to be studying the inscriptions on the wall above the doorway. The lettering was obscure and spelt out no obvious words: she let her eyes follow to the end of it where she read 'BE HALDE TO YE HENDE Qo JOHNE MORVO. She half turned to observe the artist who seemed always to be looking into the transept, although she realised that he could not see the entrance to the stairwell.

Again there were distant voices approaching from the gatehouse, but just for a moment there was emptiness about her. She seized the grill. It lifted readily off its hinges. As she held it to one side, and rested her bulky figure against the jamb of the door in order to bend down into the corner to try to retrieve the bundle, she could feel the bag containing the gun slide from her shoulder. Amid all her clumsy confusion, she heard Meg's chanting again behind her. In desperation she launched herself against the steps rising into their narrow spiral. Seated, almost jammed into the stairwell, she held the grill in a closed position.

Meg's recitation still sounded close, beginning to rise in louder tones as she found new visitors in the nave. The little man came past inquisitively. Very, very gingerly Mrs Oldberger restored the grill onto its hinges: it was all that she could do in the cramped space. Until the surge of traffic had passed her, she would have to remain where she was. It was with great difficulty that she managed to turn round to crawl on all fours a few steps higher, out of immediate sight. She scrabbled for her bag, clasping it closely to her, feeling the shape of the gun for a sense of security. The packet of money was still hidden in its corner below her but out of reach.

Real Tours crossed from the hotel to the Abbey. The sun and a sense of wellbeing brought out the whole party including its older members. As Mrs Sorenson said. 'We have paid for it, so we really ought to enjoy it, and nothing happened this morning.'

The two managers kept looking around surreptitiously for those absent.

Mrs Sorenson monopolised Brearley as they walked towards the Abbey grounds with continual and exasperating questions.

'You know, John, we really ought to see these ruins by moonlight. Just listen to this.' She pulled out a booklet from her handbag and read from it.

"If thou wouldst view fair Melrose aright,
Go visit by the pale moonlight
For the gay beams of lightsome day
Gild, but to flout, the ruins gray"
'That's what Sir Walter says.'

'I am quite content,' said her husband, 'to have a few gay beams of sunshine around right now.'

Just for a moment, Brearley wondered whether he would not be better to leave the recovery of the money until nightfall, but he felt the need for instant action. He contrived to separate himself from Mrs Sorenson and passed through the shop, leaving Macdonald outside to check the car park to see if the Land Rover had come back. 'We might need it,' he said darkly. Macdonald searched among the coaches and cars, but the vehicle was to be seen.. He followed his colleague at speed into the Abbey grounds and pulled him to one side.

'Look,' he whispered hoarsely, 'the Rover's not there but that bloody girl is sitting there in a hired car.'

'Who do you mean?'

'Molly, Molly, Oldberger, they're running. We've got to get out.'

'I want that cash, then we'll move,' Although, even as he spoke he did not see how.

'One last look round, folks,' he spoke in his Real Tours tones. 'Have you been to the museum?'

The Inspector parked in the car park in the town centre and, leaving Roger and Daphne in the vehicle, went into the hotel to find Constable Goddard dutifully at his post.

'They've all gone,' he said.

'Gone where, man?' McConachie barked at him.

'All gone to the Abbey, sir.'

'Has Mrs Oldberger reappeared?'

'Never seen her again.'

From the car the Inspector phoned Hawick to see if the woman had been sighted.

'One of the bus passengers who alighted at the hospital has described a passenger who must be Oldberger. It looks as if she reached Melrose ahead of you.'

He took his car cautiously round the town's few main streets, ending up in the Abbey parking.

'You had better stop here, Roger, until I have checked where the armed squad is. While the Americans have been in the hotel, they have been based at the station down the road.'

He spoke briefly on his phone.

'They're on stand by. The first thing we have to do is to find out if the woman has returned to the Abbey.'

He moved swiftly to the gatehouse. It was not difficult to describe Mrs Oldberger; the custodian recognised her immediately.

'Aye, Inspector,' he said. 'She came in half an hour back, and a' the ithers followed a while after.'

The police van was ordered back into position, a further cordon of the local force were posted discreetly at the gate and the museum road. The ring had closed in. Molly Oldberger in her hire car had seen the uniformed Inspector and without quite knowing why, decided to sit out of sight, sliding down in her seat.

Hawick came in again on the phone to his car..

'You had better pull Brearley and Macdonald in as well for questioning but keep the tourists happy. But for God's sake Mac, no shooting if you can help it.' His senior officer kept blurting out. 'This isn't the U.S.A.'

The Inspector thought grimly that it had begun to look rather like it with the Real Tours visitors spread out across the Abbey grounds and a murderous gun carrying woman amongst them. Leaving Daphne in the car, but taking Roger who insisted, he returned to the gatehouse and explained briefly to the custodian what was happening.

'Let no-one else in, we shall clear the grounds slowly advising all visitors to leave. If the woman comes, let her out without question. Roger, you had better stay here, because if she sees you, she will know that the game is up. I shall move round asking everyone to leave.'

'Mac, ' said Roger, 'wouldn't it be better for the custodian to go round and say he has to close early. Your uniform might cause alarm and start trouble. We can man the gate to prevent anyone coming in and check everyone out.'

Meg stood beneath the ruined tower. High above her the sun created patterns of light and shadow under the vaulted roof and in the clerestory gallery. She appreciated the new audience gathered in front of her. Deep inside her the spirit of Thomas the Rhymer stirred; her feet moved, her body swayed she began to croon. Whatever pagan elfin queen had inspired in her forbear merged with her sense of history and affection for the old Abbey.

She repeated her introductory chant:

    'Roun an roun till a' is couth,
    Rhymer gar his kin speak sooth.
    By his gift from Eildon's queen
    I see oor world with ither een'

The new visitors turned from their idle examination of the dreary Protestant columns which hid the more delicate, original pillars of the choir, to watch in fascination Meg's gyrations. Her long grey hair now draped her shoulders and the black dress below, the gold cross swung hypnotically as she moved. When she recited it was with a strength surprising from such a small frame.

'I hae the gudely gift frae him,' she said. 'And it aye comes strangly to me when I come to this kirk.'

'Times I see aroun me the light streaming through the

coloured glass of the windows, falling on the cross and the altar, and the monks walking in procession through yon arch and in their white robes, kneelin' and chantin' at their devotions.'

'Times it's dark. By the licht of the moon, I can see them coming down yon stair from the dorters, and there's yin who crosses to the Bell Stair.'

She stopped suddenly as if there was some obstruction to her vision, the images of the close-fitting stones, the wedge-shaped steps and the central column seemed to carry above them the open sky of the present day ruin.

She became aware that there were others joining the rear of the party, to her disappointment those she had encountered before. Then she saw Rabbie, the custodian, speaking to each in turn, followed by a gradual movement towards the gate. She stopped as her audience dwindled, once again disappointed in any contributions they might have wished to make.

'We're closing early,' Burns said, as with a quick look into the apparently empty transept, he passed through the door to the cloister lawn.

Meg lingered; she felt there was something incomplete about the evening, something that she still needed to say or was expected to do. The building had emptied; there was quiet except for the voices receding towards the road way. She saw the artist who had been working among the grave-stones packing up. Sam Thwaites needed little encouragement to move; he was naturally sensitive to police activity. Aware of movement on the road behind him, reluctant as he was to give up his vigil and expectations, he folded away his easel, passed rather shiftily through the gate-house, disturbed by the Inspector's scrutiny. He returned sadly to his home.

Meg looked round for the Major, had he also departed? She remembered having seen the fat woman, where had she gone? There was something unwanted in the picture in her mind. It was not just that she had not been able to utter, what should have been uttered, there was something there that should not be there. In agitation she stretched herself on the ground where the high altar would have been, pressing her body for solace against the uneven ground.

In the unexpected silence that had descended upon the Abbey, Mrs Oldberger shifted on the spiral stair, preparing to make a move. Cautiously she peered through the grill. Reassured by the absence of movement or noise, she reached for the packet and lifted the grid from its hinges.

Meg heard a noise, the almost imperceptible rustle of clothing and scraping of feet carried across the gravel. She rose slowly to stare round in puzzlement. The noise seemed to come from the direction of the grilled doorway. Was there movement behind it?

Mrs Oldberger in alarm perceived she was not alone, clutched at the grill as Meg pressed her face against it. Trying to grasp hand bag, money and grill was too much. As Meg wrenched it outwards more in curiosity than aggression, Mrs Oldberger retreated backwards up the stair, seeking distance to open her bag: she kept sprawling on the steps, while her elbows jammed in the narrows of the spiral.

Meg who had fallen back as the grid swung open on its padlock, craned her neck to peer upwards into the gloom.

'Get out, get out,' shouted the American. There was something about the mad woman that frightened her.

'I've a gun.'

Meg did not really think in terms of guns. They belonged to a reality alien to her dream world. She followed Mrs Oldberger up the stair.

Brearley had conducted as many of his party as he could to the gate that led them to the museum, anything to keep them away from the transept. Jane Marshall and her acolytes, Ruth and Beth, said that they had done it previously and, despite his efforts of discouragement, headed back to the ruins. Jane wanted somehow to regain the hegemony she realised had escaped her during the appalling morning events.

'Girls,' she said. 'It's like surviving an air crash, we've simply got to go back and look at that awful high place.'

Burns intercepted them and directed them to the exit.

John Brearley slipped behind the east end of the building to reach the transept from the south side. Gus Macdonald with a more wary instinct had noticed the police activity on the road. It was not so much what he saw, as a streetwise awareness that the traffic was not moving normally. Cars were being halted and turned round, there were no pedestrians. He was becoming more and more sure that he had to cut his losses and run. He could see no alternative way out so he, too, joined the others as they filed towards the gatehouse.

On the stair, the two women remained in confrontation. The larger had dropped her bag with the gun, clinging irrationally to the packet of money. There was not much light as her bulk blocked out the little from above, and the diminutive black figure obscured that from the doorway.

'Go away, go away,' Mrs Oldberger spoke hoarsely, retreating. A pigeon broke from the gallery above her dislodging dirt on her head.

'There's aye blood in the Abbey,' said Meg advancing, 'Blood brings blood.' There was no room for her dancing but she carried an eerie menace in her stillness. She was not really sure who the other was. It was just an alien intrusion that she had sensed at Dryburgh against which she was required to utter.

The American was beginning to panic, struggling with something unearthly. She was aware, too, of Meg's smell, the wholesome smell of the unwashed, distasteful to ideas of transatlantic hygiene. She shuffled further backwards. As the light from the clerestory began to reach her at the head of the stair, she recalled the terrifyingly unguarded parapet of the gallery. As she put out a hand she was aware that the stair branched and some dim light arrived from a different angle. She had reached the passage that led to the gallery above the transept. Reluctantly she faltered on until she was able to see the open church beneath her

There was an interruption from below, Brearley, on seeing the grill hanging open, plunged his hand into the corner searching for the packet which was not there. He heard the confusion and panting above. Mrs Oldberger recognised his figure and called out. 'John.'

He stepped back to stare aloft.

Silence fell again on the stairwell. Meg began chanting again. The footsteps below left her unmoved. She felt the need to mount higher towards the light, to speak her sibylline utterances from the gallery. Almost oblivious of the woman obstructing her, she pushed forwards relentlessly. As Meg emerged from the darkness of the staircase , Mrs Oldberger pressed herself against the stonework, anything rather than look down again. She edged herself towards the corner of the ruined tower where a flight of stairs seemed to offer escape. She fumbled her way backwards, thrusting out her hands defensively. But the old stair was a cul-de-sac leading only to space where the tower had been, and barred off from it by an inadequate wire screen The rough stone of the walls snagged her clothing and she could only find uncertain footing on the uneven treads.

There was light from the wire grill behind her, she could go little further. All she could do was to sit at the head of the short flight and fend off her adversary. Even as she sank, collapsing towards the ground, her heavy body lurched against the grill, burst its fastenings and she fell to the centre of the tower crossing fifty feet below.

Her brief scream reached the crowd that had gathered in the street. The Inspector, instructing the constable at the gate to admit and let out no-one, beckoned to Roger and both men ran as fast as they could into the ruins.. As soon as they reached the entrance to the nave, they could see the body under the open sky of the crossing. There was one figure standing beside it, carefully stretching out the arms as a cross.

'She's dead,' said the Major, as the Inspector approached. 'May she rest in peace.'

II

For Roger the scene was like the climax to a play. Not

The Bell Stair

immediately caught up by the call of any duty, he could allow himself to be a spectator. As he said to Daphne afterwards, the setting was bizarre and theatrical. Mrs Oldberger lay inert under the open sky of the tower crossing, her blood discolouring her clothing and beginning to ooze gently into the crevices of the stone floor. She still clutched a polythene bag from which a few bank notes had contrived to escape and flutter randomly across the set in the evening wind.

He watched in this frozen moment as Ian McConachie stared in astonishment at the Major, who stood at the salute like a military mourner at the head of the dead woman, as if he had just laid a wreath on a tombstone. Beyond this, stage centre, John Brearley appeared, holding uncertainly the bag he had picked up at the foot of the spiral stairway. Roger was just aware of someone moving, stage left and vanishing into the wings. Behind him there was a sort of distant murmur as if the extras, the crowd at the gate and the police outside the grounds, wanted to enter for the final curtain.

Reality returned as he recognised that the Inspector was speaking to him.

'Roger,' he had to speak twice. 'Roger, would you go to the gatehouse, tell the officer there to call for an ambulance, and instruct the sergeant that no-one should for the moment leave.' O God, the thought flashed through his mind, was he going to have to interview the whole bloody lot of Americans all over again. 'I'll have a quick look round here before anyone else.'

He bent once more over the body, still warm and gross but lifeless. The Major regarded him seriously.

'She's dead, of course,' he said. 'Couldn't be anything else, really, number four.'

Time did not remain still for John Brearley. He stood for a moment shocked by the woman's unexpected and violent fall. He felt carefully the contents of the bag that he had picked up, realising that it contained a gun and nothing remotely likely to be cash. If Mrs Oldberger had been responsible for the murders, there seemed no reason to

193

suppose that she might not be considered solely responsible for the distribution of the drugs. He repeated to himself what he kept saying to Macdonald that there was no evidence against them except Webb's, and he only had his suspicions, now that they had disposed of the stuff.

His mind raced ahead, where was Webb, was McShea safe? He must make sure that Macdonald did not panic. They must both say the same thing.

He put down the bag. 'I picked this up, it's Mrs Oldberger's.

The Inspector and the Major shifted their gaze from the corpse to stare at him.'Is she dead?' He did not wait for an answer. 'I had better get her niece.'

'I would like you to stay here, Mr Brearley,' began McConachie, but the manager had set off towards the gate, shouting over his shoulder. 'I have responsibilities as the tour manager.'

From the gatehouse the scene at the east end of the Abbey was obscured by the pulpitum. Yet the audience had become aware of the tragedy which the appearance of Roger had confirmed. There was a silence and a tension amongst them. The constable on the roadway asked them to move inside the grounds; other uniformed police like sheepdogs arrived to herd them, preventing any filtering into the town streets.

Gus Macdonald, having discovered there was no line of escape, hovered uneasily at the edge of the American group, noting the absence of his partner. When Brearley emerged from the ruins, everyone turned instinctively towards him, but he avoided all questions brusquely, pulling Macdonald to one side

'Look, Gus,' he said. 'It's the boss, she's dead. Fell from the tower. Just remember we know nothing about the drugs. No panic.'

The members of the touring party crowded round him, preventing any further private talk. He turned rather wearily towards them in his best Real Tours manner.

'I have to tell you,' he began, but then there was the wail of an ambulance siren on the road behind him. As the custodian moved to open the vehicle gates to admit it, the crowd's attention followed its progress, circling the tombstones. By the time they turned to Brearley once more, McConachie appeared with the Major walking sombrely towards them, and the manager fell silent.

The Inspector stopped and stood still. He noticed Macdonald distancing himself from Brearley; he knew that he had not succeeded in preventing them meeting. He had no need to ask for silence.

'I have to tell you,' he echoed the manager's approach, 'that there has been a fatal accident within the Abbey. We shall, of course, have to close the grounds. And I ask each of you here to give your name and address to the officer in the shop as you leave. I should also be grateful if any of you who were near the tower would try to remember if you saw anything unusual.' At present he was not going to reveal any details of the spiral stair.

He realised that he needed help: he called to one of the uniformed officers. 'Would you take the Major to the station and obtain a statement from him. Don't let him go until I have seen him.'

'He grabbed Brearley. 'Didn't Mrs Oldberger have a niece with her? Where is she? I don't wish to name the fatality until the next of kin knows.'

Brearley looked swiftly around, but then recalled what Macdonald had told him.

He stalled for a moment. 'I don't see her here,' he said.

As he spoke, he saw Molly on the road outside.

The Inspector pushed through the throng to go out by the vehicle entrance. 'Miss Oldberger,' he called. It was a task that he never liked doing, never found it any easier. He led the girl through the tombstones as he continued

'Do you think that you could manage a formal identification now? It might be easier now than later,' he added gently.

White faced and shaken, Molly joined the ambulance men and paramedic in the transept. When she had managed to stammer out the necessary words of identification, the body was conveyed to the ambulance, and the whole party left for the hospital, leaving the Inspector at last free to examine more thoroughly the staircase, the gallery and the broken grill.

He caught sight of the bag on he ground. He had forgotten that Brearley had set it down. It looked like a knitting bag, and he remembered seeing it in Mrs Oldberger's powerful hands. Puzzled by its weight, he opened it to find the gun inside

Why, he wondered, had she come back to the Abbey? Would her mind not have been set on escape after her murderous attack had been witnessed?

'Mac.' His name was called, and he glanced up to see Roger Stone approaching.

'Do you mind if I join you? I've got a personal interest in this.' He thought of his white-faced wife. 'I've given my name and address to your man.'

'No objection, Roger. Two heads are better than one in this sort of business. In any case, shortly the whole investigation squad will be here and we shall be better out of the way. Let's have a look at that stairway.'

Roger remembered as they moved into the transept. 'You know, she was here,' he said.

'Who do you mean?' The Inspector was manoeuvring his bulk into the stairwell.

'That mad woman, you know the one who chants and prophesies. When you were tending to Mrs O., I saw Meg slipping through the transept doorway. I think that she came from this stair.'

McConachie was silent. He could not turn round to exclaim, confined as he was by the twisting wheel stair, and only too restricted by its adamantine stones. The presence of his impossible cousin was the last straw at the end of a long, wearisome day when he had failed to prevent another death. As they emerged onto the clerestory gallery, he exploded at Roger.

'What in God's name was Jeannie doing here? Can she no just sit in her cottage without coming down here to complicate matters?'

He muttered angrily to himself and then, catching

Roger's surprised look at his outburst, apologised.

'It's just this,' he said. 'At the very moment we seem to have seen the end of this murderous woman, probably responsible for the other murders. Then the whole business fouls itself up. What was my cousin doing here and why was that Brearley fellow standing there, holding the bag with the gun in it? Why was the Major presiding over the corpse?'

III

They had barely time to move to the end of the gallery, where the steps led over the crossing and the wire grid was hanging by one retaining hasp, when the sound of voices below announced the arrival of the photographic team.

The Inspector collected his thoughts. There seemed so much to do. With the arrival of the professionals, Roger took his leave to collect Daphne from the car and find lodgings, while McConachie conferred with the posse of police surrounding the Abbey whose presence seemed no longer necessary. He then made his way resolutely to the hotel although the last thing he wished to do was to listen to the nasal tones of any American citizen. He found Detective Constable Goddard still at his place of duty.

'Gordon, what you have to do is to go back with the tourists to the hotel where they are staying and make sure that not one of them leaves the building. I'll deal with the managers in their separate digs but I hold you personally responsible for the others. I shall also send someone over to relieve you. Where's Brearley?'

'He's gone out, sir, with Macdonald.'

Furious with himself for not separating the two, he sent a man to the car park who returned to report the coach to be still there. Without the Land Rover, the managers could not go far. As he stood outside the hotel, he saw them approaching together.

'Mr Macdonald, I must ask you to take your party back to your Kelso hotel and tell them that they must not leave the building. Constable Goddard will go with you and I shall send over other officers. We can say at the moment that it is for everyone's security. I must ask you too, not to leave the tour hotel or your own lodging without further permission.'

Macdonald made token expostulatory noises; he did not even ask about Webb although he must have noted the man's absence.

'Now, Mr Brearley, will you accompany me to the police station.' It was not a request but an order.

There was yet another twist to the long day's events.

'Sergeant Evans from Edinburgh has been ringing, sir,' said the sergeant when he entered Melrose police station. 'Shall I get him on the line?'

The unmistakable Welsh voice came over loud and clear.

'Trail gone cold here, sir, I'm afraid. The fellow I thought would give us evidence against McShea has back-tracked. Says he was wrong, it was another man altogether. I pitched at him heavy but he stuck to his story. McShea, of course, admits nothing.'

The Inspector held his phone in unhappy silence. The Welshman continued.

'Anything fresh down your way, sir?'

McConachie took a deep breath. 'I think, Taffy,' he said rather heavily, 'I think that I'll ask the sergeant here to update you. You had better come down here first thing tomorrow morning. We shall have to go over the ground again.'

He handed the instrument over.

He could see Brearley sitting at the reception desk so he realised that the officer must still be taking a statement from Major McAlistair in the interview room. It would do no harm to let the manager cool his heels for a moment although as he eyed the man, Brearley responded with a cold and resolute stare.

The station sergeant handed him the Major's statement. He put on his spectacles to read, checked that it was set out correctly and noted that it was duly signed by a particularly neat – Alistair Peter McAlistair, Major, retd.

'I take it upon myself,' it ran, 'to make regular visits to our four magnificent, but ruined and neglected abbeys. Today I was at Melrose…' he went on at some length to say where he found fault with its maintenance and poor state of the gravestones. The sergeant interposed to say that he had been unable to cut off the flow.

However he eventually found the all too brief cogent evidence.

'I noticed the custodian asking people to leave the grounds and I decided to make my own final patrol by way of the church. I could hear voices above me. As I looked up to see where they came from, the grating overhead gave way, and this person, this woman fell to her death in front of me. Most distressing, I have to say, even though in my military career, death, violent death is no stranger to me. I consider it most unfortunate to encounter it yet again in sacred grounds.'

McConachie could imagine the moustache bristling with indignation on the sharp face.

The Major went on to say that for a moment he had thought that the woman was still alive and he had bent over to tend her until he knew that she had been killed instantly. He had heard noises from behind him and recognised the man he thought was the tour manager clutching a bag in the south transept. It was then that the Inspector had appeared.

Taking the sheet, McConachie went to the interview room where the constable and McAlistair were seated,

'Thank you for your help, Major. I am sorry to have delayed your return home. It has been a long day for us all.'

He spoke in the most conciliatory manner that he could manage; the Major, who had seemed ready to bridle, appeared mollified.

'Yes, yes,' he said. 'These things have to be done. I know the drill. All most unfortunate.'

'I need to ask one or two more questions. The voices you heard from the gallery, were they men's or women's?'

'There was not a lot of noise. I could hear movement,

and what sounded like "keep away from me!" There were footsteps and stumblings. I had the impression of two women. Definitely no male voice aloft. Come to think of it now,' he closed his eyes to recall. 'A man shouted up the staircase just before she fell. Might have been that manager's voice.'

'Thank you, Major. That was most helpful.'

It looked as if Brearley could not have been involved.

'Now, Major.' McConachie turned himself fully towards the soldier, who was sitting at attention opposite him. 'When I arrived you appeared to be stretching out the dead woman's arms to either side. Is that not so?'

McAlistair stared unflinchingly back, unabashed.

'Of course.' he said. 'Sacred ground, must have the corpse laid out like a cross.'

There did not seem to the Inspector an easy answer to this religious statement.

'Mebbe so, Major. Now could I ask if you were at Jedburgh that day the man was found dead in the, what do you call it, the chancel, at the high altar?'

'Yes, indeed, Inspector. I saw the body and thought it only right that he should be properly laid out. Abbeys make demands, you know.'

McConachie was the one who turned his eyes down. He was too tired to be contradictory about the protocol for the arrangement of corpses found on holy ground. He groped for thought, managing what he recognised as a rather stuffy answer.

'Did it not cross your mind,' then realising that this was an unfortunate choice of words, 'did it not enter your mind that this might be obstructing the police in the investigation of a crime?'

McAlistair just glared, not deigning to reply.

'Why did you not tell us this before?' Even as he asked the question, he knew what the answer would be.'

'You never asked me.'

'Now, can I ask you about Kelso?'

'Certainly, but you have asked me before.'

'Did you come across,' he once more rephrased himself,

'did you go near the body in Kelso?'

'I told you before, Inspector, I visited the Abbey briefly that afternoon, as usual, but I found no body, knew nothing about it, until you told me when you came to see me.'

All the Inspector could do was to ask him to add these answers to his statement, thank him for his assistance and bid him good night.

The younger officer was about to offer some comment on the departing witness but, catching the exhausted look on his superior's face, refrained. The Inspector summoned Brearley.

'Sit down Mr Brearley.' Suspects received a mister until they were charged. The manager straightened his Real Tours blazer as he seated himself carefully on the other side of the table. The Inspector looked at him thoughtfully wondering how he should start. He would have to approach the drug matter cautiously as he had no positive connection between the tour and the trafficking, other than what Webb alleged.

'You are having a very unhappy tour, I'm afraid, Mr Brearley, and you must be deeply upset by the death of Mrs Oldberger.'

The manager nodded, warily.

'Have you known her long?'

'Some years,' the man's voice was nervously hoarse, he coughed and tried again, 'Yes, some years, Inspector. She has come over on several of our trips.'

'Have you ever had reason to suspect that she could be violent? Is it a surprise to you to know that we now think that she may have been responsible for the two shootings?' He could see Brearley working out an answer but he went on. 'Did you know she had a gun?'

'Not until I picked up that bag and felt its contents.'

'Why did you come back to the church when the custodian was asking everyone to leave?'

That was an easy one. 'I felt it was my duty to see that all my party had left the grounds.'

'What did you do on reaching the transept?'

'I heard noises overhead and, seeing the doorway open,

I went in and shouted. I thought that I recognised Mrs Oldberger's voice. I picked up the bag at the foot of the stairs, then there was the scream and the sound of her fall, so I came out of the stairwell. You know the rest, Inspector.'

McConachie sighed inwardly. He knew it was no use asking the man why he had run to the gate.

He shifted his tack. 'I have to ask you whether you had any reason to suspect anyone in your party being concerned with drugs. We believe that both Jones, shot at Kelso, and Thornell, shot at Dryburgh were mixed up with small time drug selling. Is it just a coincidence that your touring party was present on both occasions?'

'Bloody unfortunate, Inspector.'

'Could Mrs Oldberger have been involved? After all, if we establish that she killed the two men, and the evidence of the gun should show this, then she must have had a reason.'

'I really don't know, Inspector.'

'What about McShea?'

'What about him, Inspector?'

McConachie could have struck out in irritation.

'Do you think that he could have had any connection with drugs?' If only Evans had not telephoned, he could have alleged that they had evidence against the lecturer, and use the old trick of telling one accomplice that the other had confessed.

'Did you know that Webb is a member agent of the United States Federal Bureau of Narcotics?'

He could see a reaction from Brearley as he hesitated in reply.

'I wasn't sure about it,' he said guardedly.

'What do you mean?'

'He hinted at it one day over a drink, but I was never sure whether to believe him.'

'Did he not come to see you last night at your inn?'

This time, McConachie saw that he had struck home. Brearley could control his face but not the whitening of his knuckles as he clenched his fingers.

'You mean last night?' It gave him time to think.

He looked down and continued. 'Oh yes, I think he did. We were outside with the vehicles.'

'Why did you drive off in the Land Rover?'

The reply came a little more glibly this time. 'We had battery trouble and needed to give it a run to charge up.'

McConachie now knew he had to keep the man away from Macdonald so that he could check this out. It seemed to be the one weakness in his replies. He was not sure what Graham's account of the night's activities meant, but questions about it appeared to rattle the manager.

He stood up and, as Brearley rose to follow him, he stopped him and said, 'Would you wait here.'

He returned to the main office. 'Look sergeant,' he said, 'I need to find an excuse to hold the man here until I have had time to question his partner. Would you detain him? Just say, that having found him in possession of a gun we need to make a few more enquiries before he can be allowed to go.'

Leaving the sergeant to deal with Brearley's expostulations, he collected his car and drove across country to the tourist's hotel. Goddard was in the lobby and told him Macdonald was in the bar. McConachie drew him brusquely outside.

'I have your colleague at Melrose Police Station. He was found with a gun in his hands in the Abbey grounds.' It was as hostile start as he could contrive. 'What have you to say to that?'

Macdonald's weasel face was impassive. He looked sharply at the Inspector for a moment, trying to guess what was known. He had to trust what Brearley had said to him.

'I don't know anything about that at all,' he said. 'I did not know that he had a gun.'

'It was not his gun. It was in Mrs Oldberger's handbag.'

The Inspector switched his attack abruptly. 'What happened last night at your lodgings? Why did you drive the Land Rover away in the middle of the night?'

For a moment, Macdonald wavered, biting his lip, glancing away and then back to his interrogator.

'I dinna mind.' He groped for an ambiguous, non-committal answer. 'Och, yes.' Under pressure he fell back on fragments of his home speech. 'John wanted to test something, it had not been running right.'

He stared directly at the Inspector to see how this was received.

'What was the matter?'

'I can't recall now.'

'Come on, man, it was only last night.'

'Ye'll have to ask John.'

It was a slim defence, but he glared confidently at his interrogator

McConachie altered his line of questioning again, although he realised it might only be a formality.

'Has there been, Mr Macdonald,' he deliberately stressed the Mister. 'Has there been any dealings with drugs within your touring party?'

Thoughts raced through Macdonald's head. What had Webb told the Scottish police? Brearley had said that it would be their word against the American's. In any case there could be no point in offering anything but a blunt denial. He would know soon enough if there was any undeniable evidence against them. Where was Webb? What about McShea?

He replied defiantly, 'No way inspector. Why should you think that?'

Further question elicited nothing. Eventually McConachie left him to retreat to the bar. Before leaving he checked with the constables that the tourist party were all present in the hotel and took himself home to report by telephone to the Hawick Superintendent.

'I don't think, sir, that there is anything further I can do to-night,' he said, after giving as concise an account of what he realised had been an extraordinary and lengthy day.

Even his senior officer showed understanding. 'We'll field the press. You'll ken the right schemozzle we have here. Don't say a word to anyone, yourself. The Fiscal's hopping up and down like mad, wanting every bit of paper yesterday, if not before, and itching to see someone charged. You have the whole party under observation?'

'Yes,' he said. 'I have Brearley at the Melrose station, and Macdonald and the touring party are all being watched.'

The Superintendent went on, 'The Chief Constable has ordered a conference here first thing tomorrow morning, nine o'clock sharp. You know what he feels about drug dealers, he sees them as worse than murderers. We must make sure that we make arrests. We've taken in the Land Rover and have begun to strip it down to see if it has any concealed compartments. We didn't think that we need ask anyone's permission, after all it was a vehicle involved in a crime. We'll see if we can run the sniffer dogs through the coach tomorrow, but I can't see us getting any search warrants when we have nothing except suspicions, and not with all these United States citizens. You have simply got to find some hard evidence, Mac, and we haven't much time.'

As the Inspector put down the receiver, he caught sight of his fishing rods in the corner of his study. He was very tired but he was also coldly angry. The viciousness of the intrusion of murder and drug traffickers into the rustic peace of the Borders struck deeply home to him. And he had not succeeded in preventing the last death nor been able to arrest anyone. He felt old.

TEVIOT AND TWEED

'The earth builds on the earth castles and towers,
The earth says to the earth all shall be ours'
Epitaph on tombstone: Melrose Abbey.

I

Setting off for Hawick early on Saturday morning, McConachie reflected that it had been the day he was due off. He laughed ruefully to himself as he parked at Headquarters. There was a flurry of activity in the offices, every officer conspicuous in his diligence.

At the conference the Chief Constable appeared, with the Procurator Fiscal fussing about and the senior officers of Hawick speaking importantly with low voices. As the Inspector began his report he could see that Evans had also arrived.

He gave a quick resume of what had happened the day before, on which he was occasionally questioned but for the most part his audience sat in shocked silence. The unwonted violence and death was not what their routine policing had prepared them for.

'If,' he said, in conclusion, 'we consider that the clear eye-witness evidence against Oldberger of her murderous attack on Mrs Stone also supports the theory that she murdered Jones and Thornell, it may be that we can regard the sequence of killings has ended with her death. But we have little in the way of evidence of motive. Nor can we be sure that other parties were not involved.'

'While we have the heroin discovered in Thornell's house and local suspicions against Jones, the sum total of the link between the touring group and drugs rests with Webb and the package of money clasped by Oldberger. We need to discover the source of their supplies and if and where the culprits have now disposed of them in fear of apprehension.'

When he had finished speaking, the Chief Constable spoke drily.

'Well, gentlemen, you have had an unprecedented number of violent crimes and yet I gather no-one has yet been charged.'

He regarded them austerely round the table.

'I shall, of course, leave matters in your capable hands, while I reassure the minister. It looks as if we may have reached the end of the killings but may I ask a few questions?'

'Firstly, that man Webb who might be regarded as our prime witness in the all important pursuit of the drug sellers, what is his condition?'

The Senior Hawick Officer answered. 'We checked with the hospital this morning, sir, he is in intensive care, due to loss of blood and cannot be questioned. In any case, we still have doubts about his reliability.'

'Secondly, I understand that this other woman, Jeannie, Jeannie Redpath, was present in the Abbey gallery, she'll have to be questioned.' The officers shuffled uneasily, realising that this should have already happened.

Thirdly, the drugs. You know my feelings about those involved in this pernicious traffic. I take on board what the Inspector has said but have we any evidence that any Americans are involved, other than Mrs Oldberger? Sergeant Evans, here, reports that he can find nothing on this university lecturer, despite what Webb alleges. You will all appreciate that this is a very politically sensitive matter. The fact that the touring party is from the United States makes the whole affair one to be handled with kid gloves'

He picked up his and his baton and left the room.

II

Another meeting was also taking place, this one at the hotel. A sleepy Constable Goddard joined the tourists as they assembled in the lounge, shepherded by Macdonald. As they gathered, Brearley arrived, unshaven after his night in a Melrose police cell. His partner, no great shakes himself with bloodshot eyes, made little pretence of being cheerful.

'Look, folks,' he said. 'Everything's gone bloody wrong on this tour, and we sure must offer our condolences to Molly over the terrible accident to her aunt. Molly's on the phone right now to the insurance company arranging for her body to be flown home. We have to think of ourselves for a moment. You know that we are due to fly out from Edinburgh, Sunday evening, and that, as far as I know, still stands. We shall have to clear with the police who may want to ask further questions, so I don't think that there is any possibility of going off any earlier.'

He glanced at Goddard who quickly responded. 'No question, sir, An early departure would certainly not be allowed.'

Brearley took Macdonald to one side, concealing his desperation. 'We have to go on. I don't know what game they're playing. There's no sign of Webb. For Christ's sake, pull yourself together.'

He turned to the group. 'Look,' he said to them, 'I've been helping the police with the inquiries into the accident. I need to get cleaned up. Let's meet here in half an hour and decided then what we should do for the rest of the day.'

III

McConachie took refuge in his office, but barely had he sat down than the telephone rang. The Fiscal wanted to know when he could see a detailed report. 'You'll appreciate, Inspector, I have a lot to sift through.'

'Not just you,' thought McConachie, whose immediate prime concern was whether the American party should be allowed to return to the States, and should he let Macdonald return with them.

Some of his colleagues would just sit down at their word-processors and set out their reports at speed, but he still depended on being able to dictate. There had been a stenographer at the conference so the Fiscal should have received enough to keep him happy. He had to see Jeannie and he would take in the police workshops on the way.. He needed time to think.

As he reached for his cap, an idea struck him. He checked the number in the book and rang the hotel where the Stones were lodged.

'Roger, look, do you think you could come out with me? You might make my cousin, Jeannie, she's the one they call Mad Meg, stop blethering and talk some sense. I'll send a car for you. Is your wife all right?'

'Right, Mac, the answer is yes to both questions.'

At the workshops, the Land Rover was being professionally stripped. Every part was being checked for hidden compartments, - the fuel tank, the wheels, the seating and the frame of the vehicle itself.

'It's no bin easy,' said the foreman. 'There's nae tools with the vehicle, but we have had that sniffer dog run over everywhere. He's never been the least interested. All he's done is lift his leg on ma trousers.'

The Inspector turned to Roger who had arrived.

'The dog's found nothing. The smell of diesel makes it almost impossible for it. If we can believe what Graham said about Webb and the late night drive, it could be that they disposed of any drugs they had. Webb still cannot be questioned, and I am left with the problem of the departure of the Americans.'

He pushed back his cap to scratch his head.

'Where does Mrs Oldberger fit in, Mac?'

The Inspector stood in silence for a moment. 'My guess is that she was masterminding the drug dealing with the two managers. They use the Abbeys as distribution points and where they can pick up the money without ever being seen.. She didn't trust them, so comes over to check them out. When Brearley drinks too much at Kelso, and she goes to the Abbey to stash the drugs, she's seen by Jones and shoots him to prevent identification. When she sees Thornell at Dryburgh, she realises that he had seen her.'

He stopped abruptly. He had suddenly recalled that Mrs Oldberger was included in the group of oldies that had headed towards the Tweed at Dryburgh. It did not make sense.

McConachie drove to the back of the Eildons, parked the car and together they trudged up the hill to the cottage. Jeannie came to the door to meet them, almost as if she knew they were coming. She achieved half a smile to her cousin and stared enquiringly at his companion.

'This is Mr Roger Stone, a good friend of mine. He and his wife are touring the Borders.'

She shot a sharp glance at him, holding out her hand.

'Aye,' she said, 'A've seen him afore in the Abbeys.'

She seemed in her brown dress and apron domesticated and down to earth. McConachie hoped that this time she would be a more responsive witness and accepted the offer of a cup of tea. She shooed the cat off the stove, rearranging the kettle which began immediately to steam.

'Aye, I was expecting you, but no your friend.'

She offered them the two elderly armchairs and herself drew up a wooden one within reach of the teapot. She set out the best cups from the dresser and poured the milk from the carton into a matching jug.

'Do ye tak sugar?' she asked and when they shook their heads, she infused the tea and sat down expectantly.

'What happened, then?' the Inspector asked

'Weel,' she said, 'that woman, I kent she was ill the day I seed her at Dryburgh, the big yin. It wasne richt for onybody to be on that stair. I didne ken who it was at first. I jist followed up the stair and she backed awa' from me. She shouldne hae been there.'

'Did you touch her, Jeannie?'

'Niver. Niver set honds on her. I wouldn't want to.'

She rose to attend to the tea, handing the two men their cups and offering the milk.

'And what can you mind about Dryburgh, Jeannie?'

She gave the fire a poke and did not immediately reply. For a moment the Inspector feared that she might retreat again into her private world.

'Ye'll mind,' she said, 'I whiles get ca''ed and yon day it was to Dryburgh. The spirit of the old Rhymer gars me gae and dae whit must be done. I saw that woman and I kent she was no yin of God's guid creatures. Sae, when they all stairted to gae off on their ain, I watched her. She set off towards the river with the aulder folk, but then efter a few steps, she turned back through the wee passage at the back there, then she met the ithers ganging oot.'

'I bided at the Abbey whiles they a' went for their dinner. When I saw you lot coming, I thoucht it was time to gae hame.'

It was the Inspector's turn to pause. He decided that to ask her about her outstretched position, embracing the earth, might be unwise.

'Did you see Jim again after he came out of the chapter house?'

She shook her head. 'There was a woman came and shouted for him over the wall from the hotel but he niver cam to it.'

'She picked up a scarf, a yellow yin.'

For a moment McConachie stared at Jeannie in consternation until he realised that she had reverted to Mrs Oldberger.

'You mean the large woman picked up a yellow scarf?'

'Aye,' she said, 'as she went oot o' the kirk. I saw there would be bluid on it, rivers of blood.'

Jeannie began to sway on her wooden chair, and her two visitors recognised that they would obtain nothing further from her and that it was time to leave.

'Daphne told me,' said Roger, 'that the only encounter she had had with Oldberger was in the morning at Melrose when she had, innocently enough and feeling a need to say something, asked about the yellow scarf she had seen her picking up. Why does that matter, Mac?'

McConachie explained as they went back to the car. 'She must have decided in desperation that she needed to muffle the shot. As it happened the passage seems to have restricted the sound. Only the Major thinks that he heard it. Now Jeannie's evidence explains how she got there.'

'Mac,' said Roger, 'I think we must thrash out all this tangle of facts. Could we go and walk somewhere? When I have too much running around in my head in London, I go and consult the ducks in the park. Let's find some place here near the water. I need to get the whole picture.' He shot a sympathetic glance at his companion.

The policeman's face broke into a slow smile. He might have felt guilty of neglecting the straightforward path of duty if the suggestion had come from him. After all, he had been set for the Teviot that afternoon.

'We could go and take a bit turn by the river,' he said.

McConachie took the car to his familiar parking place by the Teviot and then led the way to the riverside path. The water, which had been low during the spell of fine weather, had been freshened by overnight rain in the hills. He studied it approvingly but a little regretfully. 'Just right,' he said, and, having negotiated the stile, turned to the matter in hand.

'If I am right, Roger, Real Tours is a cover for a group, extent unknown, who distribute drugs in the course of their travels. Brearley and Macdonald run this under the supervision of Mrs O from the States. She comes over on some of the trips to keep tabs on them. In Kelso and Melrose they cache the drugs in recesses in the Abbeys, and their agents collect having put the money in earlier.. We don't know the agent involved in Melrose although we shall probably be able to track him or her down. Jones was seems to have been the man in Kelso, probably with Thornell's connivance, after all he worked in the grounds.'

'What about Jedburgh, Mac?'

'I think that we can say that Moran's death was natural. It set the party on edge perhaps. The batty Major has admitted he arranged the arms as a cross. But I am inclined to believe him, when he says that he was not involved at Kelso, although he seemed to know that Jones had been shot. Perhaps just a guess or I may have let it out. Probably when Oldberger shot Jones, she spread out his arms as a misleading connection.

'But, Mac,' Roger burst in, 'she couldn't have shot Jones,

she was...'

Before he could complete his interruption, the Inspector's attention had been abruptly distracted. They had paused at the tail of the long pool by the footbridge. The swirl of the current readily caught the eye, and he had been scanning the slow moving upstream stretch for the telltale eddies of rising trout. For a moment the policeman had vanished and he imagined himself throwing a gentle line across the tempting water.

There was already an angler at work. The man jerked his arm back and cast expertly; the silver minnow flew high to land close to them, then, as the fisherman swivelled his arm to and fro, it began its zigzag return.

Suddenly the movement stopped, they could see the line tauten and the short spinning rod bend

'He's into a fish, Roger!'

There was something wrong; whatever was hooked at the end of the line was unyielding. Roger wanted to complete what he was trying to say, but McConachie was intent on the man endeavouring to reel in.. There was clearly nothing alive at the other end, although the excited fisherman had not realised it.

'Let out your line, man. That's not a fish. You've fouled something,' he shouted across the pool and turned to Roger, who was still trying to speak. 'I know this bit of water well. There shouldn't be anything there.'

They watched as the fisherman tried slackening his line, letting it curl out into the sluggish current but when he tried again to reel in, his spinner was still caught, and the line dripped water as it tightened.

McConachie could bear it no longer. He turned determinedly to make his way back to the car, re-appearing with his waders.

'I'm not having ony foul thing in my pool,' he shouted as he struggled into them. 'The silly bugger has only got boots on.' He called to the angler as he lowered himself from the bank. 'Just keep your line tight so that I know where to look.'

He moved awkwardly without a stick but the shingle

beneath his feet was even. Gingerly he stretched out to grasp the tight line. He slid his hand down as far as he could and then shifted his position until his boot kicked against something hard and metallic below him.

Roger had moved to the centre of the footbridge to look down on him, a little anxious as the water was chest deep on the policeman's tall figure. He could not see into the water as the stirred-up mud obscured the bottom.

'Roger, can you get the rope from my car, it's in the boot. The car's open.'

He waded back to the bank to receive it and returned midstream. There he made a noose in the rope around the fisherman's line, allowing it to sink so that he could manoeuvre it with his feet about the sunken object. Then very cautiously he drew it towards the shallow water until, as the fisherman paid out his line, he could reach it with a long arm and, with Roger's help, haul it onto the bank. He freed the silver minnow, guiding it carefully back into the water.

They had little interest in the grateful fisherman, who shouted his thanks and departed.

McConachie, wet but triumphant, stared at what was clearly a heavy metal box which did not appear to have been long in the river. Roger caught his eye significantly.

'Mac,' he said, 'did I not hear your mechanic say this morning that the Land Rover had no tools?'

The Inspector sat with his large shirt-clad arms still dripping water. For a moment he did not follow his companion's remark. He was savouring the elation of having removed an intolerable snag from what he regarded as his own pool. Slowly the nature of his recovery dawned on him.

'By God, Roger, you're right. It's a car toolbox.'

It was secured by a heavy-duty padlock that he clearly could not open, but they could turn the box onto its side to allow the water to drain out. It was then light enough to carry to the car.

'We best take it straight to Kelso and have it opened at the police station.'

All at once McConachie had become cheerful again. 'Just supposing, Roger, they put the drugs into this box, drove from the hotel, - it's only a short distance away – and dumped it from the footbridge. We shall be able to identify the box, it has a serial number on it. We shall have them, Roger, we shall have them.'

'Yes, yes, Mac' Roger was at last able to speak. 'Let's hope we have Brearley and Macdonald, but there's something I have to tell you. Mrs Oldberger could not have shot Jones because Daphne and I were in The Feathers as she came in just before ten o'clock at the very moment Jones went out. She sat on the other side of the barroom until Macdonald came in and took the party to the bus-park. I followed them out as everyone there was getting worked up about the prolonged absence of the barman. I can swear that she never left the room and I think that you will find out from Molly that she and her aunt boarded the bus together.'

The Inspector stared at him. Once again, just when it looked as if all his problems were resolved, here was a new obstruction.

'Are you sure?' he asked at last. He really knew that it was an unnecessary question. Roger was a dependable witness.

IV

'I am quite sure that that it would have been impossible for any of the American party who were in the pub to get back past me to the Abbey, Mac.'

The Inspector reluctantly acknowledged it.

'That leaves Brearley,' he said. 'But the evidence from the hotel is that he was too drunk to achieve anything, let alone hold a pistol steady enough to shoot someone accurately, unless he was acting. In any case why should he? I don't know how he managed to only drive the Land Rover back We know that Webb carries a gun but he was either with the woman, Lake, or Graham the whole evening until they joined the others at the coach.'

He sighed. 'I told you about the Bournes, did I not? It seems to me likely that they, too, had a pistol, something the father brought back from Germany, perhaps, but we never found it. I think that the bullet we did find was the same calibre as Oldberger's and Webb's.'

It did not take them long to reach Kelso, passing the gaunt front of the Abbey where normality now prevailed. They unloaded the toolbox at the police station while the sergeant summoned a locksmith. As he replaced the telephone, it immediately rang again. He answered it and then, cupping his hand over the mouthpiece, turned to the Inspector. 'It's Mrs Bourne,' he said, 'She says she's worried about her daughter who has not come home.'

McConachie took the phone and listened to the distraught voice. 'It's Inspector McConachie here, Mrs Bourne, I'll come round right away.'

It was the Inspector's third visit to Neidpath Terrace. This time the street was quiet, the siege seemed to have been lifted, the blue Mini was absent. Mrs Bourne answered the door swiftly.

'I heard footsteps and hoped it was Kathy.' She regarded the Inspector anxiously.

'How long has she been gone, Mrs Bourne?' He asked.

'She missed her dinner and she niver does that.'

'How has she been?'

'The mother looked warily back. 'I dinna think that she's verra weil,' she said, ' and, mind you, she's got guid cause with her twa men killed like that. I dinna care very much for her two-timing but it didna warrant a' this.'

She wrung her hands nervously.

'Are you sure that your husband did not bring back a gun from Germany?'

She was silent.

The telephone rang in the front room, she hesitated a moment before going to answer it.

They could hear but not see her.

'Whit's that you say? An accident? Oh Gawd, no. I'll come at once.'

216

The Inspector and Roger moved spontaneously towards her as she returned ashen-faced into the kitchen.

'It's your sergeant at the station,' she said. 'He says there's been an accident to Kathy by the river.' She choked back her tears.

'We'll take you there. You had best put on a coat.'

As they drove to the new bridge, Roger saw a blue Mini among other vehicles parked at the roadside. There was a small group of people on the bridge itself staring downstream. From it, they could see the police car on the further road to which they made their way. The constable standing beside it caught sight of the Inspector.

'A woman,' he reported. 'Threw herself off the bridge. We got here as soon as we could, but it looks like too late. I think she hit the rocks.'

He directed them to the bank where, upon an improvised bed of rugs, a police officer in his shirtsleeves was bent over the body in an attempt at resuscitation.

'Woman in one of the houses raised the alarm. She recognised the blue Mini and rang the station.'

Kathy's mother stumbled over the rough ground of the bank.

'It's her,' she cried, even before the policeman drew back from the body. 'I ken the dress.' She could hardly bring herself to look at the daughter's face, before the ambulance drew up on he roadway above them.

Leaving Mrs Bourne in the care of a policewoman, McConachie took Roger back to the police station where the locksmith was at work on the padlock. The duty clerk came in with a letter.

'I did not know you were here, Inspector. It is just addressed to you and I was going to send it to Hawick.'

The name was written in an uneducated scrawl on the envelope. Just perhaps another of the useless anonymous letters, the police were apt to receive, he thought as he opened it, with half of his attention on the operation on the toolbox.

He read it with deepening seriousness evident on his face.

It ran:

Dear Inspector McConachie,

I cant go on living like this. You know most of the story, but you dinna know what happened at the Abbey. Spike and Jim had a fight. Spike had the gun and Jim knocked it from his hand. I picked it up and I must have fired it at Spike. I didn't know what to do. Jim said that he had seen that body at Jedburgh and he would stretch out the arms like a cross so the police would think it was to do with it. Kathy.

He handed the letter to Roger in silence.

The telephone went again before they could speak. This time it was the Hawick Superintendent wanting the Inspector.'

'Sir.'

'Look, Mac, Goddard has just reported that the Americans have asked if they can make a last tour round. Goddard said they had a heated discussion. Some woman determined to get to Abbotsford and none of them wanting to spend the whole day shut up in the hotel. So I have agreed but I insisted that they all go. They'll come through Kelso on a round trip.'

As he rang off, the locksmith exclaimed triumphantly as he threw back the lid. They stood together to witness the contents revealed within the toolbox. Neatly laid out in a thick and well sealed polythene bag were a series of similar, smaller containers filled with white powder. There could be little doubt about what it was.

McConachie's well-disciplined instincts only just checked his impulse to seize the packets with delight and throw them up in the air. He issued the necessary instructions for their examination and safe keeping to the officers at the station, before turning in triumph to Roger. 'We have them, Roger, we have them now.'

But then his thoughts reverted to Kathy Bourne and his feeling that once again he had failed to prevent yet another death. If only the letter had come earlier. It was Roger who broke into his reverie. 'Mac, wasn't that message about the tourists?'

He shook himself free. 'Right, absolutely right and they must be passing this way now. I don't care what anyone says, I am not going to wait until they return.'

FAREWELL AT SCOTT'S VIEW

'Look to the end, quoth John Morow.'
Inscription on the lintel of the Bell Stair:
Melrose Abbey.

John Brearley drove the coach towards Kelso heading for the road to St. Boswells and thence to Abbotsford. The Americans at the hotel had spent most of the morning in a wrangle. There had been those who had just wanted to finish their packing and stay put, but some like Mrs Sorenson wanted to press on to Abbotsford and complete the tour which they had paid for. Mrs Sorenson had not liked Mrs Oldberger anyway. Tempers were short. Dwight Graham tried to keep them calm.

'Accidents will happen,' he said, although he recognised they seemed to have had rather more than their fair share. Mrs Schumacher said that she did not think it proper to continue sightseeing after a death in the party. The younger girls were subdued. It was Molly, busy sorting out her aunt's possessions and telephoning, who finally persuaded them.

'It's no good sitting around here and moping,' she said. 'I'm right sure my aunt would have wanted you to go on.'

Brearley and Macdonald felt that they were no longer in charge. Brearley kept saying, when they had a private moment, that they had to keep going as if everything was normal. Macdonald wanted out, his one hope was to escape back to the States under the cover of the Americans. Brearley pressed Goddard to find out what had happened to the Land Rover, but all the constable would say was that it was being examined because Mrs Oldberger had used it. They had picked up from the hotel staff some story of a shooting in the Yarrow valley that might explain Webb's absence.

The majority of the party voted to make one final tour.

The insistence of the police, that in the interests of their security all had to go, overcame any remaining reluctance for the sake of propriety. The two managers accepted that anything was better that inaction. Real Tours would do its best even if the actors felt it might be a charade.

So it was that Brearley drove the coach across the new bridge at Kelso, Macdonald on the microphone explaining how the by-pass took the traffic round the town so they would miss out on a last look at the Abbey. He broke off as he became aware of the police car slowing down vehicles ahead of him. He nudged Brearley at the wheel.

'We are crossing the River Tweed, the great salmon river.' He faltered. He could see that he had lost the attention of those seated on the right hand side of the bus, as they twisted round to see what was happening. Brearley drove steadily on. At least, he thought to himself, this seemed something that he was not involved in. The police car let them past.

'It's not us, Gus, it's not us,' he whispered. 'Carry on.'

They negotiated their way clear of the town. 'That's Floors Castle behind the walls on the left,' Macdonald managed.

He caught sight of the policeman in the car behind. 'There's a police car following, J, ' he said, but he had omitted to switch off the microphone in his hand so the whole bus heard. And turned as best they could to observe.

Brearley had already seen it. 'It's Goddard, he said that we would have an escort. Don't sing out on that bloody machine. Tell them it's protecting us.' From God knows what he thought.

McConachie, now bent on pursuit and arrest, returned to the square in Kelso to intercept the coach. When no vehicle appeared, he stopped to use the telephone from which he learnt from the police on the bridge that Real Tours had already passed through the town. He could not establish contact with Goddard.

'The fool's probably got it switched off,' he said to Roger as they took to the road at speed.

'I know that it sounds silly, but I want to be the one who

catches these two. Evans has been that cocky about his drug team, and they haven't been too successful with McShea. Evans is still here with a squad from Edinburgh so Hawick have sent him out to intercept the coach, once they knew about that box. We know now for sure that Oldberger shot Thornell. He must have seen her caching the drugs, so that case looks closed. I am very upset about Kathy but at least my instincts were right, but she shouldn't have done that'.

Roger understood the unexpressed connection. The Inspector felt that he had failed. He felt responsible for Kathy's death, and the arrest of Brearley and Macdonald would be at least some compensation.

The Real Tours coach was some way ahead of them.

'That's the Edinburgh road straight on, we'll take that tomorrow' said Macdonald to cheer himself, as they swung off to the left.

Brearley was tensed up, the strain was telling. He kept seeing Goddard's face in the driving mirror, then he saw the car's light flashing and the policeman gesticulating.

He drew Macdonald's attention, as he slowed to a halt. Goddard stopped in front, stepped out of his car to walk back to the driver's window, looking rather embarrassed.'Mr Brearley, my car is short of fuel. I'll go ahead of you to St Boswells and fill up. You'll find it a slow business getting through the village so I won't hold you up. Would you stop at the garage.'

The partners exchanged glances of relief. It was only shortly afterwards that Macdonald, standing up and looking backwards to offer his commentary, saw across a corner another police car with its lights flashing.

He was becoming once more panicky. The thought of escape, however irrational, dominated him. He saw the signpost for Dryburgh Abbey at the edge of the road. The police car had not yet come over the hill.

He turned and gripped Brearley by the shoulder. 'Turn off here, J. Turn off here. For Christ's sake turn off here.'

Brearley, shocked into compliance, took the corner with a screech of tyres. He had to give all his attention to take the next sharp bend before he could spare even half a glare at his partner.

Macdonald relieved to see that the other car was not following them, picked up his microphone. The older members of the party, who had just achieved a degree of composure on the enforced outing, protested in agitation.

'It's all right, folks,' Macdonald offered weakly, 'Real Tours is taking you on a detour to, to… ' 'Scott's View,' completed Mrs Sorenson. 'I've just this minute looked it up on the map.'

'And my book says,' said her husband, 'it was Sir Walter's favourite view in the Borders and when he was on his way to Dryburgh in his coffin, the horses just stopped there like they were used to.'

On the main road, the Inspector reached the village of St Boswells. 'We should have caught up with them by now, Roger.' He tried his radio telephone again from the side of the road. 'That's Hawick, they say that they can't contact Goddard either, but the good news is that the Edinburgh police have caught McShea in possession./'

As they came out of the village, they saw Goddard in his car waiting at the exit from the pumps.

During the course of the day, Roger had seen his old friend pass through the whole gamut of emotion: there had been his sense of failure in the case, his frustration in his inability to achieve an arrest, his genuine understanding of his cousin and finally his sadness over Kathy. Now all his pent-up fury was about to be poured out on the policeman sitting there, in his car, without a trace of the coach party.

'I had to get fuel, sir, I…' At the sight of his superior's face, Goddard dried up. Roger put a restraining hand on McConachie's arm. For a moment there was a mordant silence and then the Inspector burst out. 'Where the hell are they?'

'They haven't passed me,' said Goddard, only too aware of his failure. 'I overtook them after Smailholm.'

'Then they must have taken the Dryburgh road.'

The two cars were swiftly turned and driven back through the narrow village street with its obstructive parked cars, each adding to the Inspector's anger. They crossed the Tweed to take the steep road to the left. At the Dryburgh intersection they stopped a motorist to ask if the Real Tours coach had returned to the Abbey, but he had not seen it, so they knew it had continued up the hill.

The Inspector took the opportunity to make contact with Hawick again on the telephone.

'Evans is in the other car coming off the Edinburgh road, Roger. The coach is trapped between us.'

Brearley was not far ahead of them. He had repeatedly to draw in to let on-coming vehicles pass on the narrow road. He was not now sure what they were trying to do. Rather like an automaton, he kept pointing out local interests for Macdonald to broadcast to the tourists.

'There's the Wallace Statue,' he said. 'There's Earl Haig's house. This is the village of Bemersyde.'

The tension had now communicated itself to his passengers. The abrupt swerve off the main road had unsettled them but it was the unnatural manner of Macdonald in his commentary and the uncertain driving of Brearley which confirmed to them that something was going wrong. The older wives clutched at their husbands. The Bryants and Mays conferred quietly. They were positioned at the rear of the coach where there was an emergency door. Behind them they became aware of the flashing lights of a police car following them.

At Scott's view, the single-track road is broadened to allow for a tarmacked parking space against a low wall. The visitor looks over a steep bluff, falling down in gorse, grass and woodland to the narrow defile of the river, five hundred feet below. Above it rise the three majestic peaks of the Eildons, and to their right, the Tweed valley stretches towards Melrose and into the distant hills.

As the coach approached, Brearley was prompting Macdonald who repeated mechanically, 'We are approaching Scott's view. You will see the finest prospect in the Borders, beloved by Sir Walter, and in the distance you can still make out the ruins of Melrose Abbey. You will see the finest prospect in the Borders, beloved by Sir Walter, and in the distance you can still make out the ruins of Melrose

Abbey.'

At that moment, the driver of a parked Saab chose to reverse from his position against the wall, and Brearley prepared to move to the left to avoid it. But the police car driven by Evans swung round the bend, blocking the car's manoeuvre. The driver braked sharply, forcing Brearley further to the left.

Short of the wall, the verge is only protected by a fence. The coach's wheels hit the crumbling edge and, as Brearley struggled to control the vehicle and avoid a crash, it lurched to an uncertain halt.

There was a silence, then screams and shouts. Mike May pulled up the lever to open the rear door to push out his wife and the Bryants. The coach, relieved of weight at the rear, tilted further, the front wheels sinking into soft earth until the front of the coach rested against the fence. Macdonald had scrambled to his feet, Brearley was fumbling for the release handle of the door until he realised that it was not safe to use it.

McConachie at the sight of the accident brought his car abruptly to a halt, with Goddard alongside. He could see the bearded Evans with other officers getting out of their car on the far side of the road. He was not going to let the Welshman make the arrests. It was Roger who saw immediately that the unloading of all the passengers at once through the rear door was now extremely dangerous. While the Inspector's eyes were only fixed on his prey, Roger with Bryant tried to prevent a hysterical exit from the coach.

May joined them in shouting to the passengers by name to move slowly, - it was in any case all the elderly could achieve. One by one they were helped to the ground, until they were all out. At each movement, the coach lurched more heavily against the wires until only Brearley and Macdonald were left creeping towards the exit on all fours.

Ian McConachie saw Evans waiting to pounce. He was not going to have that.

'Sergeant Evans,' he shouted. 'Would you get a rope quickly and try to secure the coach.' The Inspector did not see how this could be done but it kept Evans occupied. Barely waiting for the managers to rise to their feet, he stepped forward to arrest them, and with Goddard's help, handcuffed them and bundled them into his car.

When the chagrined Evans returned with a rope and prepared to attach it to the vehicle, the coach began to slip further as the fence gave way with a vicious twanging of wires, Slowly at first and then with increased momentum, Real Tours slid off the verge. Its loudspeaker recording system, jarred into freak action by the impact, began to repeat, 'and in the distance you can still make out the ruins of Melrose Abbey.' Only the thunderous crash of the coach's final descent brought silence.

As Roger said to Daphne when they returned home, 'those Americans certainly obtained their money's worth,' and as she said to him, 'I think, darling, that I shall leave the choice of our next holidays to you.'

* * * * *